TULE LAKE

TULE LAKE

by
EDWARD MIYAKAWA

House By The Sea Publishing Company

Acknowledgements:

Tule Lake is based on the accounts given in *The Spoilage* by Dorothy Swaine Thomas and Richard S. Nishimoto, University of California Press, Berkeley and Los Angeles, 1946.

Cover Illustration by Yukiharu Sazaki

Inside Illustration by Melanie Fergusen

Edited by Carol Van Strum

House By The Sea Publishing Company

Library of Congress Catalog Card Number: 79-87758

To my wife
Mary
and my children
**Kimiko, Isaac,
Huong, Mahn,
Keith, Kanka**

Author's Forward

It was a cool morning in the late spring of 1942 when we boarded buses that would transport us to concentration camps in desolate and isolated regions of America. We were being forcefully removed from our land and homes and from the communities we had built in the fifty years since our first generation pioneer parents had settled in America.

We were told we were being imprisoned for our own safety: the United States government was giving us a unique opportunity to prove our loyalty as Americans. I was seven years old, too young to comprehend our exile, yet I knew there was something more sinister and ominous we were being condemned for. Our crime was being Japanese.

In the years following, the evacuation remained an enigma to the Japanese Americans. We rarely talked about it among ourselves or others, and when we did, it was in a light-hearted way, guarding our innermost feelings. We pushed into the background of our lives the events of the evacuation and imprisonment behind barbed wire and machine gun towers of over 110,000 Japanese Americans, 70,000 of whom were American citizens by birth.

Until recently the majority of Americans did not know of the evacuation and many insisted it did not happen, or if it did, that it was a necessary military action. America disregarded the constitutional rights of 70,000 Japanese American citizens, yet she emerged from World War II as the protector of freedom and justice of the world.

After thirty years of silence there is now a clamor among the third and the fourth generation Japanese Americans to understand their past. TULE LAKE is a part of a continuing effort to reveal the truth about the evacuation, to relieve the burden of guilt, the self-hatred, the loss of confidence and self-respect that we have carried since those bleak days of exile. Yes, and to relieve the burden of anger and bitterness.

The history of the evacuation must, in part, be written by those of us who lived it. It is not only American history, it is Japanese American history. The generations of Japanese who were born in the camps and those following must someday know the facts about an episode that has affected their identity as Americans. Those who lived through it must learn why and how they were subjected to such treatment. The evacuation was a result of political expediency, economic exploitation, racism and hysteria. All Americans should know the truth as a reminder that it could happen again.

Prologue

On the morning of December 7, 1941, the Japanese bombed Pearl Harbor. Subsequently, the United States military evacuated 110,000 persons of Japanese ancestry from the West Coast into ten relocation centers in isolated regions of the United States. They were Manzanar and Tule Lake in California; Poston and Gila River in Arizona; Minidoka in Idaho; Rohwer and Jerome in Arkansas. My family and our friends and relatives were sent to Tule Lake in Northern California, where many of us lived from mid 1942 until 1946.

For Father it was a period of turmoil and change as drastic as the years when he first came to America in 1908 as a young man of twenty-two. Had he been born a few hundred years ago, he would have been a samurai. But he bridges the span of the three contemporary generations. He was a teacher turned farmer turned merchant. He is my father and I know him, but I do not. For the first ten years of my life he and mother were names only, existing as emigrants in a distant America.

To whom I owe myself, I am not sure, but I do know I am the last extension tying me back several hundred years. I am the first born in America, a country that my ancestors, dead and decayed, never knew existed. I am an American citizen by birth, a privilege Father and Mother can never experience: the Oriental Exclusion Act prevented all Asians from becoming naturalized citizens.

Mother and Father returned to Japan with me when I was a year old to be adopted by my maternal grandparents. In Japan when there is no male offspring, families often adopt a boy to carry on their family name. I was destined to live out a transition of my own. I lived in Japan for nine years. Therefore, I have not shared Father's hardships in changing from one country to another, moving from one time in history to another time into another history. Although I never saw the blur of his legs on pedals, I know the wheels of Father's bicycle have tracked thousands of miles of the San Joaquin Valley, delivering medical supplies to farm laborers for four or five years, summer and winter, in freezing cold and withering heat. Only depleted supplies or sickness or occasional exhaustion were reasons for turning homeward.

During the years in Japan, I learned who I was, what I was supposed to be and how I would uphold what I was taught to be truth and honor. There was love and order. When I become fragmented, I retreat to these early memories. Around the table, I see the faces of my adopted family, feet inserted in a square hole in the floor where there is a hibachi for warmth. Always it is the same -- my exercise in faith. I close my eyes, again and again. I see the peaceful furrows of my grandfather's face; my grandmother, an aura of serenity surrounding her; two half sisters or aunts; and my great grandmother. My grandfather is at the head of the table; I am seated opposite him. My grandmother and her mother are on the side toward the kitchen with my aunts opposite them.

It has been fifteen years since I last seated myself at that table. Since that day, change has become as much a part of my life as was permanence during my first ten years. I had to leave the only family I had ever known to live with strangers in a new country with different customs and dress and language.

In the house the wind was a gentle one, wafting across the garden, flowing through the pink of spring, through needles of pines, along the corridors, through opened sliding doors. For a while, I did not see my parents' faces, for I moved downwards, my eyes staring at the earth as I touched my forehead to my hands, palms outstretched upon the mat. I moved slowly up, their heads perpendicular to my vision. I bowed and righted myself over and over.

Never have I seen such sadness, hidden behind deceptive smiles, as on that day. Beneath the roof, between walls, in the house where I have lived, we sat forever. I was told that I would depart the home of my grandparents and return to America with my mother and father.

I was immune to their words. All I could see were the squares of a shoji door cast by an angle of afternoon sun into flattened shapes half on the wall and half on tatami. The filtered light through rice paper was translucent and soft white, so the lamella shadows of the thin wood frames were not in a single plane but in many.

My last day of school in Japan was set aside to bestow upon me honor and love. I arose to give the speech expected of me by my classmates and instructors. I felt no weight, no movement, as my legs carried me across the stage. I stood voiceless -- one minute -- two minutes -- then my teacher whispered, "Seichi, everyone is waiting. You must give your speech."

I concentrated on transforming thoughts to words, but my mind refused to function, to perform as it has been trained. I wanted them to understand what I wished I could understand. Beneath the shadow of the roof shade, there was silence.

Chapter 1

"How can you be so calm?" Gordie asks. "The rumors involve you!"

Dad looks up from the newspaper he is reading, focusing above the steel rimmed glasses perched on his nose. His brush of a moustache makes him appear so Japanesy -- like an "enemy alien."

"People are wondering why you haven't been arrested when most of your friends have."

"Japanese are rumor prone," Dad says.

"Don't you care what's being said about you by your own people?"

Dad makes a loud sucking sound as he sips tea.

"They say it's because you have Caucasian friends intervening for you," Gordie continues, determined to involve Father.

Father says nothing, his face showing neither anger nor calm. He is hard to read. Only rarely, in extremes, does his face respond to inner feeling. And his body is always rigid, whatever the circumstances, standing or seated, whether in church pew or on living room sofa.

"It is true. I have many friends, both Japanese and Hakujin. I do not know why I am free. Maybe it is because I have many Hakujin friends. What am I to do about it?"

"I have heard it is because you are the editor of a Japanese newspaper," Mother interjects from the kitchen. "They say the government wants to use it to influence Japanese American thinking."

"My friends, the people I trust, are not suspicious of me. I do not care what those who gossip say about me."

"I have heard rumors about you and Ben," Father continues, "because you belong to JACL. They say Japanese American Citizens League is turning people in to the FBI. Are we to believe everything we hear? Is it true about JACL?"

"Ridiculous!" Gordie says angrily. "It's stupid for anyone to accuse us of turning in fellow Japanese!"

Father nods knowingly. "It is troubled times," he says. "We have seen many friends arrested. We don't know where they are. They are threatening to remove us from our homes and land and send us to camps. I am worried . . . but not about idle rumors."

Overnight we have become the subject of suspicion and antagonism. We watch silently as friends, community leaders, family members are taken away by FBI agents. We learn that enemy aliens do not have equality under the constitution during wartime.

Public proclamations prohibit ownership of contraband articles such as flashlights, radios, cameras, and samurai swords. Our movement is restricted by curfews and zones along the entire Pacific Coast. Our identity as Americans steadily declines as we become synonymous with the "enemy race."

I analyze, then try to sever the memories that make me love one land as I do the other. To prove I am loyal, I must deny whatever I have been, even though I will always be a part of the old country.

For my brother it is not so complicated. Gordie was born and raised in America. He is Japanese by blood only. Since I first arrived from Japan, I have emulated everything about him, so I too could become an American. Gordie is big for a Japanese, and athletic. His eyes emanate friendliness and humor. He has a straight-for-ward way of dealing with people in social situations.

To welcome Gordie home from college, Mother has been preparing a delicious Japanese meal, including sushi, teriyaki chicken, and many varieties of pickled vegetables, all Gordie's favorites that are never served in college dormitories.

"Other students leaving campus too?" I ask.

"All the Japanese. Right after they heard families in different geographical areas might be sent to separate camps."

"None of it is constitutional, not the curfews, the zones, or the camps," I say. "I'd sure like to see it tested in court."

"You could get a lot of people in trouble doing that!" he says.

"Goto-san says it is dangerous to keep books and magazines in Japanese around the house," Mother says.

"Japanese are too rumor prone," Dad repeats.

Many of the books on our shelves are gone, reveal-ing a mirrored back wall where I see a reflection of Mother, standing thoughtfully near the book case. Her hair is fixed in an immaculate western-fashioned per-manent; it is still a lustrous black, framing a face that is fine featured and delicate.

Father gets up and leaves the room. He returns shortly with a yellowish letter in his hand. "It is a letter from Japan," he explains. "I received it from my father ten years ago, shortly before he died. I guess I've always been too afraid to read it." He laughs uneasily as he opens it.

He takes a long time reading it. He looks up then, his face a confused picture of relief, happiness and sadness. For the first time in fifteen years as his son, I see my father cry. He cries and laughs unashamedly as if no one else were in the room. Blinking away the silvery trail of tears running down his cheeks into his moustache, he looks up at us and says, "It is hard for me to remember my father, it has been so long ago. I never really knew him. He was a stranger to me."

In a tone of relief, he tells us the letter does not admonish him for having left Japan against his father's will. Instead, his father expresses pride in his having pioneered successfully in America.

I watch the burden suddenly lifted from his shoulders. I understand something I had not realized until this moment: we have become strangers from one generation to the next.

Because Dad believes in the promise of America, we believe also. He has done well in this country. In Japan he was a math teacher. In America he became a farmer, then a pharmacist and a publisher of a Japanese newspaper. He attributes his success to the system of government.

The memories of the old country fade. He has been a Christian for most of his years in this country, perhaps in his own intrinsic Japanese way, marching his family Sunday after Sunday to services at Parkview Presbyterian Church, where he is an elder and one of the founders.

In this living room, he has gathered us as a family twice a week for many years, to learn the most important aspects of things spiritual and worldly -- religion and language. Each of us took ten minute turns reading from the Bible.

Race was a detriment to some, but to him it seemed to matter little, for although he believed in the ideals of America, he realized also that too much faith in man's systems of things would bring him failure.

When the Anti Alien Land Laws were first enacted, he was already a property owner. With the ingenuity of a man who knows his only limitation is his own lack of imagination, he established a dummy corporation called the Ideal Brothers Corporation. He asked his Caucasian friends to be stockholders on the governing board and contracted a special law firm in San Francisco to legalize all of his land holdings. With his temperament and ambitions, he was an ideal man for this country.

I marvel at the forces that motivate Father and what he has sacrificed for his sons; Gordie's and my success are a measure of his own. It was Father's well-conceived plan that sent the two of us to college.

"You have done well, Ben," Dad said. He had called me into his study to discuss my plans. His voice was solemn, but his eyes were bright and pleased. "In nine years, you have overcome handicaps of not knowing English to get to the top of your class. You have brought honor to the family, and for this, you should be able to go to college. We are willing to do whatever we can to help you."

I remained silent, surprised. On my first day of school he had given me a book and thrust me out alone, and since then had given me little encouragement and never praise. Perhaps it was tacitly understood that what he expected of himself, he expected of others.

From the time I moved from the first grade to fourth, I progressed quickly until I was twelve and caught up with children my own age. I mastered English and became an honor student, graduating among the first five of my class. Gordie, two years behind me, achieved high grades also. It was Dad who inspired us in his endeavor to learn and achieve in the American culture.

"What do you wish to study?" he asked.

"I want to become a doctor."

"That is a good choice," he replied. "It is an honorable and worthy profession. In Japan there are those in our family who have been doctors. But in America we are a small minority. Hakujins will not come to a Japanese doctor. There is nothing the matter with that, if we do not wish to grow beyond the community of Japanese. It is true that you have the ability to become a surgeon, but your abilities are many. You speak two languages perfectly. You have been raised in the ways of both countries. There are few people who are better equipped to bridge the gaps between Japan and the United States. Perhaps you would be willing to study international law."

We must honor his sacrifices with obedience. Gradually, I made the mental adjustment and became excited by the prospects of studying law. In the fall I was enrolled at Harvard University.

I will never be able to share with my Father what it was like to be the only Japanese American in my class at a prestigious Anglo American college. Few parents have ever known the pride my parents felt at my graduation. For the most part, my college years were the happiest in my life, aside from my early childhood. It was a time to excel both in academics and sports.

It was through Dad's arrangements upon my graduation from law school that I have come to work for a Caucasian law firm in Sacramento. I am an apprentice working primarily on cases involving Japanese. There are rumors that I will be dismissed. With Gordie's forced return from the University of Southern California, where he was studying pharmacy, all of Father's plans are being scattered.

The Japanese American state workers have been forced to resign, as well as most of the young Japanese employed by Caucasians. Farmers are unable to cross restricted borders to sell their produce, yet they are told to keep producing to contribute to the war effort.

It is our custom to meet together on Wednesday noons for lunch in the Wakanoura Restaurant, across the street from Father's print shop/pharmacy. I recognize Kageyama's green flatbed that he has used to haul his truck crops into the farmer's market for as many seasons as I can remember.

I walk in to the sounds of a tinkling bell. The small, crowded room is divided into booths with bamboo partitions and shoji screens. The aroma of home-style Japanese cooking makes me anticipate my favorite lunch of tendon, deep-fried prawns on rice.

Kageyama and Father acknowledge me with a curt nod of their head. They are in the midst of a heated discussion about the publication of another of Kageyama's articles attacking the rumored evacuation of Japanese from the West Coast.

The tones of their voices are familiar, reserved for their political arguments. Masahiro Kageyama, Mother's cousin, is a Florin farmer; his mother, Hiroko or Obasan as she is known to our family, came to this country with her husband, now deceased, in the early 1890's. Masahiro was born in 1895, and aside from the time he spent in the army in World War I and a short time on a tuna boat, he has never left the Florin farm. Because he never realized his dream of attending college, he made up for it by becoming an inveterate reader and self-educated man of strong opinions. He often forgets the polite niceties when an important issue is at stake.

"I have published your articles two times before.

Now I won't. You'll get us all arrested. You accuse the government of trying to send us away in violation of constitutional rights. I can't publish that."

"How can you see it any other way?" I ask. "To incarcerate United States citizens without trial by jury. What have we done? There is nothing to try us for."

"If they send us away, it will be violation of rights. They cannot do this to us. Especially for those of us who are citizens," Kageyama says.

"That's what I mean." Father says. "You citizens are protected by the constitution. But what of those of us who are aliens? We cannot take any chances. Terao gone, Okuma, Fukuda, all arrested. It is time to be cautious."

"Cautious!" Kageyama almost shouts. "What do you know of being cautious? You who gave up security and good life in Japan to pioneer in America. What guarantee was there for you then? You made your own breaks. You stood on own two feet. You must do same now if you believe in freedom of speech and freedom of press!"

Chapter 2

On the west sidewalk of Fourth Street, a twenty-four by thirty-six inch eye watches me. The eye on the window is almond-shaped Oriental with a Caucasian epicanthic fold. It was painted by a gardener who in his non-working hours chants ancient Japanese poetry and renders the Sacramento Valley in sumi landscapes. For those who read Japanese, optician is written in calligraphy above the eye with the translation, OPTICIAN, below.

The pale asphalt street, not too long ago dust and gravel, runs north and south through the heart of our small Japanese town. We cling to our "Nihonmachi" of the San Joaquin Valley, created from what was remembered of the old country villages: a rock in a stream, a quiet pool, the soft strings of shamisen and the fluting song of shakuhachi.

I am seated in a shop entrance where the sounds and smells of the street spill into a store that supplies violins or koto, victrolas or washing machines, pianos or shamisen, radios or biwa. The musical instrument and electrical appliance store belongs to an elderly Issei, Mr. Atsumi. He is small and frail, yet hardy, a tenous touch to the past, for when he is gone, the history of transition will die with him. As Fourth Street is East and West, the eye caucasoid and mongoloid, he is a suited eight-hour merchant by day, a kimono-shrouded villager in summer evening. After dinner he sits in front of his store, rhythmically fanning the air and speaking to friends and strangers in an even tempo of Japanese. It is Atsumi's Hyogo prefecture transplanted to Sacramento.

For me there is harmony in Fourth Street cacophony: crated chickens, horses' hoofs, wagon wheels, and auto engines. Redolence of fish from river and ocean mixes with smoke and exhaust. From my back, streaming gently against the flow of street noises, I hear a woman's soft voice counting to the sometimes unmusical sounds of a student's piano playing.

"One, two, three, four. One, two, three, four." It is Alice, Mr. Atsumi's daughter. She speaks in perfect English with a musical quality that comes from talking and counting to music.

The glass eye watches but never sees; musical intruments are sold alongside electrical appliances. I have lived and walked the prefectures of Japan. I have seen frail dark brown houses built along the edges of thin dusty roads that twist and wind through villages with slow rolling carts pulled by men and women. A persistent quiet lingers where the air lacks sounds of machines. In San Joaquin Nihonmachi there are streets and sidewalks, stores sheathed in steel and glass, and high office windows that stare over streets to other windows, to trees, to sky.

Through one of the high windows I see the figure of a man in white peering into an open mouth. His glasses dangle from his ears. He drills, scrapes away film and tobacco stains, and gives hell to a patient who has neglected his teeth. I smile and mimic words I have had to listen when it was my turn to sit in his tilted chair.

"The inside of your mouth looks like the inside of a garbage CAN!" He shouts. "I ought to pull them all OUT!"

I used to wonder how Dr. Ono managed to keep

patients until I learned he could have long ago opened a "modern office" had he not provided so much of his service free. Each farm laborer, railroad worker, and farmer seated in Dr. Ono's chair gives a perspective of Nihonmachi not easily discernible from outside. It becomes clear to me why we are here, why there is a Japanese town, and why we shall be far beyond what I will know.

On a misty day, when sounds float and the air gently curls about me, mingled with the odors of seaweeds, miso pastes, and fish, the pale sidewalks of Japanese-town become the winding footpaths along the inland seacoast of my childhood.

Suddenly, there is a burst in English. "Ben! Hey Boochie!"

"Ben . . . Hey Boochie!" Tomato's face is a brighter than normal red, and his head is shaped like a full moon. His teeth are strikingly white against his dark skin. He shouts from the curb, "Join me in a game of pool! You staying away 'cause you afraid of guilt by association?"

"Sure thing." I cross the street. "They might mistake me for one of you Buddhaheads!"

Okada's pool hall is full. On a wall poster, a Caucasian soldier points out two Oriental faces for instructions on:

"HOW TO DISTINGUISH CHINESE FROM JAPANESE."

Tomato studies the buck teeth, the pale yellow color, the drool, then backs against the wall. He stretches his mouth sidewise, slits his eyes to the same angle as shown on the poster and distorts his voice, "Slanty eyes and big space between first and second toe."

Goto grunts. Tomato hisses, "Preeeeeeeeeeease, I

not . . . funny tlue, I are small . . . but sneaky and dange-
lous."

"Don't laugh! Don't say nothing!" someone says
from a table near the center of the room. "Don't want
to encourage the jerk."

It is Taniguchi. Tomato descends on him with the
quickness of a san-dan judo expert. From the skuffle Tomato growls, "I are kill dirty tlaaitor!"

Tomato is a perfect caricature of a grade C movie
villain: bow legs, strong, stocky frame, jet black hair,
darkened skin.

Dust flies. Okada barges his way through the spectators and grabs Tomato's shirt collar, babbling in hur-
ricane tempo Japanese-English which translated, says,
"Should they wish to fight, it can as well and efficiently
be done outside the premises of this pool hall."

Taniguchi struggles up and beats the dust out of his
pants. He stares at Tomato and says, "Hey, you messed
up my new clothes."

With Okada's hand on his back, Tomato swaggers
on bow legs to the bench where I am convulsed with
laughter.

"Even now things can be funny," he says. He takes
the seat next to me and quietly watches a game of pool
in progress. He says softly, "Gotta keep things funny,
'cause if people wanta see buck teeth, they're gonna
see 'em even if we're all blind, gummy-mouthed, hun-
dred-year-olds. And if they all think we're living along
irrigation ditches or under power lines 'cause we got a
submarine or round-the-world-transmitter, they'd
think it even if I was taking a high noon crap in a one-
holer in the middle of Death Valley." He leans his head
on the wall, adding to the grease from years of hair oil
and dust.

In ancient temples I have stood in semi-darkness like this pool hall. I breathe deeply to determine whether what I inhale is incense or stale cigarette smoke. It is both, for there is no way to distinguish past and present. The only real thing happening is the click and thump of balls.

"Is Death Valley in the 'Free Zone' or 'Restricted Zone?'". I ask.

"Tell you the truth." His face turns from a mixture of curiosity and suspicion to a broad smile. "Ho, ho."

At that moment, Yuji cracks an eight in a corner pocket and swings his hand exuberantly upwards, slamming his fist into the hood of a light. It clangs noisily, shaking down months of dust.

"Hey, Yuji, you're not on second base!" I smile at my wiry, energetic baseball pal, one of the best players in the league. "You got the grace of an elephant!"

"Speaking of the 'Free Zone,'" Tomato says, looking at me, "I heard Gordie left school to come back home."

"Yeh, he was afraid of getting separated." I answer. "Besides, he wanted to get back to work with the JACL. He thinks they can really help get breaks for the Japanese."

"I don't know about that!" He shrugs his shoulders and looks around the room, then shouts abruptly, "Hey, how about a table! Gotta see if this guy's still got the touch!"

"Keep your pants on." Goto speaks with the authority of an all-conference collegiate fullback. "We got money riding on this game."

"Money game!" Tomato says, puffing his face pompously and rolling his eyes up. "Listen to him! An unemployed Boochie in the winter of '42, putting out money for pool and whores like he was still back in the good ol'days. What you got, John? A rich old man you been keeping secret?"

"Two bits a game!"

Close the banks!" Tomato shouts. He jumps up with arms out-stretched. "Stop breathing!"

The games stop again. All the guys threaten to throw him out of the hall. Tomato turns to me. "Bunch of sore heads! Got no sense of humor!"

Asoo squints humorously at Tomato and rubs his chin thoughtfully. "Trouble with your kinda guy," he says slowly, "is that someone is slicing your inside with a knife, and you think it's a good time for a laugh. You think it's funny that Jap shot down over Pearl was wearing a '36 Cal ring?"

"You believe that?" Tomato smiles, his teeth flashing sarcasm.

"What you talking about, believing or not? It happened!" Asoo says.

"Whatta you mean it happened? You just like the rest of us -- you read it in the paper. You believe that stuff about how they're gonna send us into concentration camps?"

"That's completely different," Asoo says. "Nobody's gonna be sent any place, especially not American citizens."

"What makes you so sure?" Tomato needles.

"You don't seem to understand, Tomato paste! Or maybe you forgot your history lessons. This is a democracy."

"You tell us about it, Professor!"

Asoo stands back, his brows furrowed thoughtfully, and as is his habit, carefully analyzes before acting or speaking. Since his father died six years ago, he has been the head of his family, providing for his mother, two brothers and a sister while attending Sacramento State college part-time, majoring in sociology. "Well," he says, "how about those congressional hearings? Those guys coming from Washington are supposed to listen to everyone's viewpoint. How about the Bill of Rights? The Constitution doesn't say anything about us being Nihonjin. We're just Americans. Isn't that right, Ben?" He turns suddenly to me. "You're the lawyer here."

"You're right about our rights, Asoo . . . I hope. That's what they taught us . . . ."

"Yeah," Goto says, "and there's the governor's meeting. You think they'd have hearings in Germany or Japan? Why my old man's always telling me football's kid's stuff, and I'm just a spoiled weak American kid. He says if I were back in the old country, I wouldn't be giving out any lip or asking any questions about my rights. I'd shut up and do as I'm told."

"Your father says that?" Yuji asks, surprised. "He sounds just like my father. Always talking about the Emperor being a god. We're supposed to respect him even if we are Americans. Sometimes I sure don't understand those Issei so well."

"Me either," Goto says. "Spending so much time talking and thinking about going back to the old country, yet they're still here, in the same spot as thirty years ago and most of them still don't speak good English."

"Don't be too hard on them," I say. "They went through a lot, changing from one country to the other. Maybe that's how they survived."

"Eight in the corner!" Taniguchi calls out. He makes a quick back swing, slams the stick into the cue ball and watches the black ball ricochet into the corner pocket. When it disappears, he says, "They're still here . . . Japanese-town . . . . Grown men playing pool and hanging around this crappy joint."

He looks quickly around for Okada, who is in his office. "Sorry, Okada-san," Taniguchi says in a voice just low enough not to be heard from the office. "No offense meant, you understand. But this place ain't exactly the Senator Hotel."

"Hey, Tanigooch," Yuji says, "you a bakatare!"

"Bakatare!" Goto says. "Knock off the Jap talk. The FBI's arresting bakatares!"

"I take it back," Yuji turns toward Taniguchi. "You just a plain ol' American shithead."

When a couple of guys leave a table, Tomato immediately racks the balls into the triangle. On lag for break he beats me by less than a ball's diameter then proceeds to break the triangle into ricocheting fragments. He gets two stripers on the break and on his next two shots pockets the three and one. Positioning his stick, Tomato is ripple-brow concentration. Yuji says to me, "Hell, Ben, we know Japanese. We could always go back to Japan."

Tomato looks from his line, rolls a half turn, elbow between random balls. "Turn a sex fiend loose over there?"

Yuji's chalk stops torquing. "Yeah!" He mumbles in revelation. "Yeah! Why not? Didja ever wonder what they're like -- sweet and quiet on the outside?"

For the first time in forty-five minutes the balls are silent. Then Goto says enthusiastically, "The Kibei! Ask 'em! They oughta know about it! They musta got their share!"

To the right of Goto, Muratani's face tilts thirty degrees up from the table. In a whisper he says, "You wanta know? Then go back and find out."

"Ha!" Yuji laughs. "Goes to show he's never had any, either side!"

Asoo stands, shaking his head. A wry disconcerted look comes across his face, and he suddenly bends to the table picking up a line. He squints lower to shoot. The angle of the rapidly dropping afternoon light shines through the front window and over Asoo's back. The optician's eye is reflected on the glass. It stares at Asoo, Yuji, Goto, Tomato -- all of us.

Goto clinches his fists, his knuckles white. "Boy, it's been pretty strange since Pearl Harbor. You see some Hakujin you've known for years, and they're looking at you in a funny way, like they've never really seen you before. Somehow makes you feel responsible for all those planes shot down . . . all those guys killed . . . All of a sudden they make you feel like you're not American."

"Yeah," I say, "and how about Pickens and those guys, organizing into vigilante groups. They're telling everyone if they know of any spies or fifth columnists, it's our duty to turn them in, even if they are Japanese."

"Hell," Goto says, "I'm Japanese, and I never heard about any American Japanese spies until I read about them in the newspapers."

Muratani racks his cue and turns and studies me and Goto. "Why worry about them?" He speaks with a slight accent acquired from several years schooling in Japan. "They are white and easy to understand. They do not like Japanese or trust us. What is not easy to understand are those who are mixed up about loyalty, and they're not white!"

"There are some people or groups who would turn in their own kind."

"You accusing somebody of something?" Yuji asks.

Moriuchi stares tight lipped at Yuji, then turns in my direction. "Gordon Senzaki. Isn't he working for the Sacramento JACL?"

I tighten at the mention of my brother's name, but before I can reply, there is a hissing sound from Tomato. He leans over the table. "Gordie's straight as they come! And anyone's got complaints should take it to him face to face! None of this dingy pool hall gossip!" Tomato glowers and no one says anything.

Yuji breaks the silence, wondering half to himself but loud enough for everybody to hear. "Think they'll lift the ban on us from joining up?" He grunts at the end of his sentence, stabbing the cue into the cream ball. "I was pretty excited about joining up and going overseas to fight the Krauts. But when I get there, they tell me they don't need me. No reasons given. As if I didn't know."

Tomato crushes the cigarette butt under his foot. "Don't be a jerk!" He says, still angry. "No one's gonna let all the Hakujins get knocked off so we'll be the only ones left to breed with!" His hand sweeps through smoky circles of light. "For sure, we're gonna get our chance to meet our quota of 'killed in action!'"

"Saa...yy!" Asoo suggests from a far corner, "How'd you like to fight Boochies instead of the Krauts! Who knows, the first time you take aim," Asoo straightens, sights down the barrel of the cue, and fires, "and squeee ... eeeeeeze off! You might be popping the brains and eyes of an uncle!"

"Your mother's or your father's side?"

Chapter 3

Two Japanese boys sit on the top of a signboard level with the second floor windows of Nihonmachi, surveying the surrounding buffer zone of rooming houses, restaurants, hotels and business establishments that define three borders of our community. The sign is in an empty lot, visible to travelers entering the city on Capitol Avenue from the west. To the east the dome of the state capitol shines white and gold above the century old pines at the end of the avenue. The boys spit and watch their saliva sail into the brown fields. They count box cars in the Southern Pacific yards bordering us to the north. Suddenly feeling the cold, they begin their descent down the front of the billboard, pausing halfway, studying a picture of a Southern Pacific boxcars with a statement in four-foot high letters:

IT TAKES EIGHT TONS OF FREIGHT

TO K.O. ONE JAP

Eight tons seems excessive for Okuma's five-foot-one stature. He always wore black elastic to shorten his sleeves. On January 7, Okuma was arrested and sent to an enemy alien detention center in North Dakota. On February 13, Okuma died of undetermined causes. He would have been buried in a graveyard outside the center, had Father not persisted in his efforts to have Okuma's body returned to Sacramento.

To us, Okuma seemed an unlikely candidate for

arrest during the original roundups of Japanese Americans in December. Although an alien speaking broken English, he considered himself an American. He always hung the American flag in front of his store on Lincoln's birthday, the Fourth of July, and Memorial Day.

In a family photo album, there is a picture of Japanese immigrants newly arrived in San Francisco. Father stands next to Okuma. Both are dressed in knickers and long stockings, tie and vest, and both are from the same prefecture in Japan. They are members of differing social classes: Father is a descendant of a samurai family, and Okuma was the third son of a tenant farmer. They found sudden fellowship and equality in immigration.

Okuma and Father ended up living across the street from each other in Nihonmachi. For the bachelor, Okuma, there was a lonely existence, for he wanted to bring to America a picture bride, but he refused to glorify his life in America. Instead, he waited until he reached the standard of living which he thought suitable for a family man. He was about to begin formal arrangements for his marriage when the passage of the Oriental Exclusion Act abruptly doomed him to a status of permanent bachelorhood. So Okuma, like many others I know, lived alone, in the back of his store, watching twenty years of faces move past his window. I feel sure through his times of difficulty and loneliness, he had memories of rapid swellings of laughter and fulfillment, with his many close friends of Nihonmachi.

Together Father and Okuma had sat on New Years, faces flush with sake, laughing at themselves for all the times they had been foolish. Their sake-lubricated laughter was raucous and loud, with tears running down their cheeks. Father would never again drink sake with Okuma and recall together the thatch-roofed houses and summer fields, terraced and water filled, spilling down the valley between the rolling hills of their birthplaces.

Now Okuma is dead. The day his body is returned to his store, Father decides to move with Mother and Gordie and me from the gray two story house on X Street, surrounded by Sacramento Caucasians, to the apartment above the drug store where he and Mother first lived in Nihonmachi.

Mother and Gordie and I do most of the packing and organizing because Father is too busy trying to clear Okuma's personal matters and arrange his burial in Sacramento in a manner pleasing to his memory and to all who mourn not only Okuma's death, but the slipping away of our whole way of life.

I do not mind the work because it occupies my mind at a time when I have begun to resent the way Okuma died and the treatment of other Issei who were deeply loyal and proud of their adopted country.

The living room is still dark from wall paper long since faded into dusty grays, a contrast to the flowers on the table and mantle. Their deep red, yellow, and green leaves soften the gloom with their odors. The windows at opposite ends of the room filter sunlight on the floor through freshly washed glass. Gordie struggles with the lower end of a large oak desk on the incline of the stairs. Through gritted teeth and flushed face, he mumbles, "Why the hell does he have to have this desk upstairs?"

Oblivious to the commotion of moving, Father stands at the window overlooking the sights, the

smells, and sounds of Fourth Street, a perspective he
has not had since the early years of his immigration.
To his left, the street in four blocks ends on the con-
course of the Southern Pacific depot; directly opposite
is Okuma's store; and to the right, two blocks distant,
the Buddhist church. His eyes linger on the dry goods
store, the fish market, Atsumi's, the mochi shop, the
tofu-ya, and on the church a large maple stripped of
foliage breaks the facade into gnarled branches and
hairline twigs.

A noon hour bell sounds dim through the closed
window, and reminds me of the first time I walked
into the Buddhist church. Children were singing,
"Buddha loves me, this I know...." I wondered why I
was a Christian instead of a Buddhist. When I asked
Mother, there was a long pause as she skillfully
pierced a needle through cloth stretched over round
wooden frames. "There are many reasons," she answered. "But you are still too young to understand. It
is not so important what church you go to as long as
you go."

We have gone to the Bukkyo-kai often, if not for
religious services, then for funerals, marriages, festi-
vals, church league basketball, social dancing, movies,
and once in a freak summer rainstorm we held the Bon
Odori festival indoors. With many elders arrested,
those who remain in the community gather here with
their families for Okuma's funeral.

The long line of Okuma's friends move slowly past
his coffin: Atsumi, Dr. Tsuda, the optometrist; Dr.
Ono, the dentist; the labor contractor, Honda; Goto's
dad, the barber; Taniguchi, the grocer; Tomita,
Tomato's Father; Onishi, a farmer from Florin; Okada
from the pool hall. I recognize some of the farmers,

workers, shop owners from neighboring small towns of Walnut Grove, Courtland, and Locke. They are farmers for whom I have picked pears and peaches during my high school and college summer vacations.

I watch the faces carefully as they pass the coffin. They seem so distant: those who knew him well remember Okuma on a busy Saturday afternoon, his store stocked with Japanese goods. There were wind chimes, vegetable shredders, knives, ohashi, wooden crocks for pickle making, can openers, shamoji, geta, everything for the country people coming to the city for their monthly shopping tours. When his friend Onishi came to town, he was an unimpressive figure in his baggy pants, a short, bow-legged, dark colored farmer. He was among the first pioneers to settle in the Sacramento Valley. He never thought about getting choice land, but took what he could get. When Onishi returned to his old village in Japan for a visit, his seventy acres of America raised his status to wealthy land-owner. He brought his bride back to live for a decade in a wooden shack, on land yellow with shifting sand and wind that blew the topsoil away when it was cultivated. Drought ruined whatever was left. But Onishi and his wife held on through the years and made a successful farm.

Okuma lies supine in a coffin of oak and satin. Father reads his eulogy in rhythmic, undulating Japanese, relating the olden days. Through the dim light and the smell of flowers, I see Okuma and Father --faces crackling with frost in winter, necks browned and leathery in summer--pedaling their way up and down hot roads along the banks of the Sacramento River. They move slowly past farms and fields on bicycles loaded with goods for Japanese farmers and laborers.   Sometimes Father would travel with Okuma, but often times, alone.   When their paths crossed, together they would rest under the shade of a large tree, recalling old stories as the sun beat heat waves around the umbrella of leaves and branches. Then in early evening they would soak themselves red in large deep wooden tubs of scalding water before retiring to the country-sweat-smelling bunkhouses.

After paying their final respects, the crowd moves into the adjoining room, a combination gymnasium, banquet hall, town meeting room.   There, as is the custom among the Japanese, Buddhist and Christian alike, Okuma's funeral ends with a dinner, placing the natural fact of death, the climax of human experience, into the proper perspective for those who must continue life.

Although Mother and several other women did not attend the funeral ceremony because of their work for the dinner, they pay honor to Okuma by their arrangements of the food and flowers.   On Mother's kimono and obi the white of blizzard snow, the pale somberness of winter conifers indicate the season. On the tables the flower arrangements of winter ferns and green and barren branches reflect the stillness of a yet dormant spring.

The partaking of food and drink, the presence of flowers, the kimonos bring death into harmony with nature and the rhythm of the seasons.

The tables are cleared, and a desert, a delicate pink mochi wrapped with cherry leaves, is placed on the tables with pots of green tea.   The fragrance of the leaves permeates the sweet rice dough encircling the dark sweetened beanpaste inside.   Yuji-san has carefully made them in his mochi shop to honor the memory of his friend, Okuma.

The dinner following a funeral is a light-hearted affair, where sorrow is forgotten in food and fellowship and sake. Voices rise in pitch as friends recognize faces they have not seen for some time.

Honda and Onishi and Higa are seated at a table near the center of the room. Noticing their unusually dour looks, Father comes over to sit near them. "How goes things, Higa?" he asks.

"Good," Higa says gloomily into the sake glass.

"He dies of boredom waiting for the peaches and pears," Atsumi says brightly, hoping to make Higa smile.

"The good old days," Higa grunts. "Today, yesterday, tomorrow--what difference? To me they are all same."

"Ah," Father says to Higa, "it is not good to be gloomy. As Buddha says, 'to be gloomy is to fall into dark bottomless well where the light of sunshine becomes smaller as one falls deeper.'"

"To hell with Buddha!" says Higa. "What does anyone know about fruit pickers? Everyone is only interested in eating fruit I have picked. They do not care about 110 degree temperature in shade when I am soaked to drawers! They do not care about peach fuzz and dust itching my neck and back! Have they ever climbed twelve-foot ladders in hot afternoon sun?"

"What do you mean, no one knows about the fruit pickers?" I say. "Don't you remember me tailing behind you with my empty bucket?"

"Oh, hai, hai, Ben, you were always complaining about peach fuzz itching you. I remember when you wanted hot tub. You jumped in and screamed like baby! Water too hot for you Nisei!"

We laugh. I remember my soreness, the urge to plunge into the bathtub. I remember the many Higas: bands of men moving from farm to farm, orchard to orchard, working themselves from dawn to dusk in the blistering heat of summer, moving en masse to Nihonmachi in the winter, turning their hard-earned meager savings over to boardinghouse proprietors to guarantee themselves enough for each winter month's board and room in lieu of a one night gambling disaster in the Tokyo Club.

"The good old days," Onishi says. "It is hard to be cheerful with so many gone. Okuma's dead, but what happened to the rest? What's going to happen to us?"

"Who will be next?" Higa asks.

"It is sure to be Kageyama," Honda says.

Father looks quickly at Honda. "What do you know of such things?"

"It is not what I know. It is what is obvious."

"It is what he has said and written," Onishi says.

"It is more than that," Honda says.

"What do you mean?" Father asks.

"Everyone knows that there are Japanese informers."

"There are enough suspicions already," Father says. "It is not good to add fuel to the fire."

"It is not good to use each other as fuel for the fire," Honda says, "as some people are doing. It is serious matter when JACL cooperates with government . . . by giving names of Japanese."

"That is not true," Father says. "They have been working with the authorities to protect us. To protect this community we have all built together."

"It is strange way of protection," Honda says irritably. "Many of us who have helped build community are gone--arrested by FBI. We do not know why. I don't trust anyone who talks to FBI and government. Who knows what they say?"

"Your thinking is threat to our community," Father says. "We have to keep channels open."

Father takes out a handkerchief and wipes the thin sheet of sweat covering his brow, before taking his gold Elgin from his vest pocket. "It is six o'clock." He taps his drinking glass to get everyone's attention. "It is two hours before curfew," he announces. "We must begin our toasts so those who live far away can leave in time. Do not get picked up by police."

"Do not have flat tire," Honda says, "For flat tire you get sent to detention center in Santa Fe, New Mexico. Hah!" He scoffs at his own sarcasm.

"Not to be gloomy even in joke," Atsumi says.

Father wipes his glasses, handkerchief between thumb and index fingers, rotating carefully until each lens is clear, then places the glasses on his nose, pushing them into position.

"It should be remembered," Father says, "that Sacramento Nihonmachi has been characterized by long established relationships, cooperation, and customs patterned after the prefectures of our homeland." Father pauses. Although he is not tall, he is appopriately dignified in his dark suit. "It would be well to think of Okuma-san as an example of maintaining honor and hard-work for a stronger community."

The room, the setting, the people, the sounds, and smells of Japanese cooking are a curious mixture: two languages; immigrant Issei and citizen Nisei; Japanese kimonos and American suits. The American flag hangs in a cone shape from a stand on one side of the stage. On the other side the blue and gold flag of California hangs, where in better days the flag of the rising sun used to be.

Father speaks in precise, formal Japanese, as he addresses his fellow Issei. They have elected him to his third term as president of the Nihonjinkai. They trust his willingness to help, even when he grows impatient with the inability of some to grasp essentials. Perhaps it is his proficiency in two languages as well as his ability to bridge the gap between the Caucasian world and the Issei that has prevented his arrest. I wonder about his friends who were arrested, and the ones who remain.

Because many Issei believed they would one day return to the old country, they never learned English. Now, when they realize they will never see Japan again, they feel they are too old to learn. Their dream gave them strength and inspiration when they needed it, and sustained them as they built our Nihonmachi.

"I would like to toast the Issei," I say slowly, using my best Japanese, "the men and women who have provided the knowledge and endurance and loyalty that has made our community a successful, law-abiding, harmonious place for all of us to live."

Conversation fades. The toast stirs memories of years of struggle and yearnings to return to familiar customs and landscapes. As they drink in unison, Dr. Ono, the dentist, stands up. "Yes, Ben, and I'd like to thank your dad and all the men who made the Japanese Association work. They helped the new guys find jobs, and hired lawyers to fight land laws. Ever since Ushijima started it in 1908, they've been fighting prejudice. Now there are more than fifty chapters on the West Coast. Let's give old Senzaki-san and all the others a big hand for all they did."

"Thank you." Father clears his throat, visibly moved by the turn of the conversation. "Let us remember those who are not here. They are the true heroes of those years."

Atsumi stands, a serious look on his face. "You have heard story about early Japanese who came here who had only enough money to eat rice balls and umeboshi. Then he does not even have enough left for that, so he rolls umeboshi pits from one side of mouth to other for weeks while he works long hours in fields."

Higa brightens at one of the Issei's favorite stories of the hardships of pioneering. "I propose toast to man of the 'umeboshi pits!'"

"And a toast to the swindlers," Onishi shouts out, his glass pointing to the ceiling.

"Swindlers?" Honda asks.

"You did not come with us," Onishi says to Honda, "so you do not know swindlers. They sold us bridges and fields underwater or on mountain tops."

"Hai! Hai! And to those who sold us rubber boots. Boxes full. Big enough for giants."

"And donkey and pick axe and gold pan."

"And *Encyclopedia Britannica*," Atsumi laughs, "For all of us who cannot even read English."

"Fox hunting outfits! Do you remember?" asks Father , his face a bright glow.

"Red and white fox hunting clothes," Onishi says loudly. "Black boots, black cap and riding whip Okuma-san, Senzaki-san, Atsumi-san. They are very silly looking in bright new English fox hunting clothes, riding acoss San Joaquin Valley!"

Chapter 4

Monday as the beginning of the week, Sunday and Saturday as leisure time no longer have significance. Each week fades into one continuous motion without beginning or end. We would like to crank everything backwards or make the cycle stop for a short while. When we have the courage to look carefully, we know nothing is getting better. Rumors spread like flames on a windy, dry field. No one questions their origin or validity. It is said the farmers in Tulare County are lynching Japanese. It is rumored a law will be passed in Congress stripping all Japanese Americans of their birthrights.

The mayors, the police chiefs, the attorney general of California begin making statements against our loyalty. City councils and county supervisors pass restrictive ordinances, and petition Congress to enact legislation against the Japanese. The military press releases pour out, rating us as potential subversives, fifth columnists, and saboteurs.

Finally, the Governor calls a meeting with concerned and prominent Japanese to discuss the "Japanese problem."

The Governor stands almost a head taller than most of the Japanese in the room--doctors, lawyers, farmers, ministers, and Gordie, Dad, Kageyama and I. He begins, "I am here not only to express my views as a representative of the majority of Californians, but as your representative also, to hear your ideas and suggestions which you may want to offer for solving our present crisis. We hope we can come up with a plan, mutually agreed upon, which would enable us as loyal Americans to contribute our share towards winning the war."

Kageyama's face flushes as the Governor unrolls a map of California. The state is divided into zones, red for restricted, blue for free, and yellow for agricultural camps to concentrate Japanese Americans for the duration of the war. "These work camps could be set up under armed guard, for the welfare and protection of the Japanese from possible vigilante activities. The community would remain intact and share in the winning of the war. With your consent and willing cooperation, it would silence once and for all the loud minority who question your loyalty."

"PREPOSTEROUS!" Kageyama booms from the back of the room.

Startled eyes turn to Kageyama. He stands redfaced and angry. "You are suggesting we go to slave labor camps? Preposterous!"

I feel relief and shock hearing Kageyama shout at the Governor. He looks in disbelief at Kageyama. His voice is drained of friendliness and warmth.

"Slave labor camps," he repeats slowly. "Nothing of the sort. If I am correct, I believe most of the men assembled here would be willing to evacuate without protest if ordered to do so."

"They have said nothing. You cannot assume they would be willing to take their families behind barbed wire and machine guns," Kageyama says.

"The program we propose would eliminate any military involvement," the Governor says, "and give you people a chance to control your own destinies."

"We control our own destinies now. We are Americans like you!" Kageyama shouts. The room is stunned into silence.

We are ushered into the FBI office. The head agent, a Mr. Olson, asks Father for his alien registration. He looks it over carefully, then hands it back and motions for us to be seated. On his desk is a copy of the *Mainichi Times,* the latest issue containing Kageyama's article. The agent picks it up and asks Father, "What do you know about this editorial written by this man, Kageyama?"

"I am the publisher of the *Mainichi Times,* and owner and I have final say on matters of editorial policy."

"You knew what this man was saying and yet you decided to print it?"

"Yes."

"Why?"

"Why?" Father looks at the article.

"My father spent many hours debating whether to print it or not," I answer.

"Because it is my responsibility," Father says.

"Your responsibility?"

"In a democracy it is important for all views to be heard."

I notice a slight glimmer in the agent's eyes, as he is informed by an "enemy alien" about democracy.

"In time of world war?"

"I believe in this country and the freedom it stands for. It is what protects me."

"This man, Kageyama. You know him well?"

"Yes, he is my wife's cousin."

"Is this the same man who insulted the Governor of California?"

"I do not understand."

"At the governor's meeting for Japanese community leaders, a man stood up and called the governor's proposed agricultural labor camps 'slave labor camps.' Is Kageyama this same man?"

"Yes"

"Does he have any political ties to Japan, to the Emperor of Japan?"

"He does not care the least about the politics of Japan nor the Emperor." Father answers. "I have never heard him talk about anything but democracy! He is an American citizen and a veteran of World War I, and very proud of it!"

The agent questions Father about Kageyama's beliefs, his relatives in Japan, his financial interests in Japan.

"I think we need to consider the ties to the old country in the sense that all Americans were at one time or another aliens in a foreign land," I say. "We are not yet even one generation removed from Japan. We are inexricably interwoven with all aspects of Japanese life. It is the same for all those who have come from another country to search for the promise of America." I see Father wishes I had not spoken.

When the questioning is finished, the FBI agent says to Father, "There is a world war going on. It is a time for discretion, not a time to carelessly express your political views and opinions. It would be wise for you to desist printing anything inflammatory that would raise questions about your loyalty."

Father answers, "No, no, there will not be any more such articles."

Back in the car, Father says, "Drop me off at the office and go immediately to Florin to tell Kageyama what has happened. I think he should be ready to leave.

He is going to be arrested soon."

I drive south along the Sacramento River until I get to Florin Road, then head due east for several miles. In the countryside, I feel the contrasts of city and rural life and remember how much I have always enjoyed escaping to the fields lined with neat rows of vine, the contours of rich black soil.

As I enter Florin, I can see the center of town where railroad tracks and country road intersect, the dirt road bumping across tracks through a grove of eucalyptus and emerging once more into cultivated fields. The town, unchanged from decades past, is built on both sides of the road and both sides of the tracks. Within its half mile there are all the necessities of a Japanese community: Ishikawa's general merchandise store, a fish market, a tofu-ya, a red-white-and-blue striped barber pole in front of a barber shop, a garage, a feed and seed store, a boardinghouse, and a restaurant.

It is a very small western town of Orientals, a foothold for many Japanese farmers in the San Joaquin Valley. This is where Father and Mother became farmers for the first two years of their immigrant lives, and later it became a stop on Father's bicycle pharmacy business.

Some say the Kageyamas were the first Japanese to settle here. Others claim there were Issei pioneers who settled here on their way to the Gold Hill Silk Colony in the 1870's. Through the grove of towering trees, I watch the town disappear in the rear view mirror.

Beyond the trees there is no direct sun, but an overcast light reflecting off water trapped in holes and ruts. Soon the half dried mud will be transformed to fine summer dust browning a pale sky.

The Kageyama house is a mile past Florin, set at the end of a narrow road. It is a quarter mile off the highway, flanked by gnarled grape vines. The green foliage smells like spring. When I drive up to the house, I know Obasan is watching me. Now in her seventies, she has become over the years, a grandparent surrogate to Gordie and me. She always wears a simple cotton print dress with her silver hair tied in a bun behind her head. Her warm smile sends me back to all the family gatherings that have taken place here, and the decades before when Father was still a young man on his bicycle, delivering aspirins, band aids, iodine, and cough medicines.

We exchange bows. She asks about Mother and Father. Always I am struck by her -- she seems an anachronism--an elderly Japanese woman, small and delicate, yet strong and resilient like bamboo. After fifty years in this country, she speaks no English and bows as if she still lives in Japan. Framed by the front porch of her square white farm house, she looks to me a perfect mixture of rural American and rural Japanese.

I ask for Kageyama. She nods to the barn, where he is loading crates. When Kageyama sees me, he stops and smiles. Around his eyes there are gentle lines, furrowed by hot suns; the corners crinkle when he smiles.

"This is pleasant surprise," Kageyama says. "When I heard the car up the road, I couldn't imagine who would be coming. What brings you?"

"Not good news." I say. I look up at the wooden crates stacked six high on the truck bed.

He follows my eyes and before I can reply further, he says, "If you don't mind, I'll finish loading while we talk."

"Please. Maybe I can help." I grab some crates and begin stacking.

"I enjoy physical work," he says. "I don't have to do this now if I choose not to, but I cannot sit around idly wondering what's going to happen." He speaks in a matter of fact way with the same candor he showed at the governor's meeting.

I can smell the sweat of the man. His muscles are still rock hard, his face and arms are dark, a healthy out door tone even in winter. In the rhythmic swing of lifting and swaying, the boxes slide easily and swiftly from stack to stack.

"I hope I'm in as good condition as you when I'm fifty!" I shout.

"I've been doing this long time. You city guys don't get much practice. I was gone for few years when I was in army in Europe, and few years when I tried being navigator on fishing boat. But I came back. I guess this is where I belong."

When the truck is loaded to capacity, Kageyama threads two lines on opposite sides through hooks and cinches them tight. When he finishes lashing, he motions me to get into the truck. "Come with me. It's a beautiful day."

"I'd love to." I climb into the old model T flat-bed. It coughs and sputters to life, crawls slowly into motion drowning out our voices in the uproar.

"I haven't been around these fields for a long time. They're beautiful." I shout.

Above the noise he calls out, "When Dad came here, he used to say, 'You should see land then--barren--like waste land.' I often wondered what men like Dad and others saw in it. Maybe they saw nothing except chance to own land. I guess that's what it was."

I can feel every bump in the road. I hang on to keep from bouncing and hitting my head on the roof. Dusty roof, dusty seats, dusty truck: the dust is part of living and working out here.

I strain to listen to his voice above the sound of the engine. "The early Japanese took what land they could get," I say.

"It was worthless to anyone else or they wouldn't have sold it to us. When other Japanese heard about it they followed and pretty soon it is all Japanese community. They pooled everything to survive: money, seed, equipment, muscles. They didn't give up easily," he adds.

Mesmerized by the sounds and smells, by the whirring of the engine, Kageyama falls into a reverie of the past. The long rows fly by as if we were sitting stationary in the center of a long brown spoked pinwheel. He shouts, "I think he loved this land...I understand him now."

He slows the truck and pulls up under a roofed field shed. He gets out, unties the ropes, climbs onto the back and begins to hand crates down to me. We work silently, until he pauses, taking a red handkerchief out to wipe away sweat from his brows. He motions for me to sit beside him on the seat. Breathing heavily, he says, "We had to be different out here. Had to gamble and try different ideas so we could survive. One year we tried grapes. They had never grown here, but we had to try something new. It worked and pretty soon grapes began to be regular part of crops. One year we tried to grow strawberries between rows of grape vines. People laughed. They thought we were crazy. But after two years of failure, that worked too. Inch by inch we brought this land to life. Now look at it. It's valuable land. There's lots of people who would like to buy this land...or take it away," Kageyama pauses. "Of course, you didn't come to listen to me ramble on about early days."

"I enjoy hearing what you have to say."

He nods and waits for me to go on.

"The FBI. They called Dad and me for an interview at their office."

"They were asking about me?"

"Yes. Because of the editorial. Father thinks you will be arrested soon. He says you should pack and be ready to go."

"He is right. They will come. Many have been arrested who have said nothing. I was very outspoken. But I have right to speak up. I am American citizen."

As we drive back to the barn, he asks, "Do you understand Japanese people?"

I remain silent. He looks questioningly at me. "Of course you are Japanese and so you understand. But that does not always mean you really understand."

"It is possible," I answer, not committing myself.

"That is good you are cautious. Of course you do not understand what I am saying. What I did at governor's office is not like Japanese, not like myself. I do not wish to cause trouble, to question authority. So you may wonder why I am acting as I am."

I nod.

"If a man believes as I do, he should sacrifice. But to ask a man for sacrifice for half truths and lies? I cannot submit."

"But maybe the Governor is right when he says he has a responsibility to everyone. And he has information from police departments, FBI, military. Do you think it is possible there is some truth to all the rumors?"

"Truth? What is truth at time like this? Why do you talk like that to me? You think I lie? Everything was calm until newspapers and radio began to call us disloyal. Japanese live near waterways, power lines, assembly plants, highways. They had to take land no one wanted. Left-overs. Is that truth to you? And Mother...we must plan for her. She will be able to stay with you?"

"Yes, we have prepared for her," I reply, still trying to keep up with the conversation.

"My mother? The Issei? Dangerous? That is very funny. Of course she still loves old country. She has sentimental memories of childhood. That is being human. But they ignore her age and say she can't be trusted. Do you believe my mother is spy? What about your father? Is he spy? Are you spy if governor or FBI says you are?"

"No," I say. I suddenly feel incongruous. Bumping in a dusty truck along a small country road, talking with Kageyama about freedom. He looks like so many others, bending over strawberry plants, cutting lettuce with flat-blade knives under sun and heat so intense I know I could give them twenty years and still not match their endurance and stamina. And here is one of them telling me about government and my responsibilities.

"I wanted to go to college...but I didn't make it. But man does not have to go to college to become educated. I have studied much history and government. I marvel at democratic system. Yet, you and I both know Orientals are the only people in this country who can't become citizens. Man's laws are not always just. So we can't just obey blindly. When there is injustice, we must stand up against it. Do you understand?"

"Yes I do. But maybe I don't have your guts. Maybe the system will still rescue us."

"You mean Tolan hearings?" Kageyama asks.

"It is a place we can express our views."

"Don't get your hopes too high. It is also place for

those against us to speak up."

"We are innocent. We must be proven guilty."

Kageyama breathes deeply. "If there is one thing I have learned studying history, it is this: injustice breeds injustice."

"Come," Kageyama says, getting out of the truck. At the barn door he stops and says, "Ben, this may be last time I will see you for long time. They will come soon and take me to North Dakota or Crystal City. There will be need of strong voice for Japanese. When time comes, you must speak up."

He looks back across the fields he has tilled with his father, at long perfectly straight lines of brown and green, now quiet under an overcast that swallows shadows and deepens the stillness.

Chapter 5

I try to define the enemy: a group of men, an organization or many organizations. Is it an attitude, a system, or a tradition? The years I've studied American government and international law have left me with a strong faith in our system. I have attributed the discriminatory laws to the growing pains of a young country, minimizing the pain of the Issei who were never allowed their citizenship. Yet why has the Commander of the Western Defense become so powerful? He says our inherent subversive tendencies justify putting us in camps. Even in time of war we are innocent until proven guilty.

The arrest of Kageyama, an American citizen by birth, takes away my hope for the guarantee of our constitutional rights.

On the morning of his arrest, Mother receives a phone call from Obasan, saying she is ready to come. Two FBI agents arrived earlier and took him away. Kageyama had not resisted. He had left with dignity. He had shaken off the hands of the agents, walked quickly to the car and was driven off. Now she is alone for the first time since she came to America.

As we finish breakfast, Mother instructs us to go to Obasan's. "It is not good to leave her alone. Help her bring a few things now and leave the rest until later. We can all go together another time to help her finish."

The bell to the drug store rings and Mother disappears quickly downstairs. She returns with Mrs. Onishi who has come to inquire about Obasan, her closest friend from the early days in Florin. They chatter in rapid-fire Japanese, their conversation animated by gestures and undulations in their voices.

"Mother, did Obasan ever tell you about her younger years, when she came here? Weren't you close to her when you came to America with Dad?"

"Oh, yes, she became like my own mother. I am sure she could see me upset and struggling to adjust, just as in her early pioneer days. She wanted to help me feel welcome and secure. If it weren't for her, I don't think I could have made it. But Mrs. Onishi knows about Obasan's early years. She was struggling right along with her."

"Hai, hai," Mrs. Onishi nods. "When they first bought their land, their water pump brought up only muddy water, so they had to walk all the way to our farm for clear water. Obasan was a strong young woman, but she was not ready for heavy farm work."

"Yes," Mother adds. "When she finished her schooling in Japan, her parents arranged her marriage. She saw her husband only once before they were married. Three months later he was gone to America. He was still a stranger. He didn't even know he was to be a father."

"She was like all of us. She was romantic, stubborn. She wouldn't listen to any warnings about the hardship in the United States. I met Onishi-san for only short time before we married. But at least I was not picture bride like Mrs. Goto."

"Did she tell you what her first impressions were like?" I ask.

"Oh yes," Mrs. Onishi says. "Her voyage was easy because it was midsummer. She said she was so excited when she first saw San Francisco she held her baby up high so he could see land in which he would grow up. She searched the crowd on shore for face of her husband, trying to remember his features. She said she was so nervous she talked to her baby as an adult. When they met, Kageyama-san was very happy to see her and his new son. They brought him hope after a year of troubles. The men who never married suffered alone, like Okuma-san."

"They arrived at the old Yoshino farm, South of Walnut Grove, in mid August. She was told she would have to begin her job at four A.M. the next day, cooking for the six other laborers and working in the fields the rest of the time," Mother says.

"They made it so hard for her." Mrs. Onishi says. "I didn't have so much trouble my first days here. Her baby was crying all the time. She was so upset she just cried with her baby as she worked in the fields, thinning plants, pulling weeds, in August sun."

"How could she keep going?" I ask. "How could she do it?"

"She was like me," Mrs. Onishi says. "Keep dreaming of returning to Japan. Keep remembering old life. Keep hoping for change in future."

"That is right, Ben. We kept hoping and dreaming. We made ourselves do what we knew we had to do. We were tired all the time. But there was always something to look forward to."

"Kageyamas worked hard for the Yoshino's until they had saved enough together with a loan from the family in Japan to buy their own land, 12 acres, for $750. Kageyama made a small barrack. No floor. We had same thing. After two years, can afford floor, better roof. One thing at a time," Mrs. Onishi says.

"Why was Kageyama-san so hard on Obasan?" I ask.

"He wasn't, any more than other pioneer men. If they were going to make it, they had to have wife work hard as partner. I think they had a good marriage."

"Hai, hai," Mrs. Onishi says slowly. "Many women suffered when they could not make good marriage. Especially picture brides. We were fortunate, Obasan and I. Husband and wife work side by side. Share disappointments. Share happy times. Always together. It was very sad time for her when he died."

Suddenly remembering the time, Mother says, "Do not keep Obasan waiting."

"I'll drive," Gordie says, taking the car keys. For several miles, he drives grim-faced, in silence.

By this time he has become fully involved with the Japanese American Citizens League. When there were rumors men and women and children would be separated, JACL conferred with officials to keep families together and to reduce military activity in the actual evacuation of people from their homes.

"Ben," he says finally, "what do you think about Kageyama? You think he should have kept his mouth shut?"

"I think he believed it was his responsibility to speak up."

"But was it smart? He knew he was inviting trouble"

"He said he couldn't blindly accept people exploiting the system to put us in camps."

"What do you mean?"

"I think he feels his arrest is only the beginning. He cleared his own conscience by doing what he could to prevent injustice."

"Does he think he's the only one with a responsible

conscience?" Gordie asks belligerently.

"You've got him figured wrong. He thinks he's right, but I've never heard him criticize others' actions."

"You think he's right?"

"It's possible."

"Yeah."

"There may be truth to what he says," Gordie says after a long silence, "but we better cope realistically, by cooperating. We can't stand against the whole damned U.S. Army."

"We have been cooperating. Unless there's reciprocal cooperation, the effort is meaningless. We can't buy food; people are evicted from homes; people lose jobs; people are arrested, jailed without proper charges."

"That's what I'm saying," Gordie argues. "Our choice is limited. If not cooperatively, then at gunpoint and bloodshed."

As we enter Florin, Gordie slows down in front of the white church with the colored glass windows. "Lots of good memories about that place," he says in a soft voice. "Remember the time Kageyama volunteered to sing at the Christmas program and no one could talk him out of it? Oh that off-key voice! That was a great time!"

"Yeah, he still acts so innocent about it."

As we bump over the tracks, Gordie says, "Maybe in some ways Kageyama is right. If we don't let people know how we feel, they'll think we feel the camps are all right. In the right setting, maybe we could speak up."

"You're thinking about the Tolan hearings?"

"Yeah. It's open to anyone. I know a lot of JACL people from other cities who are appearing."

"How do you know it's not a kangaroo court?"

"I don't. But still sounds like a good chance to let

our views be heard."

"We don't have anything to lose."

"I could represent myself as a committee chairman of the Sacramento JACL. Would you come with me as my legal counsel?"

"Okay, but let's get someone outside the family to go with us."

"How about Asoo? He's got a sociology background, expresses ideas well."

"Tomato."

"Tomato?" Gordie asks skeptically. "Why him instead of Asoo?"

"Tomato doesn't have the education that we do, but he's got a mind like a steel trap."

"You're right. He's always acting funny, but he comes back lightning fast. And what a memory!" Gordie agrees. "I think he's our man."

As we drive up to the white farmhouse, Obasan does not come out on the porch as she had done the last time. We walk up the front steps, and through the window we see white sheets and blankets covering the furniture. We walk through the house to find Obasan sitting in the kitchen, drinking tea. She is startled when we come in. Embarrassed, she jumps up to greet us, bowing her head slightly. She smiles politely, but without the warmth we have always felt from her. She is dressed in a formal grey suit with puffed shoulders and a skirt that hangs almost to her ankles. Surrounded by boxes and a suitcase, she seems out of place in her kitchen of thirty years.

"Hello, Obasan," Gordie says awkwardly, trying to act as if everything was normal.

There are tears in her eyes. She nods and says, "I'm ready to go with you." She rinses the tea cup, and gingerly places an old dark blue straw hat over her bun.

"Okay, Obasan," I say, "We'll take these boxes and your suitcase for you. We can come back later to do any more packing that needs to be done."

She takes her final tour through the house. Here she lived with her husband, her son, Masahiro, and her first-born son, Isao, who perished in an accident at the age of ten. She once told Mother that it was Isao with his happy and friendly disposition who helped them survive those early years in America.

Gordie and I take the few boxes and suitcases and load them in the car. When we return, she tells us to drive without her to the main road and wait for her there.

We do as she asks. After ten minutes we see Obasan's head above the grape vines moving along the dirt road from the house. Then we see her walking toward us down the country road. She is dwarfed by the fields, almost motionless on a long ribbon of brown dirt with telephone poles and electrical lines disappearing into a point on the horizon.

Chapter 6

Fifteen years ago I walked into my first American school knowing no more English than I had learned in a month of studying from a primary reader.

There is foreboding in that memory as now winter skies disappear behind banks of fog. Sounds of moisture move earthward through leaves and branches. The wetness drives the cold through my clothing

Riding in the car to San Francisco where the Tolan Committee hearings are being held, I feel the same uncertainties. Tomato and Gordie and I are to appear before members of Congress to give our views of the "Japanese problem."

We speak few words on the long ride. Dad and Gordie had argued before we left. Dad feels uneasy that only Nisei have represented the Japanese community at the Tolan hearings.

The war forces us to differentiate between our generations, yet we are lumped together as enemies. Because there are differences in language and culture and age, each generation faces a question of national identity. The first generation Issei have maintained a stable and coherent community in the face of severe racial discrimination. The Nisei, who are young and impatient, live with the ways of the Issei, but they want to break away and become fully American.

After fifteen years living in America, I am still trying to understand the ways of the Nisei. Why are we being so cooperative in the face of accusations we know to be untrue? Is it our nature to overlook insults, or do we actually believe what they are saying is true? Would we behave the same way in Japan? Gordie epitomizes the new Japanese American citizen, born and raised by kind, decent people, setting aside the obvious parts of the Issei culture, yet keeping an intrinsic part of the stable, traditional values of Japan. He knows the camps are unconstitutional, yet he's been taught to respect authority.

The Federal Building is a style of architecture I have learned to associate with government functions: the fluted columns are ponderous and oversized; inside, the corridors are long and sterile. I watch Gordie, looking rather unnatural in a big-shouldered gray gaberdine suit, walk down the corridor to the hearing room. He's aggressive, earnest, impetuous and strong willed. He's outspoken about the evacuation, yet he's conciliatory, perhaps unable to believe the country of his birth would ever take away his rights.

He stands next to an American flag and looks at a poster of warships and planes and foot soldiers slogging through mud. It says in bold, black print:

IF YOU CAN'T FIGHT . . . BUY BONDS!

BUY BONDS FOR PLANES, GUNS, TANKS, SHIPS!

BONDS FOR VICTORY!

Banker' Trust Company
New York

He is mesmerized by the poster and I am mesmerized watching him, until Tomato moves alongside him:

"If you can't fight, buy bodies!

Buy bodies for planes, guns, tanks, ships!

Bodies for victory!

Bodies Trust Company"

"Never miss a chance, do you!" I say. Gordie and I break out of our nervous silence, and our laughter echoes through the corridors.

There is no life, no animation, no expression of hope or dismay in the faces assembled in the high ceilinged hearing room. Over a hundred Japanese people sit in isolated silence, staring transfixed at the white faces, talking and moving about on the hearing floor.

I listen to the murmur of voices behind the railing: These are the men who will decide our fate. They have never known Japanese, and they have never been in Japanese American communities. We will rise and be heard. We will protest and defend what lies below the color of our skin. But it will not be for us to say. They will bring witnesses to discuss all aspects of our lives, our personalities, our ways of behavior.

"It seems strange to us," says California Attorney General, Earl Warren, "...that airplane manufacturing plants should be entirely surrounded by Japanese land occupancies. It seems to us that it is more than circumstance that after certain government air bases were established, Japanese undertook farming operations in close proximity to them. You can hardly grow a jackrabbit in some of the places where they presume to be carrying on farming operations close to an army bombing base.

"Many of our vital facilities, and most of our highways are just pocketed by Japanese ownerships that could be of untold danger to us in time of stress.

"So we believe, gentlemen, that it would be wise for the military to take every protective measure that it believes is necessary to protect this state and this nation against the possible activities of these people."

When Tomato is called to the stand, there is a smooth rubber surface to his face, pliable and relaxed, easily contorted to any configuration appropriate to the circumstance. From the raised podium where the congressmen look down upon the witnesses, I think Tomato must look squattier than a normal size yellow fireplug, dressed in his plaid sport coat and shiny beige pants and oxfords. His flat-nosed smile could jar any Caucasian.

They ask him to state his name, age, religion, occupation, although they have all of these facts on papers before them.

"And your occupation?"

"A spoiled fruits and vegetable separator in a cannery!"

"Many important defense installations were found to be surrounded by Japanese. Do you think this is by accident or design?"

Tomato shrugs. "If sabotage were planned, I don't think that would be a very intelligent way to go about it."

"What do you mean?"

For half a minute, Tomato looks directly at the congressman. "Well, I guess, the last thing would be to have me do sabotage. How about if someone with black hair, slanty eyes, and this body build was caught sneaking around..." Tomato points to his face, "I think I would look pretty suspicious."

When I hear the hawk-nosed congressman from

Alabama suddenly laugh, I feel a hatred for him, for his long drawl. "The nation must decide and Congress must gravely consider, as a matter . . ." He pauses to give the matter thought, then leans forward, his early morning cologne turning an earthy sweat, and says, "and it all comes down to a single word, loyalty. Who's loyal and who's not. And herein lies the difficulty, in that we do not know who the subversive elements are. We can't tell the 'good Japs' from the 'fifth columnists.'"

I feel a flush of blood rising, and from the corner of my eye I see it on Gordie's face too.

Gordie stirs uneasily, "The science of sabotage! How could they be talking about us?"

Gordie stands, asks to be heard, and is granted permission. "Before any judgement is made regarding the loyalty of the Japanese American people, there are certain facts we feel you should be aware of. We are being accused of being disloyal in the newspapers, on the radio, at these hearings and from official sources. We resent these accusations, and we deny their validity."

"People have implied we are more loyal to Japan than to the United States because we are the same race," Gordie says. "Two-thirds of our people were born, raised, and educated here. We think, feel, and act like Americans."

Until now I have avoided looking carefully at the three men conducting the hearing. As they concentrate on Gordie and his statement, I study each of the faces: carvings from wood, lifeless, a certain sameness perhaps from eating wheaties or kix 365 days a year, thumbing through catalogues, and getting plump on chicken fried steak and scalloped potatoes. I cannot distinguish one from the other. The lines that droop from the nose, the hair lines that recede from a face of double chins and layers of skin all look the same.

"America is made up of people from many countries," Gordie says. "Japanese Americans are no different from any other immigrants. We are outraged at the attack on Pearl Harbor. We realize the aggressor must be crushed. We want to participate in the struggle.

"In this emergency, as in the past, we are not asking for special privileges or concessions. We ask only to be treated as fairly as any other Americans. We are law-abiding citizens. Whatever is decided upon in 'Due Process of Law,' in order to secure the safety and welfare of this nation, we will abide by." Gordie sits down.

"Thankyou, Mr. Senzaki, we appreciate your coming and making this statement to our committee."

Through the largest window there is dampness-- deep greens, wet blacks, saturated browns half lost in shadows and shade. It is unnerving to feel we make no impact. Gordie is especially perplexed after the mornings' descriptions of us; these he had never heard before. "It would be bad fiction if it were written in a book!" he says.

At lunch he says nothing. He cannot find the stomach to eat. He swirls mashed potatoes with his fork, in bewilderment. What we have learned about this country in school is not consistent with what we have experienced this morning.

"It would be easy enough to believe we pose a threat, if you are not Japanese," he says. "We live in a several-block ghetto where most people speak a foreign language, eat different kinds of food, bathe in community tubs, worship a Buddha, read books and magazines in Japanese scribble."

He plays with his food a while longer. "All my life I've lived here. In the past two months I've heard more about our differences, why we live where we live, descriptions of our racial tendencies, than I ever heard in twenty-five years."

"Well," Tomato says, "speaking of racial tendencies how come it is that people from the same regions look alike? I don't mean shapes of heads, eye color, but squints, pinched skin, lips that press together kinda hard and rigid like a man would be if he looked into a wind too long."

"You mean amount of exposure to the sun, geographic areas, genes?" I ask.

"Okay, I heard all that before -- even studied it. What I mean is what's ticking up here." He points his finger to his head. "It seems to me a man's *thinking* has to do with the way he ends up *looking*. Especially the guy from Alabama. Now I never seen too many of those southern jokers, but after seeing this guy, I know what they all look like. And what about those other two from Illinois and Nebraskie? One's medium fat, the other's roly-poly, but aside from the builds and different faces, you can hardly tell them apart—like they were identical disparate twins!"

"You got to be kidding," I laugh. "Disparate twins? Strange things to be thinking about on a day like this. You trying to keep yourself loose?"

"Me?" Tomato asks, as he thumps his fist into his chest. "The number one catcher of the ex-state champs? How many times did I make you a hero? Didn't you see me perform this morning? This face is like rubber. It bends instead of chipping and cracking. It stretches into the right shape when the pressure's on!"

"Speaking of pressure. I didn't get the impression the Attorney General was very sympathetic, did you?" asks Gordie.

"Not exactly. His logic is not very reassuring."

By the time I am called, the afternoon has become dull and perverse, a pale dye of sweaty faces, creased with weariness, irritation, desire for the day to end.

We are seated against the back wall. As I stand up, Tomato nudges me. "I have this feeling," he whispers, "that I'm a fetus struggling to get outa a womb some joker's filled with molasses."

The members of the committee study me with varying degrees of skepticism. The congressman from Illinois runs his right hand down the back of his head as he looks over my statistics and says in an almost obsequious voice, "You understand we must take all things into consideration." There is no jolly fat-man tone in his voice now. "We have been sent to talk to people up and down the West Coast in order to make recommendations for Washington." Two clefted shadows watch me from behind metallic rimmed glasses. "Your brother made the statement that you people resent the accusations of disloyalty. Well, what do you have to say about the performance of your people in Hawaii?"

"I beg your pardon."

"Your people in Hawaii. Did they comport themselves in a manner loyal to this country? Cars and farm trucks blocking the main roadways and intersections to airfields and military installations. Signs visible from the air. Arrows were hidden in pineapple fields as targets for the pilots. Are you aware of these things?"

"I am not," I answer. "Nor am I willing to accept yet that such acts did take place. There has been a great deal of turmoil in Hawaii, and until such accusations can be authenticated, I am not willing to make a wholesale condemnation against all Japanese."

"The report of the sabotage was from the secretary

of Navy," retorts the Illinois congressman. "Do you mean to tell us that you know something he does not?"

There is obvious sarcasm in his last sentence. I lower my voice and remove the tinge of anger. "I do not claim to know more than the secretary of Navy. However, I am a lawyer. Basic to our whole system of justice is the premise that a man is innocent until proven guilty. Outside of the report there is no substantiation that such acts did take place. You are accusing us on the basis of guilt by association. Your premise would never stand up in a court of law."

I hear my heart pounding against my ribs. I fight to gain control. Gradually, I hear the normal noises of shuffling and coughs. Out of the corner of my eye I see Tomato slumped in a chair, watching me.

I continue, "It has become the custom during the past few months to refer to anything the enemy has done as acts 'by your people.' Covert insinuations of guilt."

"Your brother has stated he would cooperate in the event evacuation is deemed necessary by the military. He said he would be willing to make sacrifices for the defense of the nation. Are you willing to cooperate?"

"I think sending all the Japanese of the West Coast into camps is ridiculous. It would be a violation of everything we have been taught about constitutional rights."

"Ridiculous! Perhaps you are forgetting if the war is lost, there will be no constitutional rights for anyone."

"I am familiar with your reasoning. It was recently used to incarcerate a relative of mine, a citizen, a veteran of World War I, as patriotic and loyal as any of you."

"If he was loyal, why was he arrested?"

"We are subject to suspicion because we are Japanese first and American second. We have committed no acts of sabotage; we are therefore suspected of planning a surprise attack. Because we are at war with Japan, we dare not speak against the movement to put us into concentration camps!"

"Concentration camps!" Congressman Wells says. "Nothing of the sort: a place of safety for the Japanese. Safe from suspicion and safe from vigilantism." He glares at me. "It would be wise, young man, for you to be careful. Do not make things any more difficult for you people."

"You people!" Tomato says as he stands up. "How come you always refer to us as 'you people?'"

"Well, Mr. Tomita," the congressman from Alabama says, "Are you willing to cooperate if you are asked to do so?"

"Wait a minute. Hold on!" Tomato bursts out. "I don't wanta end up in any camp! That's why I came here!"

Chapter 7

Where there once was the "big eye," there is now a black patch covering an empty socket: Dr. Tsuda has boarded over his optometry shop. Asoo's rooming house, Atsumi's musical instrument and electrical appliance store, the fish market, and the pool hall are all boarded up. On the telephone poles that string together Nihonmachi there are large white posters announcing in bold black letters the final instructions for an involuntary evacuation of Japanese Ameircans. They say:

THE WESTERN DEFENSE COMMAND

AND

FOURTH ARMY CIVIL CONTROL ADMINISTRATION

Instructs all persons of Japanese ancestry living in the following area . . . .

We play poker in the store room behind Yuji's father's Mochi Shop. We come in through the door off the alley where the sky is darkening. Sounds of the unemployed seep in. I hear farm workers heading to the Tokyo Club to gamble as if they were not broke, as if they were only waiting for spring strawberries to begin. Outside the Tokyo Club, there is a strange lifelessness to Fourth Street. The shops have all been picked clean by the vultures who swarmed our community like locusts, buying bargain sewing machines, washers, property, life investment inventories.

The store room is empty except for half a dozen boxes filled with mochi making tools stacked against a wall and a round table covered with a blanket. Over it hangs a hooded light. Like the unemployed patrons of the Tokyo Club, we gamble, but between old friends we pay a dime to the dollar. Someone has taken one of the Western Defense Command posters and hung it in the storeroom. Tomato breaks out a new pack of Bees and the blue, white and red chips are distributed.

Tomato follows my gaze to the poster and reads aloud, "Western Defense Command and Fourth Army . . .'" and tails off into "pheeewwweeey! That's one hell of a big organization to have going against you, ain't it?"

"Well, you know the old saying," Yuji breaks in, "if you can't beat 'em you can always join 'em."

"Except if you're a Jap," Asoo amends, deliberately contorting his face. His gold-rimmed glasses give him a sinister Oriental look.

"We're joining them any way you look at it," To--mato comments as he shuffles.

"What'd you suppose would happen," Asoo asks, "if we had decided not to go? Think they'd gun us down -- women and children and old people?"

"Naw! Not in a million years," Yuji says. "America ain't like that."

"We'll never know," Tomato says, setting the deck down for a cut.

Gordie studies Tomato's face. "What you trying to say, Tomato?"

"I'm just saying we'll never know 'cause we went along with it all."

"Right," Gordie says, "or maybe we could have gone

the way Kageyama went. And ended up where we're headed anyway, except with our families split up. What the hell'd he get by resisting -- except an enemy alien detention center?"

"Control of his own life!" I answer with a sudden surge of anger.

"Control!" Gordie points to the Western Defense Command poster. "Isolation in a detention center is control?"

"Maybe he'd rather be there than turning tail and burying his head in the sand!"

"You calling someone a coward?"

"When I heard him stand up to the Governor, I knew he was right. And his editorials. Kageyama knows the Constitution."

"Big talk," Gordie says angrily. "The Western Defense Command against a handful of Japanese."

"Hey!" Yuji says. "This here's poker time, not feuding time. We don't have to be a bunch of feuding hillbillies."

Gordie ignores Yuji's uneasy joke. "We're not free and never will be if we do the wrong thing now. That means if we have to go cooperatively to camps, then I'm willing. Just so when this whole business of war is over they won't be able to look back to '42 and say, 'See, you couldn't trust 'em then either.'"

"So you'll let them think Kageyama and any of us who speak our minds can't be trusted," I say.

"I have to do what I think will make me a free man," Gordie answers, the flush fading.

"From behind barbed wire? All Kageyama ever said was that if we protested against this whole thing, we might not be going to camps."

"Look," he answers with a hand outstretched, "it's

already been decided."

"Now that's what I call logic," Tomato says uneasily. He motions for the game to begin.

There is a long uneasy silence. The room begins to smell more strongly of smoke. Taniguchi shuffles and sprays Bee cards to the gamblers. "Roll your own." He clacks a last card in front of himself.

I take the three face down cards, and slowly shear them open. I have a three diamonds downflush. Over the edge of the cards I watch Gordie. Tomato is already watching me carefully.

He smiles when I catch him observing me. "Make it Ben?"

I give him a silent, big smile.

"What's that mean?" Tomato asks.

"For him to know and you to find out," Taniguchi says. "Okay, high card." He points to Gordie. "Make your bet."

Gordie has two sevens showing with a queen, a ten and a king. I figure him for a straight or a pair of kings or queens to go with the sevens. Either way I have him beat. Then he shakes my confidence when he comes with a big opening, as if his house is full. "Ten bucks," he says.

"Ten bucks the man says," Tomato wheezes. "Big talk for hard times! Is the man trying to bullshit us or is he on the level?" He hesitates, smiles, then flips ten blues on the pile. "In too deep to drop out now."

The store room is warm. The windows are covered with black-out curtains. Blankets hang over the door. A couple of electric heaters at either end of the room beat back the chill. When I call and raise back five, Tomato folds with a loud whistle. He looks to Gordie who is studying me with wrinkled forehead, trying to figure whether I'm bluffing or for real. When he raises me right back, Tomato looks into the overhead bulb. "When those two get at each other's throats, it's time for us humans to clear out."

I call him. "I could clean you out, but I don't want to leave you destitute so early." He turns over his cards. He's got an ace high straight to my flush. He keeps a poker face while I rake in the chips.

It is a push-pull night for me and I hang around a few dollars to the black. Goto is shuffling absent-mindedly and says, "I hear we got Tule for sure." I had not noticed the small tin button on his shirt pocket, now fully revealed when he takes off his sweater. I read it and laugh.

Goto looks at me. "What's so funny about getting Tule?"

"That button."

"Oh this," he looks down at his "I Am A Chinese" button. "Got it from Harvey Wong. Harvey's my Chinaman-football-buddy. Says if I wear it, I'll be safe."

For a few minutes, I cannot concentrate, laughing at strong man John Goto, son of a Nihonmachi barber, disguised as a Chinese. "Little John" of Japanese town. He has big face, broad shoulders, and eyes that flash into thin slits when he smiles.

Yuji deals, "Five card draw, jacks or better," he says. Between discard and deal, someone says that he has heard some new names, "Gila River, Heart Mountain and Minidoka."

Taniguchi says, "Minidoka? Holy Mackerel! Where the hell'd they get that monicker?"

"How about Topaz, Rohwer, and Jerome?" Asoo signals with index and middle finger for two cards.

"Hey," Tomato says, "I'll take Tule any day, especially over Rohwer. Whoever they are, I feel sorry for the guys who get that place."

"Whadda you know about it? You ever been there?"

"Nope! But one thing I know for sure: if the Arkies came from there and they didn't like it, it's gotta be a crummy state. And we ain't exactly going there for vacation."

"Arkies?"

"Yeah, Arkies," Yuji says. "And I hear they got mosquitos big as chicken eggs. Can you imagine seeing double A, egg-shaped mosquitos buzzing around like blimps?" He whizzes his fist in quick circles overhead.

Gordie is quiet for a long while. Then he wins, and he begins piling chips into stacks in front of him. As he gets farther ahead, he enjoys the game more and loosens up. His concentration on the game fades with the growing pile. "Heart Mountain wouldn't be so bad. I always wondered what it would be like to live in genuine cowboy country."

"Wyoming?"

"Uh huh."

"Yippy-yi-doo" Yuji shouts in a high voice uncharacteristic of a scrappy second baseman.

"Yippy-yi-doo?" Tomato repeats, "Now what the hell kinda cowboy goes around shouting 'yippi-yi-doo?'"

Yuji stops in mid deal and looks angrily at Tomato. "You making fun of me?"

"Cool off Yuji," Gordie intercedes. "It's yippy-yi-yay! That's all he's trying to say. Nothing to get offended about."

Yuji picks up the deal where he left off, flips another card to Tomato, and announces that he's getting tired of snide remarks that reflect on his Americanism. "Whatever he meant by all that stuff, Tomato's not getting his card for being a wise guy."

Tomato slams his cards down on the table with disgust. Yuji lets out a toothy grin. Tomato says, "'Yippy-yi-doo.' Now that's a Boochie cowboy for you."

"Tule sounds best to me," Gordie muses. "At least it's in California."

"Where'd you choose if you had a choice?"

"Topaz doesn't sound so bad," Asoo says.

"Sounds like a rock," I say.

"A mineral. An orthorhombic mineral, often occurring in transparent prismatic crystals, and classed as a semiprecious stone, with a characteristic color of yellow," Tomato says.

There is a dead silence around the table. We all turn around to stare at Tomato's smug face.

"Now where the shit...?" Taniguchi says.

"*Encyclopedia Britannica, Volume T.*"

"Holy shit!" Asoo says. "A photographic memory Nihonmachi Lincoln. A Boochie who's got the encyclopedia memorized."

Yuji rolls his eyeballs. "A yellow stone, huh? Oh man! They weren't subtle, were they?"

Without hearing Yuji, Taniguchi asks, "Where is it?"

"In the ground like all the other minerals."

"Utah," Gordie answers.

"Probably sitting on some damn salt beds..."

"Got to be. That's all Utah is, isn't it? I mean except for the mountains."

"Say," Yuji says. "I just remembered I know some people out there -- they're Mormons."

"Big deal! That's all there is in Utah."

"You don't understand. They're Japanese."

"Mormon Boochies?" Taniguchi says. "Japanese Mormons? Now if that don't take the cake."

I laugh. "Now what the hell would those ol' congressmen say if they heard that at the hearings?"

It is the kind of night where the biggest pile of chips shifts around. Gordie to Taniguchi to me to Goto, and when it sits for some forty-five minutes in front of Yuji, he stands up, stretches and announces he's got rear-end fatigue. He does some knee bends, squatting with both hands on the knee caps, then reaches around behind him, grabs his buttocks and massages them. He turns to the window and peels the blanket back a few inches to peek outside. "Say," he announces "it's getting light."

"Hey, how come it's always the guy with the biggest pile that notices when it's morning?" Taniguchi asks.

"You make the rules when you're on top," Gordie says glumly.

There is an all-night poker haze in the room. Everyone is quiet and numb. Tomato gets the coffee pot while the chips are counted and stacked. He places steaming cups in front of all the players.

"Thanks," echoes around the room.

Yuji slumps wearily in his chair. "New Years time the family would work from three in the morning til late at night producing thousands and thousands of mochi for the New Year crush," he says. "Never thought I'd see the day I'd be unhappy not working the long hours of the holiday season."

Tomato forces a smile and pushes his green 'wheeler-dealer' visor back. "Well, we didn't break curfew," he says and paraphrases the proclamation, "We stayed within our homes or present confinement, or roof under which we find ourselves unavoidably detained by matters of business or urgent personal business which due to

factors beyond our control forces us to seek shelter."
Tomato shrugs. "... or something like that. Anyway,
that's what we did, didn't we?"

Chapter 8

I can smell the fragrance of the cherry and peach trees, the persimmon, the plum and apricot, the iris, the lillies-of-the-valley, the roses. In a garden profuse with life, the flowers, the ferns, the vegetables and trees grow where Mother planted and tended them through the years. Early in the growing year it is neat and manicured, but in late summer the weeds and tangle slowly take over.

Her room is a similar profusion. She is a collector. In every corner there are piles of magazines dating back to the twenties and thirties, newspaper clippings about everything: birds, stamps, the Emperor's family, a picture of a young Japanese cellist, articles about lost and faithful pets, poems by some unknown, boxes of buttons, pins, pieces from jewelry, bags filled with envelopes, old paint brushes, tubes of oil paint that have dried up.

Through an open door comes the sound of a phonograph playing koto music as she sorts. She stands before her sumi painting, gazing through time and space at the land of her childhood. She carefully places the scroll along with her silk kimonos in her trunk, unwilling to let go of cherished days. She packs books, magazines, those things she refuses to part with. Perhaps there will come a time when we will have to throw it all out -- when she is gone -- but she will have left a sketch of her life.

I have a map in my hand where I have sketched out

in dark ink the broken line of roads, highways, towns, that define the ghetto boundary of Public Proclamation Number One. She traces the route with her eyes along U.S Highway 97 to Coarse Gold, backtracks quickly through Ben and Morman, through Chinese Camp, Sutter Creek and into Cool.

"It isn't far from Sacramento to Auburn or Placerville. Maybe if we had moved when the government gave us the chance, we wouldn't have to go into camps now." I help her tie heavy twine around her boxes and carry them out to the truck. She moves with the distinctive grace of a Japanese woman. The training of her first nineteen years in Japan indelibly marks the way she speaks, the way she views life.

As a boy growing up in Japan, I heard that when she was a young woman in Okayama prefecture, she and her three sisters were well known. Not only were they lovely in physical appearance, but their higher education and ability in music gave their father a favorable position in the traditional arrangements for marriage.

Father was taken by Mother's beauty at fifteen, and decided he would someday have her for his wife. Both families were supportive of the union as it would bring money to Father's samurai family, and a higher social standing to Mother's merchant class family. He had only to convince Mother.

In his youth Father was driven with a fierce determination. He took a teaching position in Mother's town and within a few years they were married.

In many ways she was well suited for him: she too set goals high and was willing to sacrifice to achieve them. Mother gave up all the comfort and leisure and elegance of her home in Japan to become a farmer's wife and drug store clerk. All the while she read and wrote poetry, played the koto and became a skilled gardener.

I drive the loaded truck across S Street. Mother's hand on my arm indicates she wishes me to stop. We take a detour to the farmer's market before depositing our load at Fourth Street. She is temporarily transformed in the market square where she has shopped twice a week for almost thirty years. Here Saturday shoppers of many races and nationalities flow through seas of crates and boxes filled with bright colored fruits and vegetables -- white radishes, green peppers, strawberries, grapes, carrots -- all of which are inspected thoroughly before being purchased.

There is the distinctive odor of dried shrimp and fish, smoked until it is stiff and chewy; the tentacles of fresh octopi turned downside up are curled and sprinkled with water.

A smile crosses her face as we recall Kageyama's father many years ago standing under the thatched roofs of the market place selling grapes, cauliflowers and strawberries. His face was wrinkled from wind and cold and hot summer heat. He was sturdy with contentment, the strength that comes from sharing in a close farming community. His square short body bent stiffly to Mother in Japanese greetings as he rapped the dust off his pants.

We pass the newly budding fruit trees. She snaps a branch and holds it, saying, "These trees remind me of the cherry blossoms soon to break open in Japan. It is most beautiful when there is a full moon. Then there is no need for light, for the blossoms glow in the darkness. If the winter is late, it is sometimes cold -- but it makes no difference because everyone is warm from sake."

Her cheeks flush as if from rice wine. "It is always sad when it is over, when all the blossoms fall to earth."

Mother seems neither sad, nor weary, nor angry, nor bitter. When I ask, she says simply, "Shikata ga nai. It cannot be helped -- one must accept what one cannot change."

Chapter 9

Farm journals and news broadcasters advertise the chance of a lifetime. The government is liquidating four thousand Japanese American farms in an emergency program to sell cheaply to Caucasians before the growing season is lost. Government loans, easy terms, and technical assistance are promised while we can't even insure our belongings or secure government guarantees for the safe storage of our property.

Kageyama understood that it would be this way when he wrote his last article, his final act of treason:

> To people who know the meaning of community life, of lifelong toil upon their land, of seeing children grow in the educational processes of a free American democracy, who see the struggles of the early years of immigration turn to success, loyalty to the country and ideals does not come cheap. It cannot be issued or revoked on the whims of a few people or organizations, nor can it be determined on the basis of race, religion, creed or heritage. Loyalty and ultimately love come from the heart, and that is not a matter for frivolous judgment.

All pretenses are dropped: fraud, forced sales and cheating become the pattern. Father stubbornly refuses to become prey to the rapacious buyers. He arranges for his old Caucasian friends to lease his store and printing equipment and rent out the house and apartment while we are away.

The opportunists still keep coming. Exasperated, he finally pounds up a sign:

THIS PROPERTY NOT FOR SALE! KEEP OUT!

Fourth Street is quiet except for the pounding of boards on store fronts that have not been shut down in thirty years. Atsumi's shop looks inhospitable with slats nailed in place and the iron gate pulled almost shut.

I feel a special warmth for Atsumi, for it was he rather than Father that encouraged me during my first years in America. His humor and his Japanese ways so often reminded me of my grandfather in Japan.

His daughter and I have been close friends for many years. I remember walking together so long ago. She was quiet. It was her way. I asked her about it. She said, "I enjoy listening to you."

I looked at her to see if she was joking, and she turned so I couldn't see her eyes. I moved quickly behind her and grabbed her head in my hands.

"People are watching us," she protested.

"So?"

She turned to see wide grins showing through windows, and she blushed.

"I could tell you didn't really mind."

"Unbelievable conceit," she said, tilting her face upwards.

"You have to act decent. Besides, all those people know we kiss in private." I looked at her slender profile moving gracefully.

"Ben," she said softly, "When will you be leaving?"

It was time to return to school, and I felt as I had for the past three years: the urge to get on my way, to get back to the excitement of traveling and settling into the routine of a new school year.

"Soon," I answered. "A week or two."

"It must be exciting for you. To go back to school on the east coast. I get awfully bored here, the same old faces, same old streets."

"I thought you liked teaching music."

"Oh, I do. I just wish I could forget the whole thing and travel. Or go to school someplace away from here to study music."

We walked in silence, along the dirty streets, the old grayish black buildings, a few weary trees reflecting the worn section of town. She looked around and said, "Look at this. You live here all your life, never leave, and you think this is all there is to the world. If I could get a scholarship, I'd sure take it."

"It may not be as nice as you picture it to be."

"You sound just like Dad. All of you think just because I'm a woman I wouldn't be capable of going away to school. Or maybe you think I just want to get married."

I shrugged my shoulders and said nothing.

"You're worse than Dad. The way you shrug your shoulders, I know what you're thinking."

She paused for a moment. A benevolent look crossed her face. "I'm sorry, Ben. I didn't mean to be so crabby." She took my hand and pulled gently. "I'm going to miss you," she said. "I look forward to the summers, but I dread the fall when you leave."

I looked at her pretty heart-shaped face. Her eyes remind me of the beautiful geisha printed on the scroll in mother's study. I have imagined Alice in flowered silken kimonos, face half-hidden by a hand-painted fan, instead of her pleated skirts and cotton smocks.

"We'll write," I answered, without conviction.

"No, we won't. You have your studies and girl friends out there. When you write, it's just out of duty. "I better keep her happy and drop her a note!'"

I began to protest.

"Shush." She spoke with the same quiet authority she used with her students.

We reached the river and walked along the bank, among trees still wearing the foliage of late summer.

"There's no need to make false promises," she said. "Besides, I have this feeling deep inside that someday you're going to end up marrying me." She had said that before in the same coquettish way. "I know you have white girl friends . . . ." Before I could say anything she went on, "But that's okay with me. As eastern as you get for nine months, you always come back where you belong."

She always seemed to know more about me than I did about her. I breathe deeply, smelling not the poplars and maples by the river, but the odors of Fourth Street.

I notice a sign Atsumi-san has hung:

MANY THANKS FOR YOUR PATRONAGE

HOPE TO SERVE YOU IN NEAR FUTURE.

GOD BE WITH YOU UNTIL WE MEET AGAIN.

THE ATSUMIS

I look through a slight opening where the shade is bent. I can see a light in the back of the store, so I knock, hoping she will be the one to answer. The shade moves to the side and I glimpse Alice's face. She opens the door surprised. "Ben!" she cries, "what on earth are you doing here? I haven't seen you for so long."

"I've been around," I answer.

"I know, I've seen you, but not here."

I nod.

"Come in, come in. We have a buyer here. Dad's trying to close a deal for selling the store." I look around, my eyes adjusting to the darkened interior. It is a dismal prophecy come true. "He's not so much interested in the store, but the merchandise."

"How's it going?"

"Not good. They know what we're up against, so they're trying to go as cheaply as possible. Below inventory, of course."

I am both angry and sympathetic. She reads my thoughts and says quickly, "It's not so bad. We're no worse off than anyone else."

"That doesn't make it okay," I say. "Only more tragic."

"Come," she says, leading me to their living area. We pass the two Caucasians sitting across from Atsumi. I dislike them on sight. We walk quietly through to the living room, small and so reminiscent of Japan.

"Can I get you some tea?" she asks. I nod, listening to the voices in the adjoining room.

The younger man sounds apologetic. "They ain't really got any right to be treating you like this. But what can a man do but go along? It ain't for the ordinary citizen to question the military."

Atsumi remains silent. The voice continues, "One thing I got to say about you folks is you're good people, willing to cooperate and all that. Why some of my best friends is Japanese and they all got a good, realistic attitude about what's happenin' to them. Got to admire you folks for that."

"Yes, yes," Atsumi says wearily. "We talk about business."

"Sure, sure, well, you're askin' too much. You got to be realistic, you know. I got so much to pay and we got to make a deal soon, or you might lose everything. I'm making a fair offer under the circumstances."

"It is not even value of inventory."

"What you got isn't new. Some of this stuff is old. They got new models now. Makes this stuff harder to sell."

Alice pours tea and says, "I've thought about you. Wondering what you are doing. You never come around much."

I nod. "It makes me sad to see the stores shut down. I'm not used to things so quiet."

"It will be like it was again some day. We will come back."

Her eyes are tired looking, darker below, but surprisingly, the same sparkle animates them.

"You sound like we're going for a little vacation," I say.

"Not really. We can't look forward to barbed wire, can we? Might as well look forward to our return. Have you heard we'll be sent to Walerga first and then to Tule Lake?"

"Yes, I heard the good news."

She laughs, almost too loud, and covers her mouth, looking into the next room.

"What's so funny?" I ask.

"I was just thinking, I am finally getting my chance to leave this place. My big adventure."

"Very funny. Into a concentration camp."

"All right. I know what you're thinking. 'She's going to have a hard time adjusting.'"

"I had no such thought, but it's probably true."

"Same old thing. Can't you see I can take care of myself?" She pauses thoughtfully, then starts to speak, and hesitates, almost smiling.

"Now what are you thinking?" I ask.

"It might be fun being in camp with you. Maybe we'll see each other more."

I like her flattery, so I return it. "Now that you mention it, I agree."

I hear Mr. Atsumi in the background, resigned and tired, "Yes, you are right."

Chapter 10

We are the enemy. Orphans, foster children in white homes, Japanese married to Caucasians, their off-spring, persons unaware of their Japanese ancestry, anyone with as little as 1/16 Japanese blood must be evacuated.

Our destination is Walerga, an assembly center northeast of Sacramento. It is a former migrant laborer camp now turned into a temporary home for Japanese until the government finishes the permanent camp at Tule Lake in northern California.

We load up the car with the last of our belongings to be stored at the church, where we will turn over our car to its new owner. We lock our house as if we were going visiting, to leave for a few hours, a day, a week end.

We carry little away with us, our heaviest burden a loneliness, a helpless desolation as we pass by deserted Japanese homes with their carefully nurtured gardens -- a touch of trees and greenery that infuse Sacramento, a city of the early gold rush days, with a quiet and simple regard for nature.

Charter buses line the street in front of the Park-view Church, surrounded by Oriental faces. They are interspersed with occasional Caucasians coming to bid farewell to friends, or government agents and police here to direct the Japanese into categories.

I see Gordie, who left the house first, busy with other JACL'ers helping people find their bus, checking attendance, and assisting the elderly with their belongings.

Many of the Issei have worn their Sunday clothes as if they were going to church. Although it is not cold, we wear our winter coats rather than carry them in the bundles reserved for kitchen utensils, basins, and other clothing. Tied to lapels are the paper tags, scrawled in our own writing, or in the case of the Issei, by their Nisei children. Gathered before a crowd of curious onlookers, we feel a strong bond; we are together in whatever awaits us.

Onishi-san, getting so old he can hardly walk, holds hands with his five year old grandson. Mrs. Onishi, younger and stronger, walks by his side carrying all of their belongings. Frail and small in her heavy overcoat, Obasan stands with the Onishis. As they are her closest friends from her early pioneer days, she prefers their companionship during the internment. With Kageyama gone, we all felt it would be easier for Obasan to live in one room with the Onishis rather than with Mother and Father and Gordie and I.

Atsumi-san sits tight-lipped on a folded stool without comment or greeting. Alice stands behind him next to her mother, as if to comfort them. As our eyes meet, I feel the hurt, the insult she feels, the compassion for her parents, the unclean self-reproach for being of this skin color, for being Japanese. Her face is sullen, her eyes soft and sensitive. We feel awkward and bulky, the way we look with our bundles. No one knows what to say for the occasion, so we speak only the necessary words. Even the children are grim-faced and silent, sensing the indignity.

The buses are loaded. The diesel engines rumble softly as they pull away from the crowd of several hundred spectators. We are acutely aware of our race. We are borne off in shame with no way to prove who we are. The buses roll through the streets of Sacramento into the countryside, a relief from the prying eyes of Caucasians.

The weather this time of year is like spring in Hayama where I grew up. There, winding roads ran through villages built scant feet from the roadside, through low wooded hills and along the beach where on clear days Fuji-san rose on the distant horizon. The mountain was peaked with snow framed by pale blue sky and water. Small crooked footpaths led to our home in the hills. I remember the breeze twisting through the trees, the smell of pine and charcoal, the soft patina of aging wood.

A short distance north off Highway 99E, we enter Walerga, our purgatory on a flat parched site, rows of long narrow barracks incongruous in a barren stretch of limitless brown.

We lose face to the worst enemy, prejudice. Such defeat bring us the greatest mortification. It has been a silent war, waged for decades, gradually being won, only to lose everything in a few short months.

When we first glimpse the center, I think the barracks are sheds. Mother's face registers disbelief. "Surely, not to live in," she says.

Father has said nothing from early morning until now. As they superficially examine us for weapons and liquor before assigning us our room, Father refuses to be searched. They try again but he backs away, raising his palm up signaling for them to stop. Not wanting to start a scene, they allow him to go on through. It was his last chance to preserve a measure of dignity. I watch him walk stiffly, head erect, towards the row of numbered barracks.

Our space is small and bare save for four cots, with army blankets hung to divide it into two bedrooms and a living room area. With the basic tools we have brought, Father keeps us busy building a porch and a walkway over the rutted ground. He believes one must make the best of all situations, never indulging in idleness.

Walerga seems a chaotic adjustment on the fringes of lunacy. Everywhere we look there are long lines: for meals, to the administration offices, for the scrap lumber piles, for the latrines, the showers, the wash houses, the hospital. Knowing this is just a temporary home, I try to look at circumstances with detachment. We stay with our friends, laughing and visiting, working where we can be most helpful, determined to make an adjustment to life within barbed wire.

In half an hour I am through a slow moving line for supper, looking for a place to sit in the packed, hot mess hall. The sounds of silverware clatter against army-style tin trays, and hundreds of voices add to the clamor.

I am resigned to taking my tray outside and eating on the front steps. Then Taniguchi calls me. At a table for six, eight Buddhaheads are crowded together, eating elbow to elbow. I squeeze in. Tomato raps his tin loudly and says, "Slop-suey again. Food was pretty good the first day, but now it's garbage slopped with shoyu and cornstarch!"

"What's the matter," Yuji asks. "Camp life getting you down already?"

"Hell no," Tomato says. "No work, no worries, everything on the house. We're living like kings, except for this stuff." He raps his fork on the tin tray again.

"Hey, you got to keep rapping that tray? Isn't there enough noise already?"

"Sorry," Tomato says. "Didn't know you were so

sensitive."

"I'll sensitive you one. Right across your flat nose."

"Say, you Japanese," Asoo waves his fork. "No racial slurs in a concentration camp. Okay?"

A car rolls past; the tiny speck on the highway catches Yuji's eye, "You know, we could have had a fine team this year. Could have taken the summer league crown, I bet." He sighs watching Taniguchi scratch himself. "What do you think, Tanigooch?"

Taniguchi ignores him, concentrating on scratching.

"What's the matter, Tanigooch? You too old for playing ball?"

"Naw," he says. "I'm allergic to flea bites. Forty flea bites I got. I counted 'em."

Tomato looks carefully at Taniguchi and Yuji, noticing their bloodshot eyes. "You two look tired. You better be getting some rest."

"You ever try to sleep with forty flea bites, knowing there's more coming?"

"Bugs don't bother me." Yuji says. "It's the density. Makes me edgy. Crowded and dusty." He thrusts his elbows out and rams them into Tomato and Taniguchi, causing Tomato to choke on a big mouthful. "Sorry," he says. He pounds on Tomato's back. "Just not used to this density."

"With elbows like that, no one would've ever got past second to Goto country."

"Speaking of Goto," Yuji says, "and Gordie. Haven't seen them around for a while."

"Gone," I answer. "Volunteered for the advance crew to Tule to make preparations."

"I heard about that. I was going to sign up until I heard all the rumors."

"What did you hear?"

"That going to Tule early was a reward for buttering the bread on the right side."

"You buying that?" I ask.

"Didn't say I believed it," Yuji says.

"Boy, we Japanese sure spread rumors," Asoo says.

"Where you been?" Tomato asks. "There's nothing holy about us."

"Hot!" Yuji complains, getting to his feet and wiping his brow with his handkerchief. "Holy cow, I feel dusty. I wonder how long the shower line is?"

In two months we have grown accustomed to the dust, the long sweaty lines, the twenty-by-twenty rooms, the mind-wearying orderly disorder.

Every Monday we wait anxiously for the transfer list that will assign us a departure time for Tule Lake. Everyone makes light of what it will be like, in spite of underlying concern. We have heard about thousands of Jews disappearing on trains in Germany never to be heard from again.

Our family is assigned space on a train that will depart late Wednesday afternoon. Packing is not difficult, although there is great ambivalence as we board the dim coaches. The shades have been pulled down and fastened, as if to keep our destination secret.

From the back of the train I hear a soft voice apologizing, "I am sorry we do not have anything better to offer." A woman and a young girl repeat themselves, growing closer until they are next to us.

She says in a low voice, "I am sorry I don't have anything better to offer you, but will you take these sandwiches?" She speaks not with pity, but with a depth of understanding that confounds me. I reach out to take the sandwich she offers, feeling the spirit of giving and receiving as never before in my life. Of all the people we have met these last months, she imparts the greatest kindness.

"They are Quakers," Mother says.

In the dingy train, the light from the gas lamp shines through the heavy, enclosed air. The car sways, clacking over steel rails. Old men and women try to find comfort on straight backed wooden benches while children and babies sleep fitfully. The faces of M.P.'s look ghostly through the light, in the swaying from side to side.

I used to sit on a stone granite bench, the world in a perfect state of equilibrium, no conflict, no ugliness, only dark pines, the radiant orange and red of the late setting sun. The train cycles through motion, motionless. A slow lurching brings me back to the present.

The train crawls slowly into desolate flatlands stretching out from the foothills purple in the setting sun.

In the morning I wake to the sounds of shades being opened. The background of soft rolling hills speckled with scrubby trees, raises the horizon a few thousand feet above the vast expanse of valley floor. Through the sage and brush, I see thousands of black barracks standing stark in the flatland, no trees, no color except for the dull gray and pale red of lava beds. The landscape is framed by wire fence, topped by rows of barbed wire.

Chapter 11

We are a dismal procession. Reluctantly we step from the train onto the platform of Newell, a small town near the Oregon border; it will soon be dwarfed by our newborn city of 20,000. There are a few towns people out to watch, wearing unfriendly expressions. We are directed to waiting buses for the final leg of our journey. It has been a long three hundred miles; a long time from yesterday to today; a long time from December to June; a long, bumpy ride along the dusty roads to Tule.

The dry heat burns the dirt loose from the earth. In gusts and whirlwinds it blows hundreds of feet above Tule, abrades our faces and filters into our eyes and throats, burning and strangling. When the spiraling wind temporarily dances away, the blue of sky descends, making bare the mountain peaks of June now spotted with barbed wire that extends across hills and valley and sky from machine gun tower to machine gun tower.

We enter the gates: there is suddenly no past. Our lives become no more than endless corridors stretching a mile and a half into the horizon. My parents say nothing, and in their silence they seem to say they understand something I do not.

In the compound there is a large crowd waiting: people look for friends and relatives and the curious come to see the new arrivals. I spot Gordie on the back of a flat-bed truck. He lights up when he sees us and jumps down off the truck with the ease of an athlete.

He takes Mother's and Father's hands in both of his and bows slightly. Then he grips my hand and smiles broadly, saying, "Gimme some skin, you slant-eyed Boochie!" We all laugh as the worries, the troubles, the anxieties are momentarily lifted. A wave of love washes over us as if Mother, Father, Gordie and I are the only persons standing in the compound.

Mother and Father weather the changes well. From the time of the evacuation orders, they have not spoken of it, but rather, have accepted it. Adverse circumstances have been so much a theme in their lives. They could survive anything. Mother looks refreshingly pretty in the early morning as she stands in the crowd, graceful and gentle in spite of the dust and confusion. A kindly Caucasian woman approaches her, taking her hand. Mother bows slightly and follows her into the receiving barrack. We are all given forms to fill out, assigned living quarters, and processed through cursory physical examinations.

There is no center to the 32,000 acres. We walk through the narrow corridors to our new home. As in Walerga we are expecting another barren room with a stove and four cots. Instead, we find partitions for two sleeping areas and a living room with a corner walled off for a kitchenette. There are flattened tin cans nailed over knot holes where slivers of light seep through shrinking floor boards. There is even wire stretched over the opening to the sleeping areas, ready to receive curtains for privacy. Pleased as if he has just turned over the keys to a mansion, Gordie scans our faces for our reactions to his work. All three of us are relieved and happy, but on Mother's face, and in her eyes, there is a glow. She is thankful we are all here together.

Gordie and I attack the further transformation of

our home with an enthusiasm and vigor lacking at Walerga. With scrap lumber that is becoming increasingly scarce, we build four chairs, a wooden couch, and closets. Father begins building a front porch again. His friends say it is his Kansas blood. Mother landscapes the front by weeding out the short tule grass and brings in fine ground lava and rocks for a path and the beginnings of a rock garden.

As I collect scraps of wood to finish a table, a figure presses toward me, pushing a wheelbarrow piled with lumber. It is Tomato, dressed in overalls. He inspects the topless table. He offers me the use of whatever lumber I may need.

"There's a shortage," I say. "What did you do, steal it?"

"You pretty choosy for a beggar!"

"I don't want to get arrested for receiving stolen goods!"

"Well, if you have to know, I'm just scoutin' around, minding my own business, when I happen to spot this wheelbarrow sitting in the middle of the compound. I stand around it for a while waiting for someone to show up. I notice I have on my carpenter's clothes, so I act official. And here I am. Now Mom can have her kitchen table and Pop can have his hard board bed instead of an aching back."

"The table can wait," I say, but he signals me to be quiet. He rummages through the lumber and roughly fits my table with pieces of siding.

"Got to hurry off," he says, "this wheelbarrow will be looking for its owner soon."

I become a spectator to the intake process, watching the new arrivals fill the hundreds of empty barracks. Masses of Japanese crowd Tule from other assembly centers, changing the lake bed overnight into a city. The slightest breezes raise clouds of dust. People scurry about to signs of whirlwind sandstorms that whip the camp. It is not without beauty, but where we are, it is colorless and somber. Along the west fence, parallel to the highway, Castle Rock Mountain dominates. Its jutting silhouette becomes the symbol of Tule Lake Concentration Camp.

I had not seen Alice at Walerga. The Atsumis had been assigned an entirely different section with separate mess halls and wash rooms. As I walk Tule, I recognize in the distance a familiar, slight figure, carrying a basket of clothes. It is Alice. She smiles when she sees me, but looks down when I look into her eyes.

"Where you headed? I'll carry it for you." I say.

"Not many places to go. To the wash house, to the showers, to the mess hall, and home again. But thankyou, I could use a lift. I'm not quite used to all this walking between chores." She smiles and hands me the basket.

"Do you have work? I mean outside of the housework."

"Yes, I've been asked to organize music lessons for children. One of the WRA women is trying to get some pianos donated to Tule."

I find myself drawn to Alice whenever there is the opportunity. We often walk together for miles around the camp, sharing our thoughts and experiences adjusting to our new life. We spend more time together than we had in Nihonmachi.

"I'm tired of camp. I want to get out of Tule," Alice says.

"How are you going to get out? You're a prisoner."

"I know, but the woman who is sponsoring the

music lessons says I have talent. She is trying to get me a scholarship to a midwestern college that wants to help Nisei in concentration camps."

"What a strange way for a dream to come true," I say. "Will your Father let you go?"

"Yes, but he's reluctant. I'm his only child. But he doesn't see any sense in passing up an opportunity.... I started the piano when I was five."

"I'm going to miss you, Alice. You know that, don't you?"

"Yes, Ben, but camp isn't any place to get serious. We're in limbo. We don't even know how long we're going to be living here. It's better for both of us if I go to school."

Not long after she mentioned the scholarship, I find an envelope penned in her hand on my desk.

> *Dear Ben,*
> *I received the scholarship to study music. I didn't want to go through the good-byes again. Especially with me being the one to leave this time. I believe there will come a time when we will be together again. I only hope it will not be long until then.*
>
>
> *Alice*

The weeks pass and I become established in my work in the legal office as part time interpreter. I gradually become used to the camp without Alice. Occasionally, I see a car flash by on the highway. I think, who gives a damn about the outside world anyway. How long will it be before I see that again?

My ambivalence accompanies uneasiness, a portent of chaos. I pitch myself in, but however high-minded my resolve, I am still a prisoner, subject to the capricious crosswinds that have blown us together to this bleak flatland of northern California. I close my eyes to the watch towers; to the newspapers and their constant barrage of hatred; to the sand and heat; to the ubiquitous tar papered barracks; to the one-room homes as dusty inside as out on a windy day; to the community toilets and showers; to the bland, starch diet; to the $14 and $16 a month wages paid for forty-eight hours of labor.

Our apartment becomes a place to sleep and to make occasional contact with family members. Mother attends classes in water color, teaches sumi, participates in shigin and making jewelry from the shells found buried in the ground. Obasan joins her, along with Mrs. Onishi and the other elderly Issei women, relaxing for the first time since their pioneer days. They are actually enjoying their imprisonment. Father becomes involved in the organization of Ward V's cooperative store and canteen. He plays go and shogi for the first time in many years. Gordie spends his time playing baseball and working as a reporter for the camp newspaper. He also keeps involved with the JACL organization in Tule.

We have become a band of roving people: children flow from one block to another, eating meals in different mess halls; boys join gangs with the toughest becoming the leaders. The traditional authority and close ties of the family slowly become a memory of pre-war days.

There are sixty-four blocks in the mile and a quarter square; in each block there are fourteen barracks; and in the entire camp there are 1200 barracks. Ward V is Sacramento Nihonmachi transferred to Tule Lake. Tomato, Asoo, Taniguchi, and their families are with us in Block 46. Goto, Moriuchi, and Muritani and Yuji live in Blocks 44 and 45.

Wherever we are, we are close together. We cannot be isolated: curtains divide rooms; thin, sound-transmitting partitions divide apartments; pencil corridors divide barracks. It is a new city, yet already it looks aged, with buildings, poles, and bodies all coated with sedimentary layers of dust and sand.

Chapter 12

Driven by a summer rainstorm, people scurry quickly into wash houses, latrines, barracks, into the canteen, past playfields of home-made rocking horses, teeter-totters, and swings. In the canteen, I look over an array of Mars, Snickers, Hersheys, and Butterfingers. I am bumped almost off my feet. Before I turn, I know the face by the voice, saying in mock seriousness, "Gomen kudasai." Gently, I catch my balance and spring back into his chest. Tomato stumbles backwards, legs pumping furiously, and smashes into a box of Baby Ruths, knocking bars flying to the floor. We catch fiery hell from Okada-san, the same torrent of garbled Japanese-English that graced his pool hall in Nihonmachi.

Back in the rain, we make a mad dash for the shelter of a laundry barrack, where we might talk in peace. Our voices are drowned by water sloshing around cement tubs where red fingers rub clothing over troughed glass textured with thousands of pimpled bumps.

Tomato smiles at the wash tubs; they are too tall for most of the short Issei women stretching to wash clothes. Obasan stands on a footstool reaching down into the sudsy water. She turns and smiles.

Tomato jabs me with an elbow. "Ben, I got a new job. With the Tule Lake Center Fire Department-TLCFD. They took me and Goto and thirty other guys on a two-week training course."

Water bangs through the pipes. "Ben, you hearing what I'm saying?" he shouts.

I nod yes.

"They had us in the classroom first, then in the field, dry-firing in rain gear, sweating and straining, keeping us moving by the drill sergeant's screamin' and swearin'.

"After a thousand dry firing runs we get ready for the real thing -- the concrete fire house. There we were, standing around hanging onto a limp hose. Then smoke from an oil fire starts billowing outa the windows. They turn on the water and the hose straightens out its kinks with water smashing out at fifty feet per second muzzle velocity. There are four of us on each hose, muscles straining, crouching, gettin' ready to charge through the door of the concrete house." Tomato stands up, crouches, arms curled around an imaginary hose. "Heads bowed, vision cut off by the rubber hats strapped under our chins, my eyes glued on Goto. I think, 'thank God for Little John Goto, the head nozzle man.' Until I went into that concrete house, I woulda said any guy who said smoke makes noises was plumb loco. There was a roar, and it wasn't only the fire. Smoke makes noises too.

"It was so dense in there I was about to panic. But I hang in there for shittin' dear life, listenin' to billows puff and churn, getting eyes and throat burned and chokin' for fresh air. Through the smoke, I see the Caucasian chief yelling, waving his arms, screaming anger, directions, encouragement, trying to get us to the edge of the oil pool so we can douse the fire with water and foam.

"We're glued to the floor for several seconds until he pokes his big face towards the nozzle, screaming at Goto to get his rear in gear. At first Goto didn't hear 'im but pretty soon he starts to turn. He swings the nozzle onto the chief's chest, knockin' 'im flat on his back, skiddin' 'im along the floor. I have never seen such blood pumpin' and burstin' red rage as when we got outside! He gave Goto the thousand gun salute! He woulda like to grab Goto's eighteen-inch neck and strangled him! Goto looked so innocent, lulling the enemy like that time he scored four touchdowns and ran over everybody for 225 yards.

"You remember?"

"Remember! Japanese American sports history?"

"Well anyway," Tomato laughs, his voice temporarily drowned out by water banging in the pipes again, "now I'm the head nozzle man." He looks over at Obasan and Mrs. Goto who is short and stocky, wearing a cotton print frock, oblivious of what transpired on a field where her son and 21 other men knocked each other silly. He waits for them to turn down the water. Impatiently he shouts above the noise. "So anyway, . . ."

"What?" I shout. "I can't hear you!"

"You are now officially a friend of," the water suddenly shuts off, "FIREMAN TOMITA!" Up and down the aisles of tubs the ladies turn to see Fireman Tomita.

"Fireman Tomita?" asks Mrs. Onishi. "Shigeru-chan?"

I pull Tomato outside. "Hey, the rain's easing off . . . Shigeru-chan! Boy, wait till the guys hear this one!"

Tomato grabs my arm in a hammer lock. He shoves me up against the barrack wall. "Keep your mouth shut! Promise? Or I'll break it off."

"Ease off. Nothing to get upset about. Shigeru-chan."

"I'm gonna break it off." He shoves me tighter against the barracks.

"Okay. Okay. I promise."

"Remember now, your word of honor," He releases my arm.

"My word of honor," I answer, rubbing the circulation back into my arm.

"Shigeru-chan! Holy Cow! Come on," he says, "Chow time."

"Hey," a familiar voice comes through a kitchen window of the mess hall. "How can you tell a piece of rotten meat from a good one? Must be a pretty thin line."

"By the color and smell."

"Smells funny and looks kinda greenish."

"Ah . . . it's okay."

"Sure looks green to me."

"It will disappear when it's cooked."

"And the rot too?"

"It's okay."

"No wonder I've been feeling sick since I got to Tule."

I nudge Tomato, "Isn't that . . . ?"

"Goto -- sure it's Goto." Tomato says. "Kicked off the fire crew so he had to get a new job."

Inside the mess hall I can see Goto smiling and grinning at his good fortune. We find Mother and Father sitting at the same table with Asoo, his mother, and five brothers and sisters. The memory of quietness and grace is lost in the sounds of 200 people slurping, clattering aluminum trays and silverware.

"Hey Shiro!" a boy's voice shouts loudly across the mess hall. "Come on, let's play!"

Before Mrs. Asoo can stop him, her nine year old bounces off the bench and charges down the aisle towards the door.

Father has always believed meals are a time for formality and grace. Mother sees him wince and nods her head in agreement, but she is sympathetic and thankful she does not have to raise small children under these conditions.

It is not always this bad. Today there are more people in the mess hall for the block meetings to discuss self-government.

Gordie has been elected from Block 46 as representative to the Temporary Community Council, a Nisei group formed to take complaints to the administration.

Gordie presides, setting up a chart that divides the camp into seven wards and sixty-four blocks. "The purpose of self-government is to make camp life an equitable substitute for all we have given up," he reads from an administration bulletin. "First we'll have elections. Issei can vote, but they cannot hold office." There is stirring and mumbling. "The elusive goal of democratic principles . . ."

"Elusive!" a loud voice interrupts. "What's elusive about learning democracy in a concentration camp?" A dignified man in his mid-fifties, Reverend Togasaki from the Puyallup Assembly Center sets the tone of the meeting, a session of complaints.

"Are you all donkeys?" Togasaki says. "Led around by nose by Caucasian? Why do they exclude Issei and turn self-government over to Nisei? We will end up like Indians on reservations."

"The Nisei are not taking over," Gordie says. "We are dealing with the WRA because of language."

"Self-government," Reverend Togasaki says sarcastically. "How do you think Japanese community function before WRA and Nisei?"

Frustrated and weary after an hour or more of complaints, Gordie adjourns the meeting with the promise he will deliver all messages and complaints to the administration.

"Hey, Gordie," Tomato says, putting his hand on his shoulder, "You better take it easy."

"Never knew democracy could be so complicated," Asoo complains.

"Didn't know *living* could be so complicated," Gordie says. "If the sun didn't shine and move those shadows, I wouldn't know this were all real."

Goto comes out of the mess hall, muscles bulging out of his tight polo shirt, looking ludicrous in his white stove-pipe chef's hat. For a few minutes we five Nihonmachi transplants sit silently on the porch of Block 46's mess hall, surrounded by hills and barbed wire.

Shadows of children play in the last minutes of a receding daylight.

"Kids," Asoo says, "playing like nothing's changed. Like this is all some kind of picnic."

Gordie's face softens after several minutes of watching. "An Indian reservation," he says, shaking his head.

A group of boys turn a corner, staying within the shadow of the barrack wall, five in single file. In the middle, a blindfolded boy, half a head shorter than the older boys, picks his way hesitantly.

"You a good sport, Uojiro, so we let you play with us," the biggest boy says. Uojiro reaches towards the blindfold in a reflex action. "Don't worry, Uojiro, you can trust us." They march towards an uneven place in the ground and the two lead boys step over it carefully. They turn around to watch happily as Uojiro steps into it and sinks to his knees. He takes off the blindfold and looks dumbfounded at his legs. A white sticky mess of flour and urine and water covers his shoes and pant legs.

The older boys burst into laughter. Enraged, Uojiro reaches into the hole and plasters the biggest boy's face with the stuff. The big boy sputters, temporarily immobilized, then grabs Uojiro in a strangling grip.

In an instant I have the leader by the collar and drag him protesting off Uojiro. Goto, Gordie, Tomato, and Asoo each grab one of the others.

"Okay guys. Time for the game to end."

They disappear into the darkness.

Thin and wiry, Uojiro lingers, head down, relieved, frightened and confused.

"You better go home too. It's getting late."

"I can't. They'll be waiting for me."

"I'll go with you."

Gordie, Tomato and Asoo depart between Wards II and IV. Uojiro leads me through the passageways to his home.

Suddenly, Uojiro breaks into a run. At the sound of footsteps a woman's voice sharply calls his name, then admonishes him for being out so late. She is startled by my sudden form.

"This man brought me home," Uojiro says. "He saved my life. He's one of the guys from Sacramento Japanese town."

"Saved your life?"

"He was being picked on by some older boys outside Block 46 mess hall."

"Block 46! What were you doing in Block 46? How many times have I told you not to go so far away from home?"

"Aw Mom, every block's the same."

"Shush, Uojiro. You do what I tell you." She puts her hand on his head and pushes gently. "Now go inside and get ready for bed."

She turns and says, "I'm Jeanne Yoshimura." I want

to see what she looks like, but I can see only her profile when she turns, her face outlined against the dim light from a window shade. She is young, but her hair is tied up in a bun like an older lady.

"It's so hard," she says, "trying to raise children in this place."

"He's right," I say. "The blocks are all alike, and we are among Japanese."

"But it's so unnatural. The anger and bitterness in the air. Sometimes the children get in such terrible fights. It's like they're trying to take it out on each other.

"Yes, they reflect the adult world," I reply.

"And the food. The change in diet is so hard on Uojiro. He refuses to eat most of the food in the mess halls. He can't stand that chowder stew. I worry about his health, but I can't do anything about it. I can't cook in camp."

"Yes, he does look frail."

"But the behavior . . . . No matter where you are, children should not be allowed to run about as they wish." She stops abruptly and stares quietly at me, realizing she does not know me. She turns, but before disappearing into the apartment she thanks me for bringing her son home to her.

From my cot I can hear the wind through one wall, the neighbors through another. I am curtained off within this cubicle, my life reduced from one hundred fifteen thousand people to ten camps, to wards, blocks, barracks, apartments, to cot. They collect and divide and categorize us into species: Issei, Nisei, Kibei, English-speaking, non-English speaking, bilingual, pro-American, anti-American. We are stabbed on pinboards to be studied and understood, by ourselves, by

Washington authorities, by the administration of Tule Lake.

The arguments that occurred at the mess hall meeting are repeated many times over in other blocks. From them prominent names surface: Honda of Sacramento; Mrs. Makino of Ward III; and Reverend Togasaki. They and a half dozen others are accused by the administration of being agitators with anti-American tendencies. They retaliate by calling those they suspect of informing on them "Inu": "Dogs." Although it is not true, they blame Gordie for submitting Togasaki's name.

Chapter 13

In early morning when the rays of light run parallel to earth, I am elongated on the ground as a shadow, and to my left is Uojiro's. He has become my companion every working morning for three weeks.

Today, I notice bald patches on his head.

"What happened?" I ask, indicating his head.

"I had a fight with my sister."

"Why?"

"Mad. I guess. Mom was out getting coal. We pulled each other's hair and scratched."

"Do you always fight like that?"

"Only since we came to camp . . . . Ben, what's 'Inu'?"

"'Inu?' Dog?"

"Yeh."

"In Japanese it's the word for dog. You knew that, didn't you?"

He nods his head yes.

"You ever had one?" I ask.

"We used to, but we had to leave him under a tree."

"Under a tree?"

"Yeah. Whenever we went anyplace in the truck, he would follow us until we got to the railroad tracks in the town. He would go under a big tree and wait for us. Everytime we came back we would slow down so Tippy-tin could jump on and ride home."

"So when you came to camp?"

"We left Tippy-tin sitting under the tree . . . . How

come the guys call me 'Inu?'"

"Maybe it's a game. What does your father have to say about it?"

"I don't know."

"You don't know? Why not?"

"He was sent to North Dakota."

"North Dakota? Your Father's in North Dakota. Well, I wouldn't worry about those guys too much. I've been called 'Inu' too."

"How come?"

"These are times of trouble. People want to find someone real to blame. Because we're together behind these fences, we call each other or the administration people names. Nobody here is to blame. Do you understand?"

"I think so."

"Hey, Uojiro, cheer up. Things aren't all bad." I put my arm around his shoulders and pull him close. Uojiro smiles up at me. He grabs me around the waist.

"When you're little, the adult world seems so big and confusing. I know. When I first came to America, I didn't understand anything. But it was funny, too."

"How come?"

"Well, the first time I saw a western toilet was on the ship. I thought you had to squat, like we did in Japan. So I got up on the seat and squatted!"

Uojiro laughs. "How?"

"You better get to school. You're almost late. Just ignore those kids and concentrate on school work."

"Thanks, Ben." Uojiro turns the corner towards the school barrack. His small, wiry body is fragile and out of place behind barbed wire. The guard tower and the soldier with the gun suddenly become excessive.

From the apex of Castle Rock we must appear to be

a thousand black creatures in sterile regimentation. The spaces between barracks are uniform. The fire-break divides us into controllable units, 18,000 people huddling around six thousand cast iron stoves.

In order to bridge the language barrier between the Issei and the administration, Mr. Moore of Internal Security asks me to accept a job as an interpreter. He is a tall lanky man with a narrow face, a small moustache, a sharp nose and kindly eyes that inspire trust. On a shelf behind him are several books on Japan, Japanese culture, and on understanding Asia.

Mr. Moore says, "The camp must serve as an equitable substitute for the life, work and homes given up. Every able-bodied evacuee must share in building the camp community."

"Then why have the Issei been excluded from positions of leadership? There are rumors that you give first priority to JACL members. They have some of the best jobs in camp."

"You don't understand. It is just a matter of having English speaking people on the committees."

"It has become a serious source of conflict in the camp."

"That is why we are screening people carefully. We are counting heavily on young people to keep things peaceful. Even though things are not perfect, we must cooperate. Do you agree?"

"Yes."

"Good. We feel you will be a real asset. Now then," he says, picking up the paper. My name is written on the top. "Do you feel loyalty to this country despite being sent here?"

"I'm not bitter."

"There are many people on the outside who do not

understand the people in the camps. It is important we establish the loyalty of the 'colonists' so we can tell the outside."

"Why is that important?"

"The hatred didn't stop when you came into these camps. Did you know it was political pressure that forced the WRA to lower their pay scales to sixteen dollars a month? There was a storm of public protest when they heard the Japanese in camps would be paid more then the American soldier . . . . It's discouraging, but it's true."

"Many people are bitter about that. There is already talk of strikes."

"Because of the wages?"

"Yes, but it's more than that. It's been building up all summer. The mail censorship doesn't help. As more Japanese are brought in, there are squabbles over scrap lumber and complaints that the best jobs are already taken. They don't like the mess hall food. People are hoarding rice and canned goods from the canteen because they've heard the WRA food supplies are running out. They're angry because they think the WRA personnel are selling the mess hall food to the canteen cooperative for profit."

In the early morning of a late fall harvest day the farm crew gathers at the dispatching station to be transported to the farm. It is several minutes beyond the time the truck ordinarily pulls through the gates, but it is still half empty. The younger guys demand a work stoppage, but the older Issei won't cooperate. A scuffle breaks out. Oshiki staggers out of the crowd with blood oozing from a gash on his hairline. He climbs back in the truck, determined to put in his day's work. A young

Nisei tough named Horie bullies the older Oshiki from the truck. Across the road Gordie burst out of the newspaper barrack and dashes over to the fight. He shoves Horie aside and leads Oshiki to the shade of the barrack. Oshiki takes his red polka dot handkerchief and gives it to Gordie to wrap around the wound.

Some fifty feet away, Honda climbs on the bed of a truck and calls in Japanese through a small hand megaphone, "Breakfast was not good enough for men who work hard in the fields." Several people shout agreement. Meanwhile more people gather around the area and send messengers to bring others.

Sunlight glitters off the public address system being hurriedly assembled on the porch of the administration offices. Following a loud blare of static, a metallic voice announces, "The failure of any crops will be place on the shoulders of the uncooperative and unwilling farm workers."

Honda begins shouting louder through his megaphone, but the microphone drowns him out.

"I am Arlin Kehoe, the Project Director," the microphone announces. "It is my job to maintain this camp in a peaceful, orderly manner. We urge everyone to forget the strike talk and go back to work. Let the small squabbles be ironed out by a negotiating committee."

"They are not small squabbles," Honda shouts. "It is matter of good breakfast so we can work forty-eight hour week."

"Why must we negotiate," Reverend Togasaki shouts angrily, "when it is responsibility of government to take care of us. We did not ask to come here."

"It is your farm. The food harvested now is what you will eat this winter."

"Our farm! That's a laugh! We're slaves!"

"You're stealing the food from the mess halls! WRA guys are making money on us!"

More and more Japanese gather, shouting obscenities at Moore and Kehoe.

"Tell your white guys we don't like them keeping our time cards!"

"Yeh! When you going to fix our shoes? You're supposed to be taking care of us!"

"Wait a minute. Hold it," Kehoe says.

"Speak Japanese," someone shouts. "Don't understand English!"

Moore steps up to the microphone. "Benjamin Senzaki. If you are present, please come to the platform."

I am introduced to Kehoe and given instructions. Together we step up to the microphone. "All harvesting including the valuable potato crop is behind schedule. Crops must be harvested without further delay."

A rumbling of disapproval flows from the crowd. When there is quiet, we inform them, "Any justifiable grievances will be taken up with the grievance committee. We cannot allow petty complaints to become a source of conflict."

"We have not received pay for July and August," Horie calls out. "A sum of $32. 50¢ a day and U.S government cannot find money to pay us."

There is a roar of laughter.

"You will be guaranteed better breakfasts, if you go to work as scheduled." He consults with Dover, the Assistant Project Director. "The morning is already half gone, so we have decided you men can take the day off. Enjoy yourselves for the rest of the day."

The crowd disappears into the maze of corridors. Kehoe reaches for my hand and pumps it warmly.

"Thank you," he says, "for helping us avert trouble. There were a lot of people out there. Wouldn't want a big crowd like that to get touched off."

"There have been reports of riots from Manzanar and Poston," Moore says.

"The crowd gathered so quickly," Kehoe says. Where did they all come from?"

"There are 18,000 of us in a square mile," I answer.

"Perhaps there should be some kind of ban on public gatherings," Moore says.

I awaken at midnight to footsteps on our porch, followed by pounding. Uojiro is at the door, panting. "Mother sent me. It's Gordie. He got beat up."

We run hard between barracks. I marvel at Uojiro's endurance: my own lungs are bursting. Uojiro takes me to a darkened area near his barracks. His mother is leaning over Gordie. He lies face up; blood from his forehead seeps into temple hairs.

Jeanne says, "I sent Uojiro. Mr. Yamato found Gordie and yelled. We came right away."

When I gently lift his shoulders and head, his arm flops to the side in a grotesque angle. I lower him back down, remove the sleeve of his broken arm and button the arm into the shirt. Uojiro leading, I carry Gordie to the emergency room of the camp hospital where his scalp is sutured and his arm set in a cast.

"Do you know who it was?" I ask Gordie when he is alert enough to answer.

"It happened so fast.... They came from behind.... I don't know for sure, but I . . . have an idea. They're anti-JACL."

"You mean the strike organizers."

"Just might be."

Mother, who was never fearful during immigration or Pearl Harbor, police curfews or military evacuation, is now frightened by an incomprehensible violence inflicted by fellow Japanese. To Father, who has overcome restrictive land laws, language and racial barriers, it is another step away from a once well-ordered world.

By the end of the week Gordie returns home and for the first time since the beginning days of camp, the twenty-by-twentyroom becomes home again. Family friends come by to see how Gordie is feeling. Obasan hovers anxiously over Gordie. His wounds awaken her fears for Kageyama.

The Sacramento buddies use our apartment as a temporary gathering place for occasional poker games. We plan our revenge, but it is no more than talk. The streets of Nihonmachi had not taught us violence. We agree to form a protection committee to prevent further beatings.

Aside from the classes she teaches, Mother curtails her outside activities, in order to take care of Gordie and prepare the apartment for winter. We completely encase the interior in sheetrock, and Mother hangs watercolors and sumi paintings of flowers and birds and the hills surrounding us. From a package she has carried from Sacramento, she papers the windows with translucent rice paper, its fibers woven over small leaves of bamboo. With this slight refocusing of attention upon each other, I suddenly realize how little time we now spend together as a family. Father has become a stranger.

Where once he kept careful account of what each of us was doing, he now is preoccupied with the Cooperative Enterprise, made up mostly of Issei. Although his position as head of the family and leader in the community has been usurped by the administration and the government, he and the other Issei are able to exercise some control and influence through this organization.

Chapter 14

Through the windows above eye level I see the sky suddenly swarm with white flakes. It is the first snowfall at Tule -- the prettiest I have seen the camp.

The administration has called a meeting of persons who represent the various interest groups and factions in Tule, in order to discuss the escalating violence. Besides Gordie, Okada was beaten, followed by an attempted attack of an active member of the JACL from Oregon.

The Japanese men come into the administration barracks, stamping their feet and swatting snow off their shoulders and chests. They look curiously at the rooms where the Caucasians work. It is warm already from a fire started well before the meeting.

I know Moore and Rothke, and I've met Kehoe. Although I do not know any of them well, I feel a kinship with them for having chosen to work here. Kehoe, I have learned, is a man of God, a man of deep conviction, who believes it is his responsibility to aid the Japanese in camps. He was a friend to many Japanese before coming to Tule. Rothke is a young lawyer who believes the imprisonment of the Japanese Americans to be unconstitutional. Moore is a career sociologist who met many Japanese in his student days at Stanford University.

I do not know the others: Williams, Dover, and Bandon. From what I have seen, most of those who are here to help us are humanitarianly motivated.

"Living worthwhile and fulfilling lives in the shadow of fear and violence is not possible." Kehoe says, the light above him highlighting weary lines of his face, "It is our responsibility to use the power of self-government to restrict violent elements to the farthest corners of the camp."

Within the boundaries of the "farthest corners" is a diversity of people few Caucasians understand. There are American-educated Nisei; Japan-educated Kibei; Issei from farms; Issei from cities; English-speaking; non-English-speaking.

Representing the diversity at the meeting are Father, Dr. Ono and Atsumi, Issei businessmen and professionals. Honda, the son of an Issei farmer, is a labor contractor, an older Kibei educated through high school in Japan. Mrs. Makino from Portland has three children; her husband is in the detention camp in Santa Fe. Togasaki, a Buddhist priest from Seattle, was born in Hawaii and educated in Japan. There are also leaders of the Japanese American Citizens League.

How well do the administrators understand the diversity?

Mr. Dover, the assistant project director, adds to Kehoe's opening remarks. "Whatever we create in Tule Lake is what we will have to live with. Tule can be a model of what people can do if they work together."

"A temporary refuge in a concentration camp," Reverend Togasaki says.

"Tule Lake is not a concentration camp," Kehoe says quickly. "It is relocation center. Things are always handled with consideration. WRA workers are here by choice rather than coercion, living under the same circumstances as the colonists."

Reverend Togasaki, feigns surprise. *Colonists!* You

believe all people, white and Japanese, live under same circumstances? You are free to come and go as you please. It is your job and you are well paid. We are given $16 a month. We are prisoners of war. Barbed wire is not for Caucasian but for Japanese."

"I cannot find it in myself to argue with you," Kehoe replies, his voice subdued. "Yes, I am free to come and go. I am decently paid for the job I perform. Against these things I cannot argue. However, do not forget, the dust which blows in your face blows in mine. The disruption you must live with, I must live with also."

"If you do not like disruption of people justified in anger, why do you not leave?" Reverend Togasaki asks.

"Perhaps," Kehoe replies, "it is in some small way to make up for a country that has failed you."

"And I ask," Dover interjects, "how long can we live with anger and bitterness before it engulfs all of us and destroys a chance to create a decent community?" Dover is a young man in his late twenties. His face is concerned and earnest. His eyes blink often when he talks.

"It is true," I reply, looking at Dover, "and perhaps that is what is wrong."

Honda rises angrily. "It is always same story, that Japanese hear since first Japanese immigrant came to America. It is true we have no choice. Caucasian always have choice. Whether Japanese should own land; whether Japanese can become citizen; whether Japanese have self-government."

Kehoe, flushed now, replies, "Understand we are not arguing against those obvious truths. We ask you to try to understand the true purpose of WRA. Our goal is to resettle all of you outside of these camps. We must work towards a peaceful camp so we can win the acceptance of the outside world."

Mrs. Makino, her voice low and without accent, says, "Why should we work to have people outside these fences accept us? They have not done so in fifty years. Ask Issei who are growing old if winning acceptance was worth the effort. Now we are told things will be better after the war. You will guarantee this?"

"Of course, we can make no such guarantees. It is only something we can hope for and work towards."

"Only a fool can believe it will change." Reverend Togasaki says. "For once we should admit truth. We are Japanese and we can be nothing else because Caucasian will not let us."

I look at Father. His face is stern, and I wonder if he, too, feels the same bitterness. Kehoe, flustered, looks around the table to the other Japanese, his gaze stopping on Father. "Mr. Senzaki," he says. "You have said nothing. Is this the way you feel, too?"

Father remains silent for a moment; his face shows no emotion. Slowly, he says, "I am not happy about being here. We did not ask to come. We came at gunpoint. For many years we have had no choice in many decisions about ourselves. I am angry about these things also." His gaze moves from the Caucasian group to the Japanese. "I am close friend of Okada who is in the hospital with a concussion. And my own son was beaten ... by fellow Japanese. It is only crazy people and fools who believe they should beat their own people."

We are fenced off from the outside world, but we are not isolated. While Gordie recuperates, news seeps into Tule from other camps. Adjustment to detention has taken a similar path in each camp. Initially, the internees were cooperative and surprisingly flexible.

Soon unrest and distrust began to develop. Internees expressed anger and frustration against the administration and victimized their fellow Japanese as the cause of their troubles. Major revolts broke out in Poston and Manzanar.

In Poston internees suspected of "informing" on fellow Japanese were sent gifts of dog bones with "Inu" written on them. Men wore dog masks in demonstrations and posted cartoons of dogs with the names of accused Japanese. Finally, two men were severely beaten. Two arrests were made, resulting in a large mob demanding the release of the prisoners. A strike was called throughout Poston. Campfires burned all night to comfort the strikers. Supporters played Japanese music to entertain them.

The administration reacted with understanding, immediately setting up negotiation meetings to work out an agreement. The strike was settled and the camp returned to normal.

In Manzanar the administration authorized the commanding officer of the military police to declare martial law. Soldiers with submachine guns lined up against the jeering crowd. They threw tear gas bombs at the evacuees, sending them running blindly in every direction. When the crowd reassembled, the soldiers fired without orders. Ten evacuees were wounded, two died. Throughout the night the Military Police patrolled Manzanar. Mess hall bells tolled loudly for the dead.

From peaceful communities that survived fifty years of difficulties, we have come to camps to learn violence.

Chapter 15

The lava is pockmarked, jagged, crumbling from centuries exposed to winds, sun, seasons. Where once it poured hot from earth like water, boiling over forest and plain, it now lies cold and hard on a walkway where children play, their airy voices singing:

> *Chi Chi Pa Pa,*
> *Suzume no gakko no sense wa,*
> *Muchi Oh furi furi,*
> *Chi Pa Pa.*

It is a cold, hard winter: the struggle to keep warm softens the edges of anger. Rumors shift to gossip about young couples caught in the darkened wash houses or the block mess chief embezzling food allowance funds. Babies are born; children attend school. Mothers continue their chores, doing their best to raise children inside a concentration camp.

In late November Gordie and the JACL leader from Oregon are called to Salt Lake City to meet with two delegates from each camp for a Japanese American Citizens League conference. The national JACL leaders were given permission by the WRA director to meet to discuss the reinstatement of the Japanese Americans' right to serve in the armed forces. JACL and WRA officials feel future resettlement of the Japanese would be hampered by the absence of Japanese Americans in the armed forces. The delegates at the Salt Lake City conference vote unanimously to petition the President of the United States to allow Nisei to fight for their country.

The temporary peace ends in January, when a War Department release states a loyalty registration will take place in all camps as a first step in forming an all-volunteer Japanese American regiment.

Rumors again sweep the camp: to prisoners who have lost all civil rights, the government will reinstate the right to fight and be killed; we will be sent to the Pacific theater to fight against relatives; the JACL "Inus" must be responsible.

"What about you?" Father says, eyeing me.

"This is a concentration camp, not a relocation center. I don't intend to fight for this."

"You are bitter?"

"I'm not bitter, but I too have to fight for what I think is right and honorable."

Mother says, "Perhaps it would be better to stay in these camps together." She glances around the mess hall. "Under these conditions, we do not have the same responsibilities."

"Our responsibilities are the same," Gordie says, carefully. "Whatever has happened to us, we are still Americans citizens. Do you want us to sit around in these camps and rot while others fight? Do you want us to be remembered for that?"

"We are becoming outcasts among our own people," Mother says softly. "People are saying we are 'Inu'."

"Because of me?" Gordie says angrily. "They're fools!"

Gordie's loud voice draws attention from those around us. A young Nisei at the next table shouts, "Fools? You're the fool. You'd have us all get killed while our families rot in these camps."

Gordie jumps to his feet, his face flushed, but before he can say anything, the front door of the mess hall slams open and Reverend Togasaki comes into the room accompanied by four young bodyguards. Taking over the front table, with his bodyguards stationed at the two entrances, Togasaki announces in Japanese, "Two days ago Army recruiting team was supposed to arrive in camp."

Tomato elbows me. "Here comes the goon squad," he whispers.

Togasaki continues, "They have not come yet, so we take opportunity to warn all people against registering. It is not wise to sign paper. Government can strip you of citizenship then force you back to Japan. If you wish to go back to Japan, do it on own terms. You do not have to register. There are many ways to resist. Many people tear up birth certificates. Do not do anything until you hear from Block Representatives who will meet to clear up issues."

"Who do you represent?" Gordie interrupts loudly.

"We represent all Japanese of Tule Lake. We are part of committee urging all blocks bind members not to register."

"What authority do you have to do that?"

"It is not matter of right, or authority, but matter of responsibility. We have been lied to and deceived since December seventh. Now it is important to be cautious or they will destroy our families."

"That is just what *you're* trying to do."

"Unlike some people," Togasaki says sarcastically, "I did not volunteer to come here. Unlike past, we must have concern for more than Nisei, but for all of us, young and old."

"Get out of here, 'bakatare!'" Gordie shouts, shaking

his fist, "And take your stupid goons with you. You've got thirty seconds!"

I glance around and see Goto, Tomato, Asoo on the edges of their seats.

"The time will come," Togasaki says, moving towards the door and signaling his bodyguards to go outside.

We have become two people now: if we register loyal, we are "Inu" to fellow Japanese; if we register disloyal, we are "anti-American" to WRA and the public. We are forced to decide by a registration we do not understand.

The announcement for registration in the *Tulean Dispatch* tells of a large meeting of the Nisei Community Council and the Issei of the Block Representatives and the Planning Board. Kehoe begins the meeting with the announcement from the Secretary of War, stating that it is the inherent right of every faithful citizen to bear arms in the country's battles.

"As some of you know," Kehoe continues, "the goal of WRA has always been to return you to your homes. With the War Department's decision to establish a Japanese regiment, we can begin a resettlement program sooner than we expected."

"Resettlement!" Honda interrupts. "What is that? WRA is planning to kick us out of camp?"

"Nothing of the sort! Resettlement will be a side effect in the determination of who is loyal and who is disloyal."

"Loyal?" Honda persists. "Who is loyal? We are here because we are disloyal, aren't we?"

"The purpose of this meeting is not to determine who is loyal or who is disloyal," Kehoe says, his voice rising. "We must determine loyalty through the use of these questionnaires."

"When do we get to see them?" Reverend Togasaki asks.

"You must give me a chance to explain," Kehoe answers. "They will first be given to Block Representatives who will give them to you. The Army will send recruiting teams for young men who register loyal and want to volunteer for combat."

Many people stand up, call out, wave their arms to be recognized. Kehoe taps on the microphone until there is quiet. "It would be fruitless to go further at this time. There will be more meetings to iron out details and answer questions."

Kehoe abruptly steps back and introduces Gordie as a representative of JACL who attended the recent conference at Salt Lake City.

Gordie begins, "We feel the action taken by the President and the War Department provides us with an opportunity to prove our loyalty to America."

In two days we are given the following questionnaires.

For men over 17 years who are citizens:

Question 27: Are you willing to serve in the armed forces of the United States on combat duty, wherever ordered?

Question 28: Will you swear unqualified allegiance to the United States of America and faithfully defend the United States from any or all attack by foreign or domestic forces, and forswear any form of allegiance or obedience to the Japanese Emperor, or any other foreign government, power, or organization?

For women citizens and for Issei men and women:

Question 27: If the opportunity presents itself and you are found qualified, would you be willing to volunteer for the Army Nurse Corps or the WAAC?

Question 28: Will you swear unqualified allegiance to the United States of America and forswear any form of allegiance or obedience to the Japanese Emperor, or any other foreign government, power, or organization?

Chapter 16

I hold my palm skyward, intercept several of the million crystals floating to Tule. I watch them touch and dissolve into tiny water points. Beyond my fingers the sky disappears in a swirling white. Flakes sail down in long sliding drifts, appearing never to collide. Snow crumbles against frozen wire; large flakes are impaled on barbed spikes.

Within a day Tule sinks a foot; within another day, two. When I see Gordie standing in a quilt of white, he seems rooted. More fragile than barracks, poles, fences -- yet hardier, more resilient, more permanent. I wait for Gordie at the window of the meeting room where we have gathered to hear a young lieutenant explain the new government program for enlistment.

The young lieutenant begins in a slow drawl. "I understand the difficult decision you men face, being asked to volunteer for service from these relocation centers."

Gordie arrives and moves back against the wall to give his full attention to the lieutenant.

"The formation of a voluntary regiment of men from Hawaii and the relocation centers is not an experiment," the lieutenant continues. "It is a broadening of a policy to return all of you to your normal place in society, a level consistent with the dignity of American citizenship."

He is one voice or many voices: a handsome man in Army uniform, clean and wrinkle-less, tiny bright bronze buttons, shoes shiny in Tule dust.

The sun has already disappeared below distant mountain ridges. "So far you have accepted all the sacrifices of a temporary nature. Now we ask those who are eligible for military service to complete the questionnaire, giving yes answers to questions 27 and 28. Those who cannot answer yes will be treated as conscientious objectors."

"How come you got a Japanese sergeant?" someone interrupts. "How come you the officer and he's the sergeant?" The Japanese sergeant shuffles uneasily.

"Not good enough?" Moriuchi suggests. "Or maybe he can't be trusted."

"Our purpose for coming here is not to hold an open forum but to answer questions on registration procedures and the all-Japanese regiment."

"How come it's got to be all-Japanese outfit? We not good enough to fight with whites?"

"The '442' is to be composed of all Japanese who will fight well and become a source of pride to Japanese Americans."

"Ho boy!" Horie calls out. "You got all the answers, Captain! Maybe we'll be easier to identify in case things don't go right."

The meeting degenerates into hostile laughter. First softly, then louder, a voice grows in chorus against the lieutenant and his program.

In the backwash of fading laughter, Horie, his fist clenched, begins again the angry questioning. "I got a brother in Camp Savage," he shouts. "They won't let him visit my sick father in a county hospital because he's a yellow Jap."

Before the lieutenant can acknowledge Horie, someone asks him why an American citizen by birth was changed from combat to alien classification at the outbreak of war.

The lieutenant looks away to a floor board. "I cannot answer that. The decision was made a year ago and is now being countermanded. Now all male citizens over 17 years are being classified 1A. And if they don't volunteer, they will possibly be drafted."

"You confuse us, Captain!" Horie shouts. "A few minutes ago you said you didn't want disloyals. Now you tell us we get drafted anyway."

"What about this part of the questionnaire? 'If the opportunity presents itself and you are found qualified, would you be willing to volunteer for Army Nurse Corps or WAAC?"

The man asking stares quietly for a few seconds. "My mother wants to know if she really can join the Army Nurse Corps or the WAAC. She's only seventy-seven!"

The officer's face turns red. He looks to the water pitcher and signals for a glass. As he reaches for it, a man in the front row calls out. The glass slips. There is sudden widening moisture around the lieutenant's crotch.

Everyone laughs deliriously. The white officer is to us what we are to those who have put us behind barbed wire. We do not care whether our actions are justified. The lieutenant turns a beet red color.

Muratani rises above the heads onto a table, waves his arms for quiet, and asks whether his accent disqualifies him from giving orders in English to Caucasian soldiers. Beyond the swaying of Muratani, Gordie's face appears, disappears. Each time I get a glimpse of him he grows a shade angrier. Muratani and Moriuchi have openly joined those who are against the JACL proposal to reinstate Nisei into the armed services. Gordie begins moving towards Muratani.

From another place in the room Goto and Asoo make their move. They converge on Muratani. Goto looks at Gordie then fingers the chair, jerking it out from under Muratani. As he falls, Gordie clubs him with his cast.

Like water poured on an ant hill, there is sudden scurrying activity. Before Gordie is lost to sight, I mark the distance, the position where he disappears. Arms and hips and posts bump me as I wade through Japanese bodies.

Then I see Gordie. He glances at me. In his eyes there is a faint flicker of a smile. I scramble to him, grab his arm and try to lead him towards the exit.

Above the chaos, I hear him. "Where you going?"

"Your arm! You got time to fight later! Damn you!" I drag him, feel him stumble on a body lying in the aisle.

Through the door where the lieutenant and sergeant have long departed, we escape the barracks. We breathe deeply the cold air of winter. We stand in shadow, feel the building jostling on footings and girders, then step beyond the icicles hanging from the eaves, our hearts pounding.

Gordie moves back to the window, stands on tiptoe. "Goto, Tomato, Asoo, Taniguchi, Yuji . . . all the guys. They're wiping 'em out." Gordie starts towards the door. "I gotta get back in there."

I grab his arm. "Hold it! They can do without us just this once. There'll be other opportunities."

"But maybe it'll be our last chance . . . all of us together."

"You'll be fighting for something bigger and more important soon."

Gordie eases back against my pull, then gingerly reaches up, touching his temple. He says, "Maybe you're right. Besides, I did get a good one here. Saw stars." Smiling, his face barely discernible from the soft light of snow, he looks through the window. The building is bouncing on its foundation, its contents rattling like pebbles in a tin can. People bolt from the barracks into the cold night air.

"It's dying out," I tell him, my hand still gripping his arm. "Time to go."

"Always the rational man, the cool head," he says. "You're right, as usual. But still . . .this damned arm!" It thuds against his side. "Shit on it all!"

We walk away, our feet crunching the snow. Gordie laughs softly. When I ask what humors him at such strange times, he says, "This is some weapon. Did you see their faces as Muratani sailed off the floor?"

"I was busy."

He laughs again. He puts his arm over my shoulder, singing softly the first line of a new song.

"My momma done tol' me . . . a woman's a two-faced thing . . ." He breaks off into a hum.

The sound of his voice disappears into the night, leaving behind only the sound of snow crinkling under our feet. He says, "Like when we were kids. Like when we fought together downtown."

His arm drops to his side. "Tonight," he says, thrusting his hands in his coat pockets, "tonight, I feel good. The kind of thing I almost forgot existed. Maybe it was because of letting go. Or maybe being in that crazy riot together, knowing that you badly needed somebody and that he was around to help you. I knew you'd come. Makes me feel good . . . but . . . it makes me feel so bad too."

"Bad? Why?"

"I really don't know. But maybe because changes are coming so fast. That this might be the last time all our Sacramento buddies are together."

"When you going to leave for the Army?"

"You know? Of course. Soon. Whenever this arm heals."

Gordie turns to look at me. "What about you? Why don't you join up too? We could go it together. You, me, Asoo, Yuji, and whoever else. We could all go together."

"I can't. They can't."

"Why? Joining the Army and fighting for this country is what we've always wanted, isn't it?"

"A year ago, yes. We were free. We were in our homes."

"Free? The way things were? People with college degrees working in fruit stands or in drug stores as stock boys -- shelving aspirins and cough medicines? Have you forgotten?"

"This is an improvement? Don't you feel bitter about being here?"

"Sure. When I saw that fence for the first time, I was angry, of course. But when it lost its edge, I saw something else. I knew our time would come, and I knew whatever alternative they offered, I would take it."

Kicking at the snow, Gordie flips up the collar of his coat, "But that's only for me," he says with emphasis. "The last thing I know is what's right or what's wrong for anyone else . . . only what I have to do."

For a long while I cannot say anything.

"And you?" Gordie asks.

"You can't stay. I can't leave. Something came

clear tonight for me too, while listening to that lieutenant and those angry Japanese. There are no disloyal Japanese in these camps, and there were no disloyal Japanese before we came here. They've put something ter-
ribly wrong on us, and I want to . . . I have to stay here
and fight it out."

We move into a firebreak, dwarfed by barracks,
fencing, and mountains. Gordie says, "Maybe it's the
best way. I would hate to think of leaving Mother and
Father in this crazy place by themselves."

Chapter 17

The riot has shattered any illusions about an ideal camp community. For Mother and Father the breakdown of order becomes a reality when Gordie receives a letter threatening his life. The Project Director, Kehoe, requests his removal along with three other JACL enlistees to the county jail in Klamath Falls until they leave for boot camp.

For the past week, Mother has begun to prepare herself for Gordie's departure in the way of a Japanese woman: she must accept that a son going off to war will not return. From childhood she has been trained to meet death courageously. There is a quietness about her, masking her sadness as she carries on her daily chores and activities.

The jail house lounge seems a strange setting to gather for our last good-byes to Gordie. There are bars on the windows, straightbacked chairs, and heavy wire screens around the entrances. Mother remains cheerful, determined to make the last moments happy ones.

For Father, Gordie's enlistment against his own wishes is another step in the breaking down of a tradition in which he and other Issei have been the leaders but now find their leadership and advice superfluous. Recognizing the futility of resisting Gordie's decision, he lays aside his ambivalence and nurtures his pride in knowing Gordie is among the first men from Tule Lake to volunteer.

"A man cannot fight well if he does not believe in

what he is fighting for," he says. "If he does not fight well, he will get killed, for the wrong reasons. You must fight well and bring honor to your family and yourself."

"I will fight well, Dad. I am an American. I know what I am fighting for."

Father sighs and shakes his head. "If we had stayed in Japan, you would be a soldier in the Japanese Army fighting against this country. But we are here, and your future is here. It is just as well. This is a big and powerful country. Japan is strong too, but it is so small. There is no way Japan can defeat America."

Father and Mother and Gordie sit in the jail lounge talking for the last time, the shadows of their heads on the wall criss-crossed with steel bars. It is from these people that I learned how to become an American.

Gordie is cheerful. His cast removed, he is ready for the rigors of combat training at Camp Shelby, where he will join Nisei from the other camps and Hawaii to form the 442nd Regimental Combat Team. I remember his impetuousness since the days I first knew him. Once when he was 11, he challenged a boy for calling us dirty Japs. I wanted to grab Gordie and run, but there was no space through the legs imprisoning us. We were encircled by a group of screaming adults egging on Gordie and the boy. Gordie fought to a draw. When it was over, he was pleased with himself. He had done the right thing. He has the same look on his face as he boards the bus with the other young men.

We all try to be formal and dignified in our farewells. Gordie grabs Mother and hugs her, and then does the same to Dad and me. The last we see of him is through glass.

Now he is gone. The cot next to me is empty. The

camp, the barracks, the apartment suddenly close in, as if a part of me has departed with him. I try to understand why he has left and why I am here; why he is called a "loyal" but a traitor to his people in camp; why I am labeled "disloyal" and an anti-administration agitator.

I have been dismissed from my job in the legal office because a person who refuses to register cannot hold such a position of trust.

Rothke and Moore call me into the office for questioning.

"We have known you since the beginning of this camp," Rothke says, "and nothing has indicated you would in any way have disloyal tendencies. We would like to know why you refuse to register."

"It is a matter of conscience," I answer. "I cannot condone something I know is wrong."

"Is it because of concern for your parents?" Moore asks. "Is it because you don't want to leave them here by themselves? If so, you should tell us, so you do not jeopardize your entire future in this country."

"Do you realize," Rothke says, "that by not registering, your parents might be risking their chances of making it in America? Who knows what the government might do with aliens who are judged disloyal?"

"What is happening in this camp," I answer, "has little to do with loyalty or disloyalty. It has to do with anger and bitterness."

"And remember," Moore says, "any interference with registration or failure to comply is a violation of the Espionage Act, punishable by maximum penalties of $10,000 fine or twenty years imprisonment or both."

"People like you," Rothke says, "with your education, your background, your position of influence, must set an example for the people. It is your responsibility."

"Yes," Moore repeats. "It's your responsibility."

"Izumi, Yuji," the lieutenant from the riot meeting reads from a list. "Tomita, William; Goto, John; Taniguchi, Edward; Senzaki, Benjamin."

"In the morning there will be transportation for you to come to the administration building and register. Registration is compulsory."

The next morning trucks arrive at pick-up points. They return empty. Registration fails to materialize.

In the *Tulean Dispatch* we read, "Non-registration punishable under the Espionage Act." We are threatened by prison terms from one side and violence and alienation on the other.

Instead of the rush for registration, a crowd of fifty impatiently stand around the Internal Security office to apply for repatriation. Several youths try to force their way through the M.P.'s barring the front door. Kehoe comes out then and reads from a notice. "It is a mistaken idea to suppose if male citizens obtain repatriation blanks, they do not have to register. Registration is compulsory for all male citizens seventeen years of age and older."

"That isn't what you said before," Horie shouts.

"It was mistaken information," Kehoe concedes above the voices. "We are now setting the record straight."

"You are changing the rules of the game!" Moriuchi calls out. "That is what you Caucasians are always doing. Give us repatriation forms!"

There is shouting and demanding of rights.

When the angry youths quiet down, Kehoe says, "please be patient. All of this anger you feel is a result of not understanding the issues. Don't be rash. We will meet again with the Planning Board and clarify the registration procedures and inform you as soon as possible. Please return to your normal activities. It would be foolish to have to call in the Military Police."

Temporarily, anger subsides. I respect Kehoe for avoiding a confrontation. Perhaps it is the mention of the Planning Board. Along with the Cooperative Enterprise, this is the only group where the Issei have influence in camp decision making. The eight elected Issei representing each ward are known for their leadership in their former communities. They have the respect and admiration of a large segment of the Tule population. The Community Council, the Nisei self-governing unit of Tule, has profound confidence in the Plannning Board members, working closely with them on administrative issues.

Father has been gone long hours into the nights, working feverishly with his fellow members of the Planning Board to stem the anti-registration tide. They have prepared a statement urging those who wish to remain in the United States to give registration careful thought. "It is matter," the statement says, "that should not be influenced by the emotions and dire feeling of the moment but by careful and reasoned thinking. We feel parents should act as consultants to their children."

The administration withholds circulation of the statement because they feel parents would have detrimental influence on the Nisei.

"They are our children," Father says exasperatedly, "and as parents we have a right to guide them."

"This is different," Kehoe says. "We are not talking about cultural or religious matters, but of political loyalties in this country. Because the Issei might not understand the problems, they might give advice that could result in tragic consequences."

Father replies, "We are trying to work with you, and you are telling us what we can or cannot discuss with our children?"

"On these particular issues, because of their political nature, we feel only we can clearly explain them. We urge you to accede to our feelings."

"You wish us to change the statement to read, 'Registration is a matter of individual choice and final decision should be left up to each person?"

"No. Because it is not an individual decision. Especially in the atmosphere that prevails. It would be too easy for people under emotional stress to make the wrong choices. We must all work to clear the air so that the correct collective decision is made."

Although there is frustration there is a feeling among the Board members that they have contributed towards turning the tide of anti-registration.

The next day Father pales in anger. The administration, convinced the resistance to registration is traceable to pro-Japan agitators, is embarking on a policy of identifying, arresting and removing the disruptive elements. Two members of the Planning Board are sent to an isolation center in Moab, Utah.

Father resigns from the Planning Board along with all other remaining members. The Issei generation has been effectively removed from any decision making processes.

In the evening the matter of non-registration is discussed between the three of us. I cannot register, but because of the threat of Father being removed and sent away to an isolation camp, it is decided they should register Yes-Yes secretly.

A new list is circulated. It again gives the names of those male citizens over 17 years of age who have not registered. I am named along with Tomato, Taniguchi, Asoo, Goto, Yuji and others who in the confusion have not yet decided what to do. A single truck will be dispatched to Block 44. At that time those eligible will be taken to the administration building to register.

When I awake from restless sleep in the early morning, I stare at the yellowing gypsum above me, stained with dust and moisture and smoke. Save for Mother's and Father's heavy breathing on the other side of the partition, it is deathly quiet. A camp of 18,000 people within a square mile as quiet in the early morning as farmlands in Florin. I remember the green fields of strawberries in the spring time, the rows upon rows of grape vines so carefully tended, the wood-framed farmhouse, its warmth and simplicity and the peculiar odor of a wood-burning stove mingled with Japanese cooking. I remember the weather-beaten barn where in late December the men of the nearby families would take turns pounding sweet steamed rice into a smooth, sticky dough to be made into the mochi for New Years festivities. As young boys, Gordie and I long anticipated the day when we would become man enough to take our turns with the wooden sledge hammer. We were finally allowed to do so. I remember the pounding, the sudden jolt of the heavy blows into the rice bin, thinking we could have hammered day and night without stopping.

I turn and look at Gordie's empty cot. "Sabishii." A loneliness floods over me. I try to understand. Perhaps it is the camp, a world unto itself. Perhaps remaining here while others go off to war is wrong. Perhaps I have made a mistake. Perhaps I am wrong ... perhaps I have irrevocably committed myself to a course of action I will spend the rest of my life regretting.

I am idle again, as I had been in the months before evacuation. After we return from breakfast, I sit quietly and watch Father across the room. The early Tule Lake mask of acceptance and resignation wears thin: his face takes on a dark brooding. He is short-tempered with me over the least problem. When he can't find something in the apartment he accuses me of misplacing it. I haven't heard him laugh for weeks. He lashes out at Mother as if suddenly she were responsible for everything.

Mother is openly sad. The deceptive cheer of Gordie's last week is gone. She is alone now and weary. Strangely, instead of feeling compassion, I am angry at her for her weakness. She had left me many years ago in Japan -- her own baby -- then came back and took me from my home in Japan to Sacramento.

My anger spills over to Father who is aging before my eyes. So much of what happened is his doing. He was the one who decided to come to America. He was the one who decided to leave me in Japan and then return to get me. He looks to me a shadow of the man he used to be.

I struggle for self-control. I know that what I feel is destructive. This is not a time we can afford to be negative toward one another. Above all else, we must be together or we will lose everything. I get up abruptly to escape this room with the rice-papered glass windows.

I go straight to Block 44 where the army trucks will arrive with armed soldiers to take the guys on the list to register. It is still early, but the fifteen boys from 44 are lined up and proudly waiting to be taken. Their hair is shaved into bozu haircuts with white bands tied over their temples and foreheads. Their legs are exposed from their white shorts to their socks, mimicking the recruits in a Japanese army boot camp. They have rolled bundles with bedding, clothes, and tooth brushes at their feet.

In the crowd that has gathered to watch I find Goto, Asoo, Tomato, Yuji, and Taniguchi.

"Crazy bastards," Goto says. "You can bet they wouldn't be so enthusiastic if they were back in Japan. I've read about those nuts."

"Even if you don't agree with registration, that sure is a crazy way to go about letting people know," Taniguchi says.

"Yeah," Yuji says. "There've been times this year when I've wondered what I am, but when I see those crazy guys standing around dressed like that, I *know* I'm not a real, live, Japan-type Boochie."

"But you can't blame them for feeling that way." Asoo says. "No one asked to come here."

Goto frowns, but before he can say anything, we hear truck engines on the firebreak road. They roll into the corridor. There is an army command jeep and three troop trucks. A captain and a lieutenant from the MP detachment, both in battle fatigues and helmet with 45's strapped to their hips, jump out of the jeep and signal for the troops with bayonets to come out and fall into ranks opposite the Japanese boys. When they are at attention, the captain turns and begins reading off the names of the required registries.

After the names are read, he announces, "Unless those whose names were read come voluntarily to register, they will be taken at bayonet point."

"Get out of here, Gringoes!" someone shouts from the crowd. A rumble of anger flows through the several hundred people. A couple of guys near us pick up chunks of lava and hurl it towards the soldiers. Before anyone else can follow, Goto bellows in his big voice, "Hold up, you crazy bastards!"

With his muscular six-foot frame, Goto stands above the crowd, intimidating everyone.

A spokesman for the Block 44 guys steps out of rank and announces, "We of Block 44, due to the injustice of forcing people into concentration camps and then requiring them to sign a loyalty oath, collectively refuse to recognize registration. It is a device conceived by Washington to persecute prisoners of war. We refuse registration and will suffer the consequences."

When he finishes, the crowd cheers their heroism.

Tomato says, "Well, if you don't agree with them, you gotta admire 'em."

"Who knows? In this crazy place." Taniguchi shakes his head.

The spectators shout "Bakatare" and "Bastards!" The soldiers surround the boys and march them into the third truck. All the while the Block 44 boys shout to each marching step, "Banzai! Banzai! Banzai!"

Moved by their courage and pleased with their rebellious display, the crowd cheers them as they are driven away.

"What a nut house!" Tomato says.

"Rather clever." I say. Tomato frowns at me.

"Clever? Yeah, clever protest against government injustice, but they had everyone worked up. We coulda had a riot! No telling what those soldiers would do if those rocks hit them. They looked pretty trigger-happy to me."

For a few days the arrest inspires a small movement towards registration but then stops again. Petitions continue to urge non-commitment and a general camp-wide strike. With the war and the world outside temporarily forgotten, fire sirens sound daily and mess hall bells ring, calling meetings to remind everyone that the only things of consequence are in this mile and a quarter square enclosure.

An announcement is made in the *Tulean Dispatch* that an Army representative has arrived in camp from Washington with official explanations of procedures. The following statement is released:

Nisei and Kibei who answer 'No' to questions 27 and 28, and who persist in that answer, cannot anticipate that the Army of the United States will ever ask for their services or that they will be inducted into the armed forces by selective service.

A 'No' answer on question 27, accompanied by a 'Yes' answer on 28, is not regarded by the War Department as proof of disloyalty in the individual, or as bearing on that question . . . [but] these men have the minimum chance of being called into military service.

The 'Yes' answer to both questions speaks for itself.... In case it is so filed, then they are liable to induction for general service elsewhere throughout the Army of the United States, in the same manner as any other inductee within the country.

We are suddenly given a way to break the stale-mate. The officials assure us that we are exempted from military duty if we answer no on questions 27 and 28. We can protest with No-No answers without worry of punishment. For those who are still confused and undecided, the No-Yes answers would relieve them of military service without being labeled "disloyal."

Registration can proceed as planned. When it is over, we hear from outside press and radio that our camp houses thousands of disloyal Japanese American citizens who are potentially dangerous to the war effort.

The registration results in splitting the evacuee population in each of the ten relocation projects into two groups:

1) Adult citizens who swear they have no allegiance outside of the United States and are willing to serve in the armed forces, answering questions 27 and 28 affirmatively, are known as "Yes-Yes's." They also include aliens who are willing to abide by the laws and do nothing to hamper the war effort.

2) A minority in each camp, who either refuse to answer the registration questions or answer them in the negative. They are stigmatized as politically disloyal to the United States and potentially dangerous to its war effort.

We become known as the "No-No Boys."

Chapter 18

As spring ripens into summer, flowers and gardens sprout between barracks. It is our first spring in camp. In the awakening, stone paths, rock gardens, wooden foot bridges transform the drabness of camp into a multitude of miniature replicas of springs in Japan.

Along the original fence, green tule sprouts like bamboo shoots from winter-plated ground, and two hundred feet beyond, another fence rises out of hardpan with its own set of towers, spotlights, and machine guns. Between the fences there are several tanks lined up, their 12mm cannons facing the center of camp. A few hundred yards from the tanks, there are new barracks to house the battalion assigned to guard the Tule Lake Segregation Center.

Once again, within a span of a year and a half, the Japanese community, 115,000 people in ten relocation projects, experience the turmoil of uprooting and change. Following pressure from the American public and the U.S. Congress, Tule Lake has been officially designated a segregation center to house those Japanese who have been stigmatized by the registration as politically disloyal to the United States. In less than 20 days over 6,000 Tuleans leave while over 9,000 "New Segregants" are transfeered to Tule from the nine other camps. Almost 4,000 more arrive by spring.

The inner face of Tule changes. During the first relocation, our communities have remained intact, but now they will be dissected and divided. The young people leave to attend colleges, go in the service, or re-settle in the midwest. Our camp becomes a haven for the very old, the very young, the confused, the bitter, the angry, the disloyal, the loyal Tuleans unwilling to move again. Buses come in and out taking people to the train station in Newell and delivering new arrivals.

Names that have established reputations in the other camps will soon replace those who are departing: Ansai and Shiozawa from Manzanar; Baba and Hiura from Poston; Abe from Heart Mountain; Koike from Topaz; Funo from Santa Fe. Along with the known troublemakers, many thousands of other men, women, and children join 6000 old Tuleans who remain. Word from Santa Fe comes that Kageyama will be interned at Tule Lake as a disloyal troublemaker. The emptiness left by Gordie's absence and the departures of friends is somewhat assuaged by the news of Kageyama's coming. Obasan's insecurity and loneliness are suddenly lifted and replaced with energetic activity in preparation for the reunion with her son.

With a special pass we accompany our Sacramento friends to the train. Yuji and his family will resettle in Chicago, and Taniguchi and his family are assigned to the Topaz camp.

Newell reminds me of Tokyo's Shimbashi station. People are again dressed in their best traveling clothes, their coats and suits smelling of moth balls. Their suit-cases, bundles, and packages are labeled for Chicago, Minneapolis, Minidoka, Topaz, Denver. Children climb and balance on long wooden saw horse barri-cades. Others walk the station tracks, struggling to keep from slipping off the thin rails. The people have difficulty forcing themselves to board the train. The soldiers, without malevolence, carrying rifles without bayonets, prod the men and children into coaches.

Underlying the warmth and cheerfulness as friends bid each other goodbye, there is a sadness. They have not only left the communities they have built together, but now they must depart from the lifelong friends of those communities. We assure each other that we will all return to our old communities to take up life anew, but we are not certain how or when or whether it will ever really take place.

When the train disappears,those of us left standing on the platform reluctantly board the bus back to Tule. From among our closest friends, only Goto, Tomato, Asoo and I remain. We are here for varying reasons which even we do not understand.

Asoo's family has decided that declaring loyalty would force them to resettle out of camp in the midst of a hostile American public. To people such as the Asoos, the choice is not between Japan and America, in a political sense, but between Tule Lake and the rest of America, in a security sense.

For Mr. and Mrs. Goto, who insist that their son register No-No, the attraction of Tule Lake over the rest of America is enhanced by the potential reward of a disloyal label if Japan wins the war, and by their belief that Japan is winning the war. They hope to return to Japan in victory.

To the Tomita family and many others like them it is bitterness and disillusionment over the abrogation of rights and the economic losses they suffered, that resulted in their declaration of disloyalty to America, by refusing to register. They have no real sympathy for or interest in Japan.

As we pass through the double layer of fencing, Tomato groans, "We must be nuts! Coming back here when we could be getting out. We gotta be crazy!"

"No crazier," Asoo says, "than going out and getting shot up when our families are rotting in a concentration camp!"

The bus stops outside the motor pool, and Goto gazes for a moment at the MP's standing by the gate. They wear helmets with M-1 rifles slung over their shoulders; a young lieutenant also wears a 45 strapped to his hip. "Look at those guys. Whole damned army sent to guard us. Old men, old women, children and the rest. How the hell does a man stay sane?"

"In a looney bin?" Asoo says. "An insane asylum?"

"Hey Asoo," Goto says. "You some kind of heavy-weight. How about keeping things light and funny!"

"It's his sociology background," Tomato says. "You know, all that stuff about defining groups and inter-group differentials in economic and cultural trends and social organizations with particular emphasis on patterns of social and demographic changes."

"Listen to him," I say. "You never cease to amaze me. You sound like Asoo. Where'd you learn that kind of talk?"

"*Encyclopedia Britannica*, Volume S."

"You got that memorized too?" Goto says. "How the hell you know so much about so much?"

"Didn't go to college and get my head all stuffed up with garbage."

"Hey!" Goto says. "Don't go insulting me. I went to Cal Poly to play football."

There is no one left on the bus but the four of us. The morning sun shines in through the windows. We sit in its warmth, unwilling to leave the bus for the monotony and drabness of camp. The sounds of farm trucks rolling out of the motor pool seem distant. Lazily, I watch three trucks idle in the compound while workers clamber onto the rear flatbeds. As they load up, each truck edges to the gate and stops while identification of drivers and crew members are checked. The third truck pauses for a long while as the main gate MP looks into the cab, his face flushed and angry, the voice loud but still drowned out beneath idling engines. Suddenly the engine is shut off and I hear clearly the angry exchange.

"Your identification or you're under arrest!" The MP steps back, his bayonet slanting into the face of the driver. "Get outa the truck!"

The driver hesitates, but his partner nudges him out. The door opens and the driver reluctantly steps down from the truck.

Goto straightens up quickly, leans toward the glass. "Hey!" he exclaims, "it's Horie!"

"Horse shit!" Horie spits out in his tough voice. "We been passing through these gates two times a day for a whole year. You guys seen my identification a hundred times."

"New regulations. Orders from Colonel Griffin."

"I'm a U.S. citizen just like you," Horie retorts. A half circle begins to form around the three.

"This ain't a Boy Scout Camp, Jap."

Horie grits his teeth and clenches his fists, his muscles tightened, ready to take the soldier on, rifle-bayonet and all.

The growing circle of onlookers shoves the soldiers and Horie closer together until the point of the bayonet is but a few feet from Horie's nose. The guard house is behind the MP. He steps back into it to use the phone.

A voice from the tower magnified many decibels booms out, "Disperse immediately! Get back in the trucks! Go back to work!"

But the outer fringes continue their pushing, forcing Horie and the corporal closer. I wedge my way to them through the crowd, Tomato right behind me. A rock flies in from behind and clatters off the corporal's helmet. There is a sudden movement from the corporal's right, and he turns quickly with his rifle thrust out, his face a mixture of panic and anger.

When Horie takes a step towards him, the corporal whirls around and pulls the rifle back as he would to thrust it into a kill dummy. His panicked eyes bulge out, and in an instant I am on him, catching his kidney area between my shoulder and head.

Dust blows into my face, coating my tongue and mouth like fine grained sandpaper. Heavy footsteps and blurs of khaki quickly surround us. Horie is roughly dragged to his feet and removed from the mob. Two huge MP soldiers take my arms and half-lift, half-drag me out of the crowd. The Japanese shout angrily to release us. The soldiers line up and counter their anger with demands to disperse. They use the butts of their rifles to shove the crowd back. Many of the onlookers leave, intimidated by the soldiers.

We are taken to a stockade type guard house with barred windows. We are placed in separate rooms. The MP's tell me I will be held for questioning.

"How long?" I ask.

"Indefinitely."

"You can't do that. I'm already a prisoner."

"Shut your mouth, Jap!"

I become a distant observer of the commotion at the front gate. After half an hour of heated discussion among soldiers, Japanese, and administration personnel, a new driver is assigned to the truck so the workers can resume their trip to the farm. Eventually, order is restored and the trucks pull out.

I sit on the edge of a wooden cot covered with a thin straw mattress, staring at the sheet-rock walls, wondering how I have landed behind barred windows. I hear in the distance the soft whirring of wheels racing toward the camp. Truck number three races down the road through the gate, bumping roughly, its human cargo jouncing like loose crates in a boxcar. Almost running down the main gate MP, it heads directly to the hospital barracks. A stretcher is brought out by orderlies and a body is taken quickly inside.

Word is sent to Mother and Father. On Wednesday they arrive for a visit.

Tired and weary, Mother and Father urgently quiz me about my involvement in the gate incident. I reassure them I have been told I am not being held for complicity, but for questioning.

"What happened at the hospital?" I ask Father.

"After the trouble at the main gate, an inexperienced driver missed a turn and ran the truck into an irrigation canal. Several people were injured, but no one seriously except for Higa."

"Higa? From Walnut Grove?"

"Yes."

"How is he?"

"He is in a coma. They do not know whether he will live."

"People are very upset about what happened," Mother adds. "They blame it on new MP's who hate the Japanese. They say the unnecessary harassings at the gate caused accident."

"This is not a concentration camp. They should not

treat us like we are prisoners of war," Father says. "There are meetings being organized to bring the matter to the attention of the administration and the military commander."

"But everyone is saying that new military commander is a hard man who does not like Japanese. They say he was sent here after he was injured in the Pacific theater."

Father slowly turns his head from side to side, his body bent and rigid. "So many changes in camp," he says. "Dr. Ono is gone; Onishi has left; Taniguchi family is in Topaz. It is becoming a strange place."

Mother's face brightens up. "But there is good news too. Yesterday we received a letter from Masahiro in Santa Fe. They are sending him to Tule Lake for sure. He will be here any day now, " she takes a letter from Kageyama out of her purse.

There are black censor marks throughout the letter, but I can read underlying anger in his account of Santa Fe and his transfer to Tule Lake as a troublemaker.

"Obasan is very happy about the news," Mother says. "When we read the letter to her, she cried. It has been over a year and a half since we have seen him, and letters have not come often. I am so glad he is returning. She has been so lonely since Onishis left."

The image of Obasan and Masahiro that remains dominant in my mind is an old World War I photograph. Obasan stands in a field next to Kageyama who is home on leave. He is a young man of twenty-two dressed in his U.S. Army uniform. She wears baggy, dusty pants and a loose work shirt. Her arms are wrapped from elbows to wrists in rags from an old sheet. Her head is covered by a white sun bonnet, and she is holding a long wooden basket carrier full of ripe strawberries. Her face is serene, yet already contoured by years of hardship and austerity.

Once again buses transport the new arrivals to Tule, just as a year and a half ago they brought us. Some men are dressed in suits with the jackets slung over their arms and shoulders; others wear working clothes. Dressed in cotton print dresses, the women appear harassed by travel and children. The boys are unusually clean, their shirt tails tucked in, and the girls are neat and fresh in summer cotton prints.

I am excited by the flow of strangers from all areas of the West Coast. Daily from my cell I search the crowds for Kageyama. On the fourth day of my jail vigil, I am certain I see him: the slope of the shoulders, the quick, purposeful walk, head held up and back as if surveying crops before harvest. I want to shout out to him, but sound is lost in distance and wind.

While I wait to be questioned about the incident at the gate, Higa continues to lie in a suspended state, clinging to life. He becomes a toxemia to the camp as feelings of bitterness and betrayal are heightened by his life and death struggle. Although I scarcely know Higa, I have seen him many times from afar, his back bent to the sun as he cuts cauliflower and cabbages, or strawberries.

On the seventh day of his coma, he dies. Suddenly, he is no longer faceless. He becomes more important dead than he ever was alive. Conflict erupts over who should conduct the funeral services and burial. His old Sacramento friends want to take care of him because he was a part of the Nihonmachi community for years before the war. The "New Segregants" from the other camps as well as Reverend Togasaki and Honda claim his body belongs to all of Tule Lake and his death is a concern to everyone.

Seizing upon Higa's death as leverage to gain political power, the "New Segregants" claim the decision should be left up to the people. Because the situation must be quickly resolved, the machinery to select representatives to negotiate with the administration is organized. Within a week representatives are chosen from the blocks to elect another body of representatives from the seven wards.

Kageyama is selected from Ward V and then is chosen chairman of the final negotiating committee. He has been in the camp for a week, and aside from a very brief reunion with Mother and Father and Obasan, he has ridden his reputation to a position of leadership in the camp.

My thoughts of Higa and Kageyama are interrupted by the heavy footsteps of an MP, who takes me to the military command barracks.

I am now to meet the new army man who heads the military unit dispatched to our segregation center. When I am brought into the room he is bent over, reading a manilla file lying open on the desk. He does not look up, but curtly motions me to sit in the vacant chair opposite his polished six-foot desk. "Colonel William Griffin, U.S. Army," shines in bright brass from a triangular block of dark wood. While I sit patiently, he reads about who I am, what I believe, how I have behaved during the course of my life, especially since the bombing of Pearl Harbor.

When he finishes, he looks up expectantly, anxious to see how my physical appearance matches my records. Without surprise, he leans back in his chair and says, "You are a United States citizen, but have lived in Japan as a child."

In the past year and a half, I have been given so much factual data about myself from "dossiers," that I no longer feel obligation to confirm, deny or reply.

I watch him as carefully as he watches me. He is an intimidating older man in his late forties who does not smile often.

"You are bilingual," he continues, "and up until the time of registration you have no record of political involvement nor any acts that could be construed as disloyal. You have a brother who is loyal, parents registered yes on questions 27 and 28, yet you are here, a disloyal involved in a serious altercation."

His voice is flat, without inflection or emotion, yet tinged with curiosity. "You are a Kibei of sorts, are you not?"

"Of sorts."

"You are the only immigrant people who have ever sent their children back to the old country to be educated and then classified them with a name. I would like to know exactly what a Kibei is."

"A Kibei is similar to an Issei because he knows the culture of both lands. He is sent to Japan to be educated so he will have the advantages of both places. When the promise of America was not fulfilled, many people decided their children should not have to endure similar disappointments, so they did what they could to prepare them for life either in this country or Japan."

"And how has it worked out?"

"Not always well. Quite often the Kibei feels like an American in Japan and a Japanese in America. Values and culture and prejudices often conflict."

"I see. That helps to explain some of the attitudes." Then with the back of his hand he taps my "dossier" several times. "Valedictorian of your high school.

Harvard, '37.' Boalt Hall Law School, '40.' Registration, '41.'"

"Attention . . . Port arms! . . . Shoulder arms! . . . Parade rest." From outside comes the peculiar sound of hands slapping against the stocks of rifles. Then there is frantic running to "Kill!" They thrust their bayonets into the kill dummy.

Leaning forward, the colonel says, "Why have you made the choice, 'disloyal?'"

"I have been uprooted and placed behind barbed wire as a resident of this camp for a year and a half, without a hearing, without charges, without recourse to the normal channels of justice. Everything I have been taught this country is not. Everything I have been taught democracy is not."

Momentarily taken aback, Griffin leans slowly back in his chair, then says, "These are rationalizations of your own. This is wartime. It was all done through legitimate channels."

"Nothing was done through legitimate *democratic* channels. We have been falsely accused; given a trial by public opinion; given mock hearings by kangaroo courts; found guilty by military tribunals. And you ask me why I have chosen to refuse registration. In my opinion the registration is one more civil outrage forced upon Japanese-Americans."

"You have the nerve to insult the greatest political system ever devised by man? I fought and almost lost my life for this country. You refuse to answer the call of your country in wartime. Are you telling me you prefer to live under totalitarianism?"

"We, the Japanese Americans, are *already* living under totalitarianism. We have been betrayed by democracy. In our case this system of government has been perverted by special interest groups."

Griffin's face is red with anger. "Democracy has not failed!"

"If democracy has not failed, then what has failed is man's ability to truly govern himself."

"Your talk verges on treason! The registration is a simple procedure. It is a means of determining political loyalties. YES -- I am 'loyal.' NO! -- I am not!" he shouts, banging his fist on my life history. "Any man who chooses freely to complicate his own life and situation does himself and his country a disservice!"

He rises impatiently, paces the room, returns to the table, and pushes a button. "In an effort to understand your ways, I have taken time from a busy schedule to hear you out. I have neither the time nor inclination to interview each of 18,000 individuals for their explanations of loyalty or disloyalty."

From the colonel's office I am taken to another barrack where I will be fingerprinted, processed, and released back into camp. While I am waiting for finger-printing, the sounds of a ball game drift through the open window. The familiar crack of ball meeting bat, the rapid shuffling of feet, the staccato voices shouting encouragement bring back old memories of Sacramento. I remember the year we won the summer league city championship. It was late summer. I had been given the starting assignment for the championship game. My arm grew weary and numb as I approached a hundred pitches. I had been beaten one in ten starts, and once again I won. I felt the strain, the release of energy, the Americanness of playing ball, the pacifying knowledge that on the baseball diamond we were all equals. Now baseball becomes the common ground between soldiers and the young Japanese of the camp.

After waiting another couple of hours, I am finger-printed and released into a sudden Tule dust storm.

Chapter 19

Outside the military compound, I blink to clear my eyes of dust. Two young men walk towards me.

"You are Senzaki-san?"

"Yes"

"Please come with us.

"I've been here for thirteen days. I want to go home."

"Please come with us," the other says. "There is important meeting about funeral for Higa. We have been assigned to wait for you and bring you to the meeting."

"Who asked you to come after me?"

"We have been told to say nothing. Please follow us."

The wind drives clouds of dust between the dim shapes of barracks. The two young men fade into shadows, leading me from enforced isolation into further uncertainty. I feel like young Urashima riding through the depths of the ocean on a turtle's back. I return to a world that is strange beyond understanding.

In the murky glare tanks loom ominously, standing guard over Japanese gardeners, old farm ladies, babies, lawyers, doctors and college students.

The two men lead me to a block manager's barrack in Ward V. As we approach, we are watched suspiciously by several youths, some of whom are familiar to me. Inside, it is dark in contrast to the glare outside. Before my eyes adjust, a man is beside me. I cannot make out the details of the face, but the form, the smile, are unmistakable.

"Ben," Kageyama says softly.

"Masahiro," I say, relieved and surprised.

He grips my hand in both of his, squeezes tightly. "It has been a long time," he says, the smile twitching slightly in an effort to control his feelings.

I become aware of several others in the room. Kageyama says quietly, "We will talk soon." He releases my hand and goes to a chair.

When everyone is seated, Reverend Togasaki explains, "We are meeting to arrange for Higa-san's funeral. Higa-san's death has caused very sad feelings in camp. Many people wish to have a public ceremony to honor him."

Togasaki introduces me to the men around the table. Five of them are familiar old Tuleans. Seven, including Kageyama, are outsiders from other camps.

In the glare of the single window, Kageyama peers at us, his eyes obscured behind dark sockets. There are few changes apparent in him: age is deceptively masked by smooth flesh tanned a dull, oiled copper. His gray streaked hair is the only sign of years.

"We are trying to reserve the main firebreak for the thousands who want to attend Higa's funeral," he says. "But the military commander accuses us of using Higa's death to cause unrest in camp."

"They do not know about feeling of community," Honda says. "They do not live with us."

"It is a waste of time to negotiate," Togasaki asserts. "Griffin fought against the Japanese in the Pacific."

"We must try to negotiate," Kageyama says. "We are not yet in a position to dictate terms. We must show cooperative side. We will have our way later."

"You are new to this camp," Togasaki says.

"I am Japanese," Kageyama replies. "I am from Florin area. I am part of this camp."

"We will have our way," Honda says angrily.

"We will lose if we are forced to use violence."

"It is violent time," Reverend Togasaki says. "We are victims of America's prejudice and violence. I am not afraid to behave same way." There is a look of disdain on Togasaki's face.

"Do you mean ambushing your fellow Japanese in the dark?" I ask. "When the victim is outnumbered three or four to one?"

"It is violent time," Honda says. "Everyone is affected."

"Japanese against Japanese? In the darkness? The work of cowards!"

Kageyama intercedes, "These are strange times created out of hatred. We must try to understand what is happening and respond in right way, or we will have serious trouble."

"Serious trouble?" Togasaki asks. "It is possible for things to be worse?. No one should be surprised there is social disruption and violence. Don't blame it on Japanese." Togasaki's face is flushed with anger and bitterness. The silence of the others implies agreement.

"We are branded as 'trouble makers,'" Honda says. "When only crime is to stand up against injustice. We see the stupidity and hypocrisy of those who pretend to administer our lives. Whoever heard of self-government under dictatorship?"

"You have heard of Mitsutomi?" Shiozawa says, his dark face creased with wrinkles.

Mitsutomi was the catalyst for the Manzanar strike. He was suspected of beating a JACL leader. When he was arrested, a crowd gathered outside his residence and demanded his release. At the gathering they issued "death lists" of "inu," most of whom were JACL collaborators with the administration. The project director met with them, but ordered the military police to be ready. The trouble escalated into a full-scale riot with the soldiers wounding eight Japanese and killing two.

Shiozawa, so nondescript for the size of his reputation, says, "It was a case of loyalists winning favors by using other Japanese."

Kageyama shakes his head from side to side. "So many stories of Japanese turning on each other. Why?" he asks, looking around the room. "Because we have foolishly put trust in Hakujin we know so well. We let them direct our lives and use us until we have become traitors to each other."

"And it is our responsibility to take these matters into our own hands and beat people into agreement? Make black lists and become judge, jury, and executioner? My brother almost lost his life because of that kind of thinking."

Honda jumps to his feet, but before he can reply, Kageyama orders him harshly to wait. "It is a mistake for us to argue," he says, his hands above his head, palms out. "This was not our purpose."

He rises and motions to the hot plate in the corner where a tea kettle is gently steaming. In a sudden movement and clatter of china, he says in a quiet voice, "I did not wish for us to argue. We must work together."

Green tea is passed around the table. When tempers are calmed by the warmth and ceremony of sharing tea, Kageyama says, "We are falling into useless argument, like trying to decide whether we should have come to camp or resisted. We are here and that is what we must deal with. We must work together to settle serious problems of strike, funeral, and people's grievances."

Everyone remains silent, their eyes lowered. Kageyama gazes thoughtfully into his cup as if reading something in the leaves. "True," he admits, "there is no denying there has been much violence. It is unhealthy because it is what is called displaced. It must be used constructively. As newly appointed chairman of the Body of Block Representatives, I and other leaders from this camp and other camps have been called in to settle serious troubles as arbitrators. Our right to do this has been questioned by administration, so we have had election to prove we are true representatives. The election has proved our right."

"Only by slim majority," Togasaki interjects. "Fast election where many old Tuleans did not vote."

"True," Kageyama says. "But it was an election. We must work with what we have. Higa is waiting. We must act quickly."

Ignoring the shifting and mumbling, Kageyama continues. "It is important now to have a go-between to help negotiate with the administration and military. I wish to nominate Senzaki-san for committee approval. He is someone who will represent the commitee but also talk to both sides of the fence."

I turn quickly to Kageyama, surprised and uneasy.

Several people start to speak. Togasaki says sarcastically, "You wish to make the business of 18,000 people a family matter?"

Kageyama replies evenly, "It is more than that. Do you know of anyone in camp who is better qualified? Senzaki-san is fluent in English and in Japanese. He is a lawyer, which is a very important discipline to all of as long as we are unlawfully interned in these camps. We do not have time to hesitate."

Following the tradition of Japanese elders making an important decision, the discussion goes on for another half hour. Finally, they give reluctant approval of my appointment.

After another hour of meeting, I summarize the three main points they want me to negotiate. "Number one, you want me to ask them to stop the continuous harrassment by the military police at the gate. Number two, you want Corporal Elmendorf prosecuted for his responsibility in the accident that killed Higa. And third, I should have them focus on the basic grievances of living conditions in camp."

Togasaki nods yes and says, "Until the following grievances have been investigated, the farm crew will continue their strike: shortage of ambulances; defective fire fighting apparatus; broken plumbing in the latrines; overcrowding; scarcity of jobs; lack of unemployment compensation; poor food in the mess halls."

After the resolution is written up, we adjourn the meeting. Kageyama comes over to me and says, "We will get together to talk soon."

Outside in the brightness, I am clapped on the back by a familiar hand. Tomato, Goto, and Asoo are waiting for me. "Good to see you again, Ben," Asoo says loudly. I feel a lightness and warmth I haven't felt in days.

Goto explains, "Saw you walking through the firebreak this afternoon with those two teen-agers, so I decided to stick close, just in case. After you went inside, I brought Tomato and Asoo to keep watch."

"I didn't know I was being watched over so carefully. Thanks, you guys."

After dinner at Block 46 mess hall, we go to Tomato's place, because his mother and father have gone out to the Japanese movie. As Tomato builds a fire, we pull up chairs in a circle around the stove. There is a smooth spot on the floor surrounding the glow of red coal through the cracks of the stove. Light and heat radiate from the stove, but there is darkness behind, in the corners and along the wall, wrapping a blanket of cold air over my back. Outside, the small, square windows of other barracks glow in the night.

"Did they give you a hard time?" Tomato asks, looking at me.

I shake my head. "No. Besides, Kageyama was there. I was very happy to see him again. But I was glad when I came outside and spotted all of you. It's pretty easy to think we're living in some kind of foreign country."

"How was jail?" Asoo asks. "They beat you or anything like that?"

"Naw," I laugh. "Boring and lousy food, but good treatment. They just left me alone."

"I always wondered what it's like to be in jail," Goto says.

"What did they want with you at the meeting?"

"They want me to negotiate with the administration."

"Oh?" Tomato says, raising his eyebrows.

"To settle the farm strike, and take care of Higa's funeral. And take care of the same old complaints about living conditions."

"Two autumns, two strikes," Goto says. "That's all? Same grievances been going on for a year. And what's so complicated about organizing a funeral?"

"It's only a part of it," I explain. "Kageyama's concerned about the violence. He says we were once peaceful and cooperative people. We have ceased being 'true Japanese.'"

"'True Japanese?'" Tomato says, "What kind of Japanese is that? Tule Lake kind? California kind? Kibei kind? Nisei kind? Issei kind?"

"Peaceful and cooperative people!" Asoo says with a frown. "I know what those guys are saying. I went to a meeting for 'true Japanese' the other night."

"Well," Goto says, "you got something against 'true Japanese?'" Asoo nods his head. "After that meeting I've been thinking a lot about the past. I have to admit, I liked it a lot -- the pool hall and the boardinghouse, and the bath house that would make you warm on the cold days. Remember our ball team and dreaming about getting in the Pacific Coast League? And New Year's when we had more food in the house than any other time of the year. My brothers and sister and I would spend the whole day eating mochi, sushi, and drinking soda pop like it was water. We used to hang branches of pine on the doors to offer gifts of thanks to the local patron gods." Asoo laughs. "Can you imagine that? It was good, okay, but listening to some of these 'true Japanese,' you would think we didn't have any troubles until we got to this place. I guess I don't see things the same way. My father was a working man. When he was alive, things were always tough. When he died, everyone paid our debts or canceled them, so we wouldn't owe anyone anything. Seems kind of like they treated us better after he died than when he was alive."

"Now take your uncle, Ben" he continues, straightening in his chair. "Sounds like he had things pretty good, owning a farm and making a success of it. A guy gets in a good position and he sees only what he wants to see, maybe ignoring the unpleasant things. He acts like we're something special, like he's surprised Japanese have conflict. Me? I'm surprised too." Asoo puts his index finger to his chest. "But I'm not surprised too. None of the community liked it much when we had to get help from welfare to raise my brothers and sister. My mom got a lot of criticism. Seems to me, instead of talking behind our backs, they could have helped us. Kageyama's bitter because he lost so much. I didn't lose much, so I'm not so upset. In fact, things in some ways are easier than they were when I was a kid."

I am surprised at Asoo for being so open, for I have rarely shared intimate conversation with him. Since Gordie left, I am drawn more closely to Asoo, Tomato and the others.

"You crazy or something?" Tomato says. "Maybe things weren't so perfect back then, but at least we didn't go around in the night beating each other."

"Yeah, I know," Asoo answers defensively. "I know." He leans forward on his elbows and looks over at me. "You know what I'm trying to say, Ben?"

"I know what you're saying."

Asoo looks away, then settles back in his chair. "You can't say all those guys in the camp had a square deal."

"Not all of them," Goto says.

"When I try to see things like some of the trouble-makers, I'm not surprised at what's happening. Some have been wronged not only by Hakujin, but by Nihon-jin too, so some of these guys are just giving it back."

"Sure thing," Tomato says. "Getting back at every-body. Doesn't make any difference who the damn it is. Maybe things weren't so bad for me like they were for you." Tomato stops, looks from Asoo to me. "But I'm no college samurai either, just a Fourth Street pool hall

Boochie trying to make the best of things."

"Well anyway, I'm kind of pissed too," Asoo says. "But not so much I would even think of filling out repatriation forms. I'm still an American, and there isn't anything happening here that makes me feel like going back to a place I've never been. I didn't choose to stay out of the Army by registering No-Yes because I don't believe in this country. It's because I'm the head of the family and I have responsibilities to five other people."

"Crazy bastards," Tomato says. "Those guys go around telling everyone to fill out repatriation forms. And Honda," Tomato adds. "Seemed like an okay guy in Sacramento."

"I think I know why he's acting so crazy." Goto says.

"You know him?"

"Not well," Goto replies. "But my dad does. And besides, when you spend time in a barbershop you know everybody there is to know, and hear most of what there is to hear." He looks to me with a half smile and adds, "Get to know more about Nihonmachi in a hot tub than on a college campus. No offense meant, you understand?"

"None taken," I laugh.

"Yeah," Goto continues, "I remember him okay. He liked my dad. He used to come over and spend a lot of time talking. In the early days he used to work at Southern Pacific as a boiler washer in the railroad roundhouse. We were only a few blocks from the station. Outside of my dad, I guess he didn't have too many friends. I heard he was hard to get along with. One day he got in an argument with the division head of the roundhouse and got fired. After that he found a job working in a grocery store, for pretty low wages. He had to take what he could get.

"Honda had to pay a kick-back from his low wages. He was so sore about it that he would complain to my dad about the store owner taking advantage of his fellow Nihonjins. Being that he was not the kind of guy to sit around and take a lot of garbage, he decided to organize and report the kick-backs to the union officials. Somehow word got out, and Honda was thrown out."

"That's when he got into the labor contracting business?" Tomato asks.

"Yep. After that things got brighter for him, but he was still bitter at the treatment he got from those 'uppity Japs.'"

"Labor contracting?" Asoo says. "So that's where I used to see him. Those summers we were picking fruit."

Tomato's eyes brighten. "Remember those summers out there picking together?"

"Do I remember? How could I forget?" Goto says. "100^0 in the shade! Lugging twelve-foot ladders around ten hours a day! Dust and peach fuzz grinding into the sweat!"

"Yeah," Tomato says. "What a joke! Remember the old guys we used to work around? We'd hitch out to Courtland to pick pears . . . . We thought we were pretty tough . . . thought we'd show those old fruit pickers how to work."

"Uh huh. Remember the legs running up and down ladders?" Goto says.

"This sixty year old was heading down the ladder with a full bucket and mine wasn't even half full at two in the afternoon!" Asoo says.

"Oh boy," Tomato says. "Those wild men practically *ran* up and down, shoving their ladders around.

They made me feel like I was seventy!"

"They sure showed us a thing or two." Asoo laughs.

For a long time the four of us sit in a barrack of Tule Lake, laughing, faces glowing red and warm, not wanting to move, or let go of a past that seemed so good.

Chapter 20

Since the day he died, Higa has lain in his coffin on public display. The room is sodden with the odor of wisteria, lilac roses, and greenery, crowded around the casket. To guard the body against disturbance, a twenty-four hour watch is set up, with visiting hours designated from noon of each day to midnight. For a short time in midmorning, the sun squeezes through the window from above the adjacent barrack, shining softly on the death-tarnished face. For the first time since the beginning of Tule Lake, there is remorse for a victim of violence.

The Committee distributes a bulletin to the camp announcing that the funeral will be a camp-wide ceremony, attended by friends and family, fellow workers and all others who feel a personal loss in the death. The bulletin demands that the Project Director attend the funeral and bring a letter of condolence to read at the ceremony.

When the ultimatum reaches the Project Director, he accuses Kageyama of exploiting the death to gain political power. Kageyama laughs and responds with a public statement. "We, Higa and I, and many others like us, have come from the same rural farming area of California. We are tied together by more than geography: we have a kinship of spirit. In death Higa has profoundly moved the people as he never did in life. His funeral is an atonement for all the abuse he and the men and women and children of this camp have suffered for the past two years and the past forty."

Contrary to the plans of the Committee, the ceremony will be restricted to the Japanese. *The Tulean Dispatch*, a newspaper printed in the evacuee area, informs us that the administration will not comply with our demands. The newspaper expresses the Japanese opinions openly in both the English and Japanese sections. It says the Project Director will not make a personal appearance. A letter of condolence will not be sent. The funeral cannot be held in the main firebreak.

The younger members of the Committee construct a stage in the main firebreak. Reverend Togasaki speaks in clear and concise Japanese to the several thousand people who gather to honor Higa. The public address system amplifies Togasaki's voice up aisles down roads between blocks, and finally, into corridors, reaching the administrators.

"Higa is symbolic because he is an innocent man forced to return to the soil sooner than he would have, had he not suffered persecution. That is why he must be remembered. The mistakes and injustices that contributed to his death cannot be repeated."

From the distance comes the muffled sound of an approaching engine turning onto the road at the southwest corner of the firebreak. At first, it is so soft, it doesn't distract from the priest, but as it rolls closer, the motor renders Reverend Togasaki's words inaudible. Close to the stage, the jeep stops and a Caucasian climbs out and takes a camera from the back seat. Attempting to be inconspicuous, he tiptoes slowly across the crunching hardpan. From one angle, then another, and another, the man takes pictures of the crowd, the stage, the priest, and the casket.

"It is appropriate," Reverend Togasaki continues,

"for all men to return to their origins in the earth, especially a man who worked with the soil." The eulogy is punctuated intermittently by shutter clickings.

"But it is ironical that instead of being buried in the land in which he was born or that which he spent most of his life tilling, he will lie in a tomb in a distant concentration camp. When the war ends and we leave, he will remain, a testimony to our time spent here."

The camera man tiptoes around the back of the stage and reappears, taking pictures of the crowd and the priest from a different viewpoint. He goes back to his jeep and shifts the gears. The noise fades as the jeep disappears behind the far barracks. Suddenly the entire firebreak is silent. Reverend Togasaki's mouth is still working, but he is only heard by those in the front rows. The lights strung from the poles down the center of the block are no longer on. The administration has shut off the Tule Lake power.

Because it is a solemn occasion, no one seems to know whether or not to interrupt Togasaki, who is too intensely preoccupied to realize what has happened. After several minutes, someone near the front calls out, "Gomen kudasai! Gomen kudasai! We cannot hear you. Someone has shut off the electricity for the microphone."

Puzzled at first, Togasaki makes arrangements for those in the rear to raise their hands when they cannot hear him. After several interruptions, someone gives him a megaphone. His concentration and rhythm disturbed, Togasaki struggles through the remainder of the funeral, hoping to be heard and understood. After his eulogy we go to the high school auditorium for tea and food.

A meeting is arranged between the administration

and the Committee of 7 in the conference room at the administration barrack. The long corridor is flanked by offices on both sides. On one wall is a poster with a finger pointing at me. Behind it an eye stares at me as the other squints into tight wrinkles. The face has a white beard with a red, white, and blue stovepipe hat on top. The top row of letters are blocked out by the bottom chord of a truss. Right below the beard, the sign commands in bold, black letters, "NEEDS YOU!"

The new Project Director, Charles Burrell, is sitting at the head of the long table. His face is thin and dark, his complexion weatherbeaten and haggard, perhaps from living in this desolate place as long as the rest of us. His voice is hard and cold, the result of serving as director of our foreign and artificial communities during the hysteria of wartime.

Kageyama says, "We are 18,000 Japanese people placed behind these fences against our will. We are being guarded by a handful of Caucasians disguised as benevolent administrators, who insult us by their inhumane treatment, boycotting Higa's funeral and turning off the electricity in the middle of his eulogy."

"My attendance was demanded. As head of a segregation center, I do not accede to demands."

There is a stale brittleness to the unsmiling faces in the circle, as if they had been carved in place long ago. Our meetings remind me of the "Tanuki" in the folk stories of Japan. The Tanuki are not ordinary badgers. They are peculiarly talented in changing identities whenever necessary. On such occasions the Tanuki sit and think and tap their stomachs: tim-tim-tim.

"You claim to represent the people of this camp," Burrell says, his face flushed. "Your election victory was by a scant majority. Therefore, how do you or the men sitting in this room make claim to represent the people?" The reference to the men is followed by an uneasy shifting in the chairs.

Suddenly Kageyama is on his feet, bristling at Burrell's condescending attitude. He leans forward, his palms flat on the table. "However we won the election does not make any difference. We are Japanese and whatever we do is for the welfare of all Japanese. True, many of us were elected by scant majority, but at least I am not given appointment by Washington!"

"I am in charge of this camp, and whatever happens here is my responsibility. Therefore, I will administer with an objectivity you do not have."

"What?" Kageyama asks in disbelief.

"You are a 'disloyal.' Among the men who sit here claiming to represent the people of this camp, there are only four old Tulean 'loyalists.' That means thirty-three per cent. The rest of you are either 'disloyals' from other camps or old Tulean 'disloyals.' Therefore, you are not an objective representation. I will see to it that the fifty-five per cent old Tulean population is represented fairly."

"This is big joke," Kageyama says angrily. "How can you, a white man who lives in your little segregated community at far end of camp know what needs to be done for the people? I am from Florin! You have no contact with us except at meetings and in the administration offices! You are so insensitive you forbid public ceremony for Higa when several thousand people are in mourning. Is this concern of man who claims to administer camp?"

Kageyama's face shines with an oily sheet of sweat. As the conversation veers and drifts, flattens and bursts, the sun comes out at last. The men face the center of the table, their masked expressions blotched with dark patches: tim, tim, tim.

"Work stoppage!" Baba, formerly of Poston, interjects.

Burrell waits. "The farm work has gone on since spring. A lot of Japanese work and sweat and now it's harvest time and the crew decides to strike. Can't you men see you are just hurting the people? It's *your* food lying in the fields ready to rot. You men have misled the people by encouraging this strike. What will you say to them in the winter time?"

I think of the fields of the Tule Lake farm: rows of crops stretch so distant they converge into vast reaches of green. Dry, dead, useless land, reclaimed within a year from surface dust to rich productive farm lands waiting to be harvested.

"If administration took better care of people's needs, there would not be work stoppage," says Abe from Heart Mountain. "Food they give us in the mess halls is not enough for hard work in the fields."

Moore of Internal Security interrupts. "The mess hall situation, the 'disloyal' issue, the funeral, and self-government: these are all separate issues. Lumping them together only confuses things. On the one hand, there are complaints about food, and on the other, the strike threatens to ruin crops lying in the fields. There is a war going on. There is a food shortage."

"We are not interested," Baba says sarcastically.

Williams rises, knocking his chair backwards. "No matter what's said here or anywhere else, that food is going to be saved, if I have to call in the Army to do it! Then you'll have to requisition your food from them!"

Soon it will be my second winter in Tule. Did we

ever see the mercurial orange sun set in the pines from a stone bench? I rise and move across reeds and seashore-hardened juniper, over rocks turning black for the night. I hurry along the small graveled paths winding through the hills, the desert of Tule a distant mirage.

Chapter 21

Walking the borders of Tule, I hold my breath against the choking autumn dust. Kageyama lives away from the zones of "loyalty" and "disloyalty," in a far corner of camp where in a month many of the eight thousand new transferees have been assigned living quarters.

Inside, the room has been converted into an office divided by plaster-board partitions trimmed in black wood. Against the wall there is a wooden desk that was made in the carpenters' shop. A curtain of patchwork rice sacks hangs from a wire stretched across the sleeping compartment. Through a slight opening the bed remains unmade. Otherwise, Kageyama's apartment is neat and tidy.

Since my release, I have seen Kageyama twice, both times at meetings, in the presence of other people. In such situations he keeps a distance between us, concealing the person I knew at Florin. Today he smiles warmly and questions me exuberantly about the family, life in Tule, the shutting down of Nihonmachi. The year and a half we have lived in separate camps is erased by the closeness I feel being with him now. The wrinkles around his eyes have spread and deepened, making him more threatening in anger, but more gentle when he smiles.

Now, as before the camps, he makes no pretenses. He speaks what he feels, whether it is his love for the land or his own beliefs of justice or democracy.

"Will you be living here for long?" I ask. "Or will you move to Block 46 with Obasan and Mother and Dad?"

"They have assigned me here. It is better I stay here. Mr. Nye was right: trouble seems to follow me. It would not be safe for Mother and your mother and father for me to be too close."

"You mean we are in the same camp and we cannot be together as a family?"

"It is strange, I know. It is a crazy world they have created for us."

"By they, do you mean Nye, Burrell, Griffin?"

"Yes, but others, too." He gets up and walks over to his desk.

"What others?"

He hands me a newspaper. The front page stares up at me. It is a copy of the *San Francisco Examiner*. Across the page is written:

WAR EXTRA!
18,000 JAPS ON STRIKE IN STATE!
ARMY GUARDING FENCED IN NIPS IN TULE LAKE!

"And this," he says, handing me a copy of the *Los Angeles Times*. It is a cartoon captioned: "HONORABLE DR. JEKYLL AND MR. HYDE," showing a bucktoothed, slant-eyed, stupidly grinning simian "Jap" lighting a bomb. Kageyama stands silently awaiting my response. I say nothing and hand back the newspapers.

"We have crowded World War II off the front pages," he says sardonically. "It is almost 1944. Over two hundred Japanese Americans have already died in Italy. Almost four hundred have been wounded. They are calling the 100th Battalion the 'Purple Heart Battalion.' Soon the 442nd will be through training and will go to Europe. Meanwhile, we have come here like good little Japs, and they still write about us like this."

It is the first time I had ever heard Kageyama use the word, Jap. Coming from him, it sounds especially disgusting.

"Isn't it amazing," he asks, turning away from me, his voice dropping as if he truly cannot believe his eyes, "what can happen when people give in to something they know is wrong?"

"And you have always known?"

"From the beginning."

"Do you think the men of the 100th and the 442nd are wrong?"

"No. Of course I cannot say that. All of us must do as we believe. But we must not forget that compliance has put us behind these fences."

"And World War I was a different time and a different set of circumstances?"

"Let me see," he says. "How old was I? Early twenties, like Gordie. I was a young man going to war to defend my country. Only this time we are at war against the land we have come from. And when I went to war, I did not leave my family sitting in a concentration camp."

Dressed in rumpled, olive-green trousers and a faded navy blue sweater, Kageyama turns his back to stare at the stove and the tea kettle steaming on it. "Age makes a big difference in how a man sees the world. When you are young, there is a lot worth gambling for. But for older people who have had their homes and land and communities taken away, there is nothing left to lose but self-respect. Without self-respect, I am nothing."

He picks up the *Times* and *Examiner* and dumps them into the trash. "The Japanese Americans are the envy of many Caucasians. They have laughed at us, but their laughter turned to jealousy when they saw our accomplishments. These newspapers are proof of what I am saying. They know we will be back, and they're preparing for us."

Kageyama hands me a hot cup of tea. The heat stings my fingers as I try to balance the cup on the arm rest. "Santa Fe has made you very bitter."

He looks at me curiously, as if he is not sure I am serious. "Santa Fe," he says slowly. "Those of us who were.... It is painful to think about. It was very lonely. I had too much time to think. Yes, I became very bitter. My bitterness was self-destructive. I decided I had to survive, no matter what happened. I would not let them break me. Since I could not get rid of my bitter feelings, I decided to express them where it was most appropriate. I became a 'trouble maker' for survival."

I look out at the dust, the pallid colors, barracks, fences, the constants that go almost unnoticed now. I think he is right. While we wait for the end of the war, we must work to preserve what we have left.

I express agreement, and he smiles, his mission accomplished. For several minutes he sits nursing tea. He sets the empty cup on a corner of his desk and begins thumbing through pages of a note book. "Mr. Burrell claims we are not true representatives of the people. But he is government puppet. We must pull Japanese together before Hakujins completely run our camp."

"It does not look very promising."

"We stand at the base of the ladder. We have a different perspective from the Hakujin who sits at the top. We see chaos that he can't see. We can be crushed by his stupidity, so we must not give up."

He reads again from the notebook, his tone businesslike, "Now that matter of Higa's funeral is over, we must consider next important item, the settling of farm work stoppage. Since it is grown by us, it is our food, so we will save it. However, not until we use work stoppage to achieve other goals that are equally important. The Committee of seven have polled the people for the issues that we all have in common such as coal shortage, improvement of living conditions.

"We must make it clear to everyone we are not involved in strike, but work stoppage. If it were strike, administration could terminate farm crew and call in the Army. We don't want that to happen. I think Mr. Burrell was receptive to negotiation. He has taken a conciliatory stand."

He stops, looks out the window, and says, thinking aloud, "I know how WRA operates these camps. I've been inside Santa Fe and Tule Lake, and I have fought every inch of the way. I've learned by experience, so now I must share my experience. I did not choose to be in this position. I'm being forced into it."

"I believe you have misinterpreted Burrell's reaction to the meeting. There didn't seem to be anything conciliatory about his attitude toward the Committee."

"And because I am here," he continues as if he had not heard me, "I don't intend to let trouble-shooters run this camp like a place for aliens without rights. Washington's choice of Burrell only reflects antagonism and hatred of public. They are not interested in how we are treated or how we feel, but only in making us enemies of this country."

He shifts his gaze from the window to me. "Do you agree?" he asks abruptly.

I quickly sift over what he has been saying. "To what?" I ask.

"Burrell," he answers. "What about him?"

"He did not take a conciliatory stand on the farm crew's work stoppage. I believe he has other plans."

"Why do you say that?"

"You have said it yourself. He is a trouble-shooter. His role is to maintain discipline, not to set up ideal self-governed communities of citizens in exile. He is not here to reconcile, and he can't afford to lose something as important as the farm strike. But there was something in his attitude."

"Good. You are careful observer. You may be right. It is important I be on guard, especially when I am dealing directly with the man. What you have said will make me more cautious."

He leans back in his chair. "But tonight, that is different matter. We must get people behind our cause. I have report to be presented at public hearing. This report outlines what we have talked about now and for the past days." Kageyama hands me the report. "I want you to present this."

"Why me?"

"This is only one meeting among many."

"True, but task of building Tule Lake, the Segregation Center, takes much groundwork."

"You are original Tule Lake evacuee. We must appear to be representative of all people. Administration believes we give only view of transferees. You help draw original Tuleans and transferees and administration into position of closer harmony."

The room is crowded with people standing closely

packed, and others outside listening through the windows. The late autumn insects find their way into the assemblage and flicker around the dull light bulbs, raising the tempo of senseless activity. I present the material in Japanese and English, emphasizing the need for all Japanese to be united. When I mention the burial of Higa an angry older man interrupts, "What about Higa's tombstone?"

I hesitate. Okubo from the carpenter shop says the tombstone is made of oak and needs to be engraved before it is placed on the grave site.

The angry questioner demands to know why the tombstone was made of oak instead of marble or granite. "Wood will not last. When all of us are gone, there will be nothing to show where Higa is buried."

I break in, explaining the position of the Committee and their attempts to achieve some necessary reforms.

"Compensation!" the same guy yells out. "What about compensation for Higa-san's widow?"

Ueda, who had been appointed to a special committee to look into proper compensation for the family, comes to the platform. "The administration has decided Higa's widow will receive 70% of the monthly wage that Higa made on the farm crew."

"70% of $16? That's eleven dollars and twenty cents a month!"

Kageyama jumps to his feet and holds his arms up for silence. He explains, "There are many things that must be worked on. The Committee can do only so much at one time. The people must be patient."

"Patient!" a voice calls from the rear of the room. People move to make way for the speaker. It is Reverend Togasaki. "All we have heard from commitee since election is promises," he says in Japanese. "Talk of better living conditions, better food, but we get nothing. Food is worse and strike threatens to wipe out vegetables for winter."

"If we are united and have peoples' support, all things will be settled for good of majority. We will meet again soon with administration," Kageyama replies patiently.

"You have been fooled. They have deceived you and they will do it again. Many Hakujins are getting rich while we talk with them over conference table."

"How do you know this?"

"We have organized our own investigations and committees." A man hands Togasaki a sheet of paper. "For past month of investigation, mess halls spend 18¢ to 20¢ a person for food each day. WRA regulations say all Japanese are allowed 45¢ per day for food. Where is other 25¢?" Togasaki asks. He takes a newspaper from his back pocket. "In newspaper there are many articles about Hakujins who have left Tule Lake. They say they leave because camp is too crazy and Japanese are sneaky and violent. These are lies! They use lies so they can leave Tule with money they have stolen from food allowances and movie projects. They steal money from prisoners who make $16 a month."

Kageyama tries to interrupt. Honda, standing near Reverend Togasaki, shouts, "The people need new representation!" He looks around the room. From several locations, groups of young men begin shouting and stamping their feet.

It takes ten minutes to restore order. On the platform we wait, watching the crowd of angry faces shouting epithets and obscenities.

As the raucous noise begins subsiding, Kageyama

booms in a loud voice, "Committee is working on settlement of strike. You can judge work of Committee when we are finished. If people are not happy, they can elect new representative body."

"You will get your chance," Togasaki says. "But you do not have much time . . . many things are going to happen."

He turns to leave with a score of young followers behind him.

Chapter 22

The door to the stove is slightly ajar, filling the room with smoke from the untended smouldering fire. Through a watery haze I peer around the meeting room at the familiar faces of administrators and Japanese. We rub our eyes and blink until someone is called to stoke the fire and open the windows.

The head of the War Relocation Authority opens the meeting for negotiation as 10,000 'colonists' stand patiently outside, waiting to hear the latest decisions to affect their lives. Nye and the other four Caucasians are the only whites surrounded by Japanese negotiators and the more "potentially explosive" Japanese packed elbow to elbow outside. They have become virtual prisoners of those they've imprisoned -- but the Army is no further away than the phone in the next room.

"Representation?" Kageyama says. "You keep bringing that up, over and over again. What do you know about it? You don't live in 'colony' -- as you Caucasians call it. Yet you tell us we know nothing about representation for Japanese."

"I didn't say that you know nothing about representation of the Japanese," Nye says. "I'm simply asking whether everyone is represented. Almost fifty per cent voted against you."

"And you," Kageyama says, staring sardonically at Nye, "are here because you hold good paying position, appointed by some Washington friend who does not know a Japanese from a Chinese from a Korean, who thinks all Japanese look alike!"

Faces flush at Kageyama's audacity. "Why is it, Mr. Kageyama," Nye says heatedly, "that the feelings of the people are so whipped up? Wherever you are, there is trouble. And certain others in this room. Trouble from 'troublemakers!'"

Kageyama starts to answer, instead takes a deep breath as if he is about to swim under water.

He is interrupted by Burrell. "It isn't the nature of you people to advocate violence and noncooperation. Doesn't it strike you as strange that you bring trouble wherever you are?"

Beneath Kageyama's sun-darkened skin, the redness rises up his face like coffee rising in a glass tube. He says with sarcastic patience, "It is strange we are forced into all-Japanese communities, then into concentration camps, and then are told what we are like by people like yourselves, and newspapers, and officials and sociologists. It is interesting to hear about ourselves from you. Someday you might like to hear what we know about you!"

I look at Burrell, Nye, Dover, and Moore. Deep shadows mark Nye's nose on his lean, bony face, and symmetrical circles indent Burrell's sallow cheeks.

Wearily, Kageyama says, "Because you are on top, you are in position of control."

"Control?" Burrell asks. "Who's on top? The only things I'm concerned about are the people and the camp. And the food lying in the fields rotting while you people strike. This camp is our responsibility. We have to do whatever is necessary to save the crops."

"Your responsibility . . . you must do whatever is necessary. You are from Washington, D.C.!"

"You don't seem to understand our position," Nye

protests. "WRA is caught in the middle. From the time the Army began transferring you people, WRA has had responsibility to both you people and the government. WRA has been given the messes to clean up."

"It's been a difficult job," Burrell adds. "There has been a lot of confusion. Especially here. For every train at any of the other camps, there must have been several that moved in and out of Tule Lake. It isn't our fault. I suppose if you had to find fault it would have to be Washington's."

"Then . . . what we have to say should be listened to," I interject. All eyes turn to me. "It is the gap between the promise of America and its fulfillment: the fulfillment is nonexistent, like the ear you give us." The four Caucasians watch me now with curiosity. "You ask why it is we are different from the 'loyals,' why some are fighting in Europe while others remain here. We are no different. We have had forced upon us a choice we did not wish to make. You have chosen our alternatives for us, just as you have chosen not to hear what Kageyama has been telling you. You refuse to listen to us, however many times, however many ways we tell you. You make us accept the intent of your prejudice which forces us into positions of inferiority and self-hatred, into compromise and confusion that makes busboys from engineers, fruit market clerks from architects, stock boys from those with college degrees, and now concentration camp inhabitants whose sons and brothers and husbands fight for this country overseas.

"Until you understand the indignities you thrust upon us," I continue, "you are not qualified to control our lives. Look at what we are doing now: sitting around this table discussing absurdities."

I pause, and in the interim I hear the ten thousand now surrounding the barrack on three sides. "If you should look outside," I say to the four, "at babies being nursed, at the old hardly able to walk, at the masses of people, would you see them as clearly as if they were white?"

Burrell laughs uneasily. "This is ridiculous," he says. "White? Japanese?" He rubs his right hand across his brow. "Many of you in this camp are American citizens, just as I am, and Mr. Nye, Mr. Dover, and Mr. Moore. Our goals are the same as yours. We are in the same boat together."

"We are like rabbits," Kageyama replies in a drawn-out tone. "We are victims of predators, like rabbits. It is as Senzaki says: you do not know you are predators."

"But that isn't the relation between Japanese and Caucasians," Nye says. "We are all a part of the same country, governed by the same government. Whatever is done is for the best interests of the majority of people exclusive of race or national origin."

Kageyama laughs a deep chuckle. He continues for fifteen or twenty seconds and other Japanese break out in a smile, the first indication they are in the room. But as quickly as he stops, they too stop.

I, too, smile and unsmile as if I were thinking an unseemly thought in the midst of a serious Sunday sermon. They do not understand, so I return to the immediacies of camp life. "If you're so interested in doing what is in the best interests of the greatest number, you should open channels to alleviate the bitterness and frustrations of the living conditions, the strike, the food, and the hospital."

"We will investigate the suggestions," Burrell

replies, "as we have always done, but we will only take action after we have completed our investigation."

"We have heard that before," I answer, "yet nothing changes. If those conditions are not changed for the better, there is danger of violence. I am not threatening: I warn you of an explosive situation that exists."

Mr. Nye's face remains intransigent. "We cannot accede to demands, in view of the fact that we have always run things in an orderly and democratic way."

"And what you say about violence," Moore interrupts, "it's obvious the people are pretty well whipped up. Somebody is responsible for getting them upset."

The temporary lull of laughter is gone from Kageyama's weary and exasperated face. "You insinuate we are responsible. You make me laugh. All of you!" He spits out sarcastically. "At your hands we are sent around like cattle, then you observe the people are whipped up and tell us we are responsible!" Kageyama's expression is one I have seen on all of us, on the thousands waiting outside for word of their destinies being decided around another conference table.

Inside, we have reached an impasse, so we adjourn to the barrack porch, unwilling conspirators in the deception of those thousands, already so many times deceived. Nye, Kageyama, Burrell smile as if the meeting has produced an amicable solution to the problems and grievances. First Nye with an interpreter, then Kageyama tell the people, now cold and shuffling, how we must work together, how we must have faith in the government, and the importance of cooperation between the people of Tule Lake and the administration.

"Now," Kageyama announces, "in ending the

meeting and as a gesture of respect, in the tradition of the Japanese, we must bow." And as bamboo on windy days of winter, thousands of people move earthward. They hover a moment, then rise slowly as a gust whips by, and bend again in another flurry. Like a colony of ants unexpectedly abandoning a nest, the compound empties. Ten thousand Japanese reverse their direction and disappear into the maze of barracks.

Chapter 23

A shrill, head-splitting flute willows its way through the eerie grayish sky. Pointed hats and robed figures move softly to the rhythm of strings of koto and wood tempo. Silently we watch the Meijisetsu ceremony commemorating the birthday of the late Emperor Meji, grandfather of the reigning Emperor Hirohito. Thousands sit or stand, their faces crimped against the fragile landscape of ice.

In the evening I smell the persistent and now familiar odor of men gathered together for a final meeting of the Committee of Seven. Secretions of salt, stove and cigarette smoke cling to their oily faces. The speech ranges from Japanese to pidgin English. A man stands, crosses, and uncrosses his arms and shouts out until he is recognized by the chair. When he is given the floor, he says loudly, "How do we know who can be trusted?"

"These are names," Kageyama answers, waving over his head a fist full of papers. "It was responsibility of each block representative to hand in names of men so we can choose permanent representative body."

"Who is to decide which people are chosen?"

"We have picked selection commitee to select permanent members from names submitted."

"Committee of Seven was chosen by majority. Now new committee is picked to select permanent representative body. Already too many people don't know which committee is for what!" By this time the man's face is flushed a burnt bronze.

"Hai! Hai!" someone shouts. "Already so many that some on committee don't know what for. We don't need more committees!"

Kageyama waves for silence. "Selection committee must pick body to replace Committee of Seven. Many members wish to resign."

"Who?"

"Shiozawa-san, Koike-san, Senzaki-san. And I too wish to resign. I cannot do what I wish. There is still much organizing to do for Buddhist Center."

As louder, angrier voices compete, the room becomes an echo chamber of sound.

"Longer than month camp on passive resistance! Still there is no betterment of living conditions! Buddhist Center not needed!"

Kageyama slumps into his chair wearily. Abe, representative of Ward III, stands. "Appointment of permanent body by selection is subject to public review. Thereby selection by majority is assured."

The crowded room makes me dizzy, its air polluted with body stink and smoke. For a long while I watch, sound shut off, the rising and seating of many different men, of people shuffling in and out of the barrack.

The bulbs that light the room are dim, casting shadows against the farthest corners. A door opens; the rush of cold air and shuffling indicate the urgency of the man responsible for the disturbance. Everyone turns as the face of Horie comes into view. "They are stealing Tule Lake people's food," he shouts. He searches out Kageyama and says with increased belligerence, "The Hakujins and Army are trucking away food and giving it to backstabbing strike breakers! We must stop food stealing!"

Kageyama stares at Horie, trying to read in the

youthful face how far he can be trusted. "How many?"

"Two trucks and four jeeps of soldiers."

"Go back," Kageyama directs. "And watch what is happening. Count the trucks and take the license numbers." Horie turns, begins working a new path through the crowd. Half-way to the door he is stopped by a command.

"Avoid trouble at all cost! It is bad time for violence!"

How many minutes or hours go by after Horie leaves I do not know. His face lingers in my mind, to be extinguished by the first sounds of gunfire. The lights go out and the room becomes chaos. People scrape over one another, pushing and shoving and grunting as every man and woman simultaneously tries to squeeze out into the night.

Sensing the futility, I do not move. The advancing sounds of gunfire, whining engines, the accompanying tremor from tanks rumbling between Tule passageways swamp the porous walls. Jeeps with searchlights move between buildings. Shafts of light break along the walls, through each window. The crunching of tires stops, and a spotlight flashes onto the post inches above my head like a high-noon sun in a black sky.

The spotlights pin us against the wall. We are unable to move until the helmeted soldiers peel us from floors and walls. We are arrested and taken for the night to the Army clothing store warehouse where we get a couple of hours of rest on wooden floors.

In the morning chill, we are taken before Colonel Griffin. His color is antiseptic, his face rigid and inflexible.

To the assembled prisoner-evacuees he tells of the newly instituted regulations that will govern meetings and the general behavior of Tule Lake "colonists." We listen to the same voice we have heard for decades.

"Until the camp returns to normal conditions, all of us will have to suffer the inconveniences of regimentation."

Tomato raises his arm. "Would you please define for us what you mean by normal conditions?"

"When the camp is able to function as a self-governing community. That means, when the work crews are purged of troublemakers, when military intervention is no longer needed to keep order."

Tomato mumbles softly, "So that's normal conditions."

"Why were we arrested?" Kageyama asks. "Why the gunfire, the soldiers, the tanks?"

Griffin looks at Kageyama, then to each of the rest of us. Suspiciously, he says, "You don't know?" He studies the faces. "Some of your young toughs attacked the military and government personnel at the food warehouses."

Kageyama sighs heavily.

"Some of the men escaped. Others were captured and put in the stockade. The rest of you were arrested so we might find out who inspired those men to attack."

"They did it on their own," Kageyama replies.

Griffin looks over to Kageyama. "I have heard about you."

Kageyama starts to answer, pauses, then changes his mind.

"In fact, I have heard of all of you. You have made yourselves my business. Those boys were pretty worked up. Some one must have put them up to that attack. Who was responsible?"

Kageyama turns to look at the faces of the Japanese,

studies them a moment, then turns back to Griffin. "All of us here were in the meeting hall. None of us had anything to do with the attack."

"I realize that," Griffin says, impatiently. "But one does not have to be at the scene of the crime to be guilty."

"Guilty!" Kageyama intercedes. "We are guilty?"

"I didn't say that."

"No, you didn't. No one has ever said that. But we are here."

"There are obviously troublemakers . . . ."

"There are obviously troublemakers!" Kageyama mimics.

Griffin turns red at Kageyama's insolence. "I will not get into fruitless arguments. But I will do whatever is necessary to get rid of the rebellious people."

"With tanks, machine guns, armed troops against a people defenseless and already behind barbed wire?"

"This is not a concentration camp," Griffin says, "but for some of you there is obviously need for one."

"There would be little trouble if there were relaxing of military and administration controls. There is shortage of coal crew members, and it is getting close to winter. Already many barracks are too cold for children and old people. There is garbage scattered about barracks and compounds because Army has refused to let crews work at full strength."

"In the future," Griffin says, "a forty-eight hour work week will be expected of all workers. A full day's work."

Griffin's face is intransigent. His voice becomes monotone. He cannot hear us any more than the congressional committees could, or the governor or the newspapers or radios.

"You are trying to make us responsible for the discomforts of the children and old and the invalid," Griffin says, coldly. "It is not our doing. It's your fault. We must purge the work crews to get the agitators. You have only made our job more difficult by not cooperating. Until the situation is straightened out, it's up to you to care for the young and old."

In a tired gesture Kageyama rubs his hand across his face. He is more weary, I think, than if he were trudging from the fields in summer. But he, too, persists as if there were no other direction. "It is impossible for us to go back to the people and tell them that."

"I don't understand."

Kageyama winces.

I intercede, try to explain. "Because of the Army policies, those who are cleared are suspected of treachery to their own people and are being called 'Inu' or informer. We can't build a community. Ending the screening and re-instating all crews is the only way we can progress."

Griffin looks me in the eyes and says, "You are only one of two original Tuleans who sit on the Committee. This camp is made up of forty-five per cent original Tuleans, and you say your committee represents the camp. What distortion! This camp is being run by disloyals and troublemakers!"

I feel my face turning hot. "Considering that 'disloyal' is a term manufactured by you to categorize us, it is hardly justifiable that you make an analogy of disloyalty and the problems that have torn apart the camp. For decades we have survived in trust and cooperation without you. With you we live in chaos."

"You bring chaos upon yourselves. It is Japanese who kill Japanese. You wreak violence on each other.

It is precisely because there was too much leniency, too much effort by the administration to lean over backwards trying to help you people. Now, it is coming to an end. As of last night, I have and will run Tule Lake until it is conclusively proven I am not needed."

I am momentarily frightened that he is right. Then in his shiny white-sheathed face, I read that he is wrong more than I have ever understood what is right.

Griffin continues, "Until further notice no disloyals will return to any work crews. Anyone who further disrupts camp life will be arrested and put in the stockade with the original rioters. Certain essential work crews will be cleared of troublemakers. Until this is finished, your people will have to put up with the inconveniences."

He scrapes his chair back and stands. "Day after tomorrow there will be a camp wide meeting. I will address the colonists on the new policies. The meeting will be in the main firebreak and all able bodies among the 18,000 colonists will be expected to attend."

Within forty-eight hours Griffin is on stage, dressed in khaki, his trousers, stiff and creased, his hat a regulation inch above the brows. There is a deathly stillness, a silence vibrating like a frayed string in a typhoon. Griffin stands at attention, reading from a sheaf of fluttering documents.

From the temporary stage he addresses an empty firebreak.

Splinters of ice rise on the wind, condense into misty clouds that temporarily obscure him and sweep the sounds of his voice away from our barrack walls. " . . . military jurisdiction . . . threats to the welfare of decent people . . . imposing wills over the majority . . . the best interests of the greatest number . . . anarchistic

activity . . . the safety and welfare of every resident . . ."
He talks to himself, to soldiers cordoning off the stage,
to jeeps rolling in and out of snow flurries.

For forty-five minutes I hear his angry echoes. It is
the hundredth day without the light of sun. In the gray
light there is silent laughter, rumbling like tumbleweed
through passageways, walls, and floors. As the P.A.
voices fade in the afternoon, the laughter grows louder,
throbbing.

I become aware that I am being hunted even before
I am informed by messenger. Pain shoots through every
nerve ending. I consider how perfect the night is for an
escaping fugitive in a concentration camp: moonless,
everyone having retreated into darkened barracks, all
light bulbs extinguished as if on signal.

I blindly follow the silent, swiftly moving form. He
tells me we are now under martial law. I don't know
who it is that leads me insanely through the night.
Without fear I listen to accelerating engines. I am doing all that is humanly possible to escape, running wildly, chaotically, disappearing again and again. A spotlight straightens itself against the opposite barrack wall
of the corridor. I am brought away from my wild running. The shadow in front of me falls, rolls, disappears
under the barrack, gesturing "Down!"

The light moves frictionlessly over tar paper, and I,
too, roll into the dark. When it is quiet, we roll out and
continue.

He leads me to another barrack. I slide after him
through a door barely open and I see the warped batts
and sagging tar paper on the wall.

For a long while we stand with our backs against the
walls, listening to our lungs heaving, our hearts pounding.

From a black corner, Kageyama says in a whisper, "I didn't know if we could get to you before Military Police. Already Shiozawa and Ansai have been arrested and put into stockade."

I wonder where I am -- Fourth Street, Ward V, I, IV. Who searches for me? Even insanity must be cyclic -- an abyss.

"Maybe it would be better to surrender," he says, in a voice thinly washed with the fear of the hunted.

For a long while there is no response to Baba's suggestion. Then someone says, "Prisoners in stockade are beaten. Maybe we stay in hiding."

"Where can we hide? They can find us easily."

From the darkness comes Tomato's cocky voice. "There's 1200 barracks. Pretty hard to find eight of us among 18,000 Japanese who all look alike."

Funo, ignores Tomato's humor. "Not all Japanese friend."

"We could hide between ceiling and roof," Baba says, this time bolder. The fear of alleged cowardice before his people is greater than his fear of the hunter.

Kageyama spells out a plan. "We should stay in hiding, avoid arrest. We will go to other blocks, find Committee friends and be buried under barracks. We will keep in contact by messenger, continue to negotiate, and make good representation for people."

From blackness, to deeper blackness. We will contact each other through earth.

He continues, softly, sanely, "It will be impossible for army to search under ground, under one thousand two hundred barracks. They will have to dig up every square foot of Tule Lake. We have no worries. The Nihonjin are not worth that to Hakujins. We will be safe and still dictate policy, make arrangements to free stockade prisoners, make for overall betterment of living conditions. Kato, go to Block 54. Find Hirotomi. Have yourself buried under a barrack where they cannot find you."

"Senzaki go to . . . ."

I am confined to a box hidden under a barrack, buried. There is no proportion. I struggle to turn from left to right, supine or face down, but I cannot move. I am in earth. The two feet that entomb me are the closest I have ever been to breaking surface into the light of day.

Remarkable that the daylight is scant inches away from blackness. I was told long ago of light traveling millions of years connecting star to distant stars, and I did not understand. It is as comprehensible as the twenty four inches of crust that have become to me the difference between life and death as I know it.

To measure the number of days I have lain here, there is the counting of meals: the times I am unearthed by someone removing the boards over me that I might breath fresh air and relieve my insides.

How long it is since the time I was exhumed to defecate and urinate, to cleanse away the stench of me in a box whose volume is half again my own, I cannot say.

I am a reeking, decaying, waste matter, a part of earth as few men will ever be. My skin grows fleshless without sun. I float in a sea of soil and minerals.

There is a muffled sound--tapping on wood through soil packed loosely upon me. A voice slides down the rubber tubing. "Army has massive search to find five of you."

"Five of us?"

"Yes. Tomita, Muratani, Moriuchi, and Baba were caught before getting buried in hiding place. Now they are in stockade. Army is going from barrack to barrack, one end of camp to other. Soldiers come behind to make sure no one slips through. Squeeze everyone against east fence. They find no one yet. Soon they come here. When you hear sound of Hakujin moving bed and chairs, you know they're soldiers. Don't mistake them for friends. Don't reveal where you are hiding."

He disappears with his footsteps. New footsteps approach and stop directly over me. In my total distortion there is a soldier standing on me, his feet buried in my face and chest. I laugh softly, my body convulsing, while he searches blindly, not thinking of the excavation he has made me make for myself. I restrain my laughter. His footsteps roam quickly back and forth. As I hold my breath, my face swells.

He leaves me undisturbed in my grave. I try to run back to Fourth Street, to Okayama, but bump into the box where time is disfigured.

"Senzaki! Senzaki!"

"Yes! Yes!"

As if I hadn't answered, the voice continues. "Kageyama sends message. It has been nine days. Little change. More people in stockade. Most crews cannot have enough people to work. Food is same, bad. Army won't make change until five fugitives surrender. Koike, Kageyama, Ansai, Kato having bad time in box. If nothing comes of hiding, they wish to surrender and go back to top of earth. Kageyama asks how you feel about it."

I start laughing . . . jolting, ripping laughter that aches; I want to laugh, to roll over and over, yet I can only move inches against the sides of the coffin. The sounds fill my wooden box until I am submerged in decibels that threaten to cut off my breathing, to drown me like cold water inundating my lungs, my skin and pores, my being.

I don't know how long I fail to answer. I cannot concentrate on a question I do not understand.

"Senzaki-san! Why don't you answer? Can you hear me? Senzaki-san, can you hear me?"

Another pair of feet move over me. "What is matter?"

"I don't know. He doesn't answer when I call."

"SENZAKI-SAN! SENZAKI-SAN!" the voice calls out in panic. "The tools! Something's wrong. Get him out!"

Earth scrapes, nails screech from wood. The last board. A cold blast of air washes over my skin, my arms, my face.

Panicked arms and hands lift me. Soon a doctor is working on me.

"He has come close to suffocating. He soon would have died."

I am startled at my complacency. I had believed death would be a violent struggle. Yet on the fringes, in place of struggle, there is a gentle drift from one state to another.

Next will be the stockade. From death to life, from soil to air, from a blanket-lined wooden box to a barbed wire stockade in a concentration camp.

Although I do not travel, I am on an endless journey.

Chapter 24

After two days in the hospital, I am taken to the stockade and imprisoned in the "bullpen", a confinement within the stockade within the concentration camp.

We are separated from the cold ground by a layer of water proofed canvas, a couple of blankets and clothing, and yet each rock and pebble imbeds itself in my back. For twenty-four hours we have lain in bullpen pup tents, the slanted canvas sides our only view. We have not talked, nor barely moved about. It is confining, but compared to my live burial, the tent is infinite freedom.

For the first time during the day, Kageyama makes a sound other than snoring or breathing. He rasps his throat as if he is preparing to say something. After another several minutes, he asks, "Do you often think about Gordie?"

I do not answer, but he waits patiently, knowing he has lots of time.

"I do," I answer finally. "Why do you ask?"

"Did you know him very well?"

"Yes and no. No, I did not know him until he was eight and I was ten. I don't know what he was like before then, what he did, what interested him, except, of course, what I was told. He was a stranger when I saw him, sitting on the tatami. I wondered, 'Is he my brother?'"

I try to bring into focus images growing misty and

dusty with time. I recall the more recent years. "Yes, I have known him well since that time."

"And he is well?" Kageyama asks in a concerned voice.

"Yes," I reply. "In his last letter he said he hadn't been injured. 'Vedi Napolic e poi muori,' is a proverb he wrote. He said it means, 'See Napoli and die.'"

It was a long letter. I choose to relate that part as if it spoke for the whole letter. We lie silently for some time.

Our conversation does not intersect, but runs parallel. "I, too, was ten," Kageyama says, "and that is when he died. It has been so long, he is hard to remember."

"Isao?"

"Isao," he replies softly. "Yes, Isao."

He turns to look back up at the canvas. "Strange," he muses, "you were ten when you met your brother, and I was ten when mine died."

"You have lost a brother and now I will also." I think about the small flag hanging on the wall of our barracks home that announces, 'SERVING OUR COUNTRY,' and in the center a star that designates Gordie. The thought makes me uneasy. I think of more pleasant things. I laugh when I think of the first time he saw a Japanese toilet. He didn't know what to do with the hole in the floor, so he waited until he suffered stomach cramps.

Kageyama looks up, his eyes focused on the past. "He is hard to remember," he repeats, his brow rippled. "But he was noisy, and always getting into trouble, so there are some things I can easily remember. Hah!" Kageyama's blanket heaves with laughter. "I remember one day when he was going to school and found a mother snake and her babies. He put all of them into a bag and took them to school. They got out, and it took hours to restore order. He became notorious for that one. Mother and Dad did not think it was funny then, but now, when Mother thinks about it, it makes her happy." He smiles broadly as he finishes the story. "Those are things we remember," he continues as if thinking aloud. "Because after that, there is no progression or change. I think that is what death means. He must live in time forever as a small boy."

Kageyama does not seem to mind when I ask him about Isao's death. Because it happened forty years ago, he talks about it easily, without hesitation. "It was in August, the hottest time of year in Florin. Sun does not shine but beats into land. Flies buzz around garbage can. It is like their buzzing is the only living thing. We were walking through hot fields and we saw a small glitter on the ground. They were small silver cylinders with strings attached. They looked pretty, so we took them home.

"Near the barn -- you remember where we loaded truck last time -- there was trash burning. Isao threw one of silver things into fire and when he turned away from heat, there was loud noise from behind. He stared at me, looking surprised. Then he fell forward. I looked at the back of his head and then I noticed deep red where pants where ripped open. There was hole where buttock used to be. Mother ran out of house screaming. She did not know he was going to die. Isao was taken to hospital, and Mother was told to stay home. She obeyed. Many times before Isao died, he called for her. She was not there, and for that, she still cannot forgive herself. She does not understand he has forgotten and forgiven. He will not remember her absence. And he will never forget the love between mother and children. Still, many times she thinks, 'if there had not been a fire; the carelessness; if I did not stay home.'"

It is late afternoon. He lapses into silence that extends into dusk and into night and into an unrestful sleep.

A boot thuds against the tent pole a few inches from our heads, and the tent shudders. Following several shattering blasts from a shrill whistle, someone shouts, "All right you bastards! Outa the tents and onto the feet! You ain't here for a vacation!"

Startled, I jump into the cold air and begin fumbling with my shoes. Kageyama turns and studies my frantic movements. In a calm voice he says, "Maybe we will be here for a long time. Much to endure. Do not be too anxious."

While we fall in for roll, I hear the sounds of bitter cold: breath turns into crackling, ice splinters. The brittle ground splits under the weight of men shuffling in the semidark.

"Abe!" the sergeant shouts, pronouncing the name as in Abe Lincoln.

"AHH . . . BIHH . . . HERE!"

There is an indecisive, pause then a stumbling over the pronunciation of Kato.

"Here!"

"Baba!"

Another pause, then Baba says evenly, "BAH . . . BAH!" He waits a few seconds. "HERE!"

The sergeant stares unbelievingly for a moment at Baba's dusky silhouette, and shines a beam in his face. "A straight answer," he growls irritatedly. "HERE or NNnn . . ." he stammers, then stops, open mouthed.

Back to the list, he keeps his record perfect by mispronouncing Tomita.

"TOE . . . ME . . . TAA . . . NOT HERE!"

Even in the darkness the sergeant's red face shows. "Once more," he says angrily. "The next man . . . ."

He calls Horie, Kageyama, Funo, then he calls out "Sen zacky!"

Following a short silence he repeats, "Senzacky!" I don't answer. He bellows furiously, "SENN ZACKY!"

Footsteps move in around me, and someone jabs a rifle butt in my stomach. I double over, and a soldier raps me again from behind. Face flat, I listen while a voice tells me I must learn respect for authority and respond when my name is called.

From close to me, Kageyama says earnestly, "Answer to your name, Ben."

When I stagger to my feet with Kageyama and Tomato's help. The sergeant demands to know why I did not answer.

In the icy air, I am sweating and chilled. "I didn't know I hadn't. I didn't think it necessary."

The sergeant eyes me suspiciously. "Don't bring trouble on yourself," he says, turning away.

I start to laugh. Bring trouble upon yourselves! Do you wish to come to the top of the earth after nine days? In this center ring of three layers of fencing, am I here?

None of the soldiers makes a move towards me. I laugh hysterically while they stand around dumbfounded, waiting for the laughter to subside, waiting for the morning to shed its darkness. The pain from the rifle butt is long gone, replaced by aching muscles.

For two days there are no more rifle butts in my stomach or roll calls. On the fourth day we are taken individually to the commander of the stockade. The regulations governing our behavior are explained, warning us that any attempts to cause disruption while in the stockade will result in more bullpen confinement. Good behavior might mean eventual release back into the camp, surrounded by only two fences.

There are 250 of us in the stockade: Nisei, Issei, and Kibei, loyals and disloyals, young and old. Uprooted, we adapt and accept, undecipherable kanji to our captors, arranged neatly in columns from right to left, top to bottom.

We are nameless people: our lives, our heritage, our homes, our families have been reduced to the numbers hanging from our lapels the day we left Sacramento. It is indeed advantageous to remain innocuous in the stockade. This is relatively easy because the population changes steadily as the purges continue in the camp. Releases. Detainees. Releases. The population graph of the stockade rises, drops, rises, drops. From the steady changeover of prisoners, we hear rumors and news of the camp.

The Resegregationists, under the leadership of Togasaki, have gone completely underground to avoid arrest and incarceration. In an attempt to establish their own innocence, they point to persons in the stockade as the leaders of the anti-administration, anti-military forces. Prominent in their accusations are Kageyama, myself, and others.

After a rise on the graph to a high of over 300 prisoners, there begins a steady decline, and in two and a half months, we are one hundred and fifty. Four weeks later, we are twenty-five. Activity within the stockade slows down to a boring routine of lying on our cots. There is no work or play or people coming and going to occupy our thoughts. Although our numbers are small, I avoid others. I rarely speak even to Tomato and Kageyama. There have been no stockade releases for over a month. Still we wait patiently, hopefully.

Although I have rarely looked at him or spoken to him, I know the man next to me, Kodama. He is introspective, silent. I remember having seen him on a basketball court in Walnut Grove or Brighton, or Courtland. He seems a harmless, peaceful person. I am perplexed by his presence in the stockade. To my knowledge he has not been active in the politics of camp, nor taken part in other activities that would justify his being here.

He has a hard time remaining in one place for any length of time. Sometimes he sits on the edge of his cot, elbows on knees, rolling and unrolling pieces of paper. He lies down, gets up, slumps against the wall, gets up and walks heavily out into the night. In an hour or two he comes back inside, stuffs his coat in his foot locker, and instead of lying back onto his cot, sits on the edge facing me. For the first time since we have become cot neighbors, he is going to speak to me. I look at his face. He averts his eyes, looking to the floor beneath me. His face is broad, expressionless, mild mannered.

I look away, stare at Shiozawa and Kato across the aisle, two sleeping army blanket lumps.

I study the two lumps, the forms, the shadows, the steady movement of breathing, waiting for Kodama. "Ah . . . mmmm," he says, clearing his rusty throat. "How long's it been?"

I study him for a moment. He is keeper of the stockade calendar. I look to the slashes he has been marking on the end wall of the barrack, and make a quick count of the groups. "Fifteen weeks exactly."

"Wow!" he says, whistling softly. "Been that long, huh?"

"Un-huh."

"Wow!" he repeats in simple, genuine amazement, as if he had never taken a count before. He takes a handkerchief out of his back pocket and blows his nose. He folds it back up, puts it away, and rubs his hand over the back of his neck.

"Say," he says thoughtfully, "did you ever think about how it is we got here?"

"The bullpen? The stockade?"

"This crummy camp and the stockade, yeah. I ain't done nothing to get the bullpen yet. Yeah! How's it a nobody ends up in a no-place place like this? A guy whose old man and old lady's just day workers."

For the first time Kodama stops and looks me in the eye: a quick glance that shifts back to the same spot on the floor. "You from Sacramento? You used to play church league basketball?"

"Uh-huh. Spent most of my life there. Or at least a lot of it."

"Me too. Well almost . . . Locke. You know where that is?" he asks, looking again at me. "South from Sac, along the Sac River. You know, where all them Chinamen run those gambling houses."

I nod my head that I know.

"I'm from there. At least that's all I can remember. I guess I'm from there 'cause that's what my old man told me."

I smile. "I suppose you're no different from any of the rest of us. We can only know our origins from what we are told by our parents."

"I guess you're right," he says and smiles for the first time. "Hey," he says suddenly, " I got something." He gets up and gets a package of gum from his footlocker and offers me a stick of stale Wrigley's Peppermint.

For a while we chew silently. Kodama takes the wrap-per and rolls it into a tight roll, folds it into a school-boy -wad and flips it into the center of the aisle.

"Hey! Kodama!" Moriuchi says. "Somebody's gonna have to clean it up."

Kodama ignores Moriuchi and stands up. "Jumping Jiminy. They never told me anything. My old lady never told me why they came to this country. I don't know when they married, how they got here. Don't know anything about what they did, how come I was born here, and how come I had to go to Jap school. How come they always want me to learn English when they're always talking Japanese at home? Holy Moley!" he says, sitting back down heavily and shaking his head from side to side, "I don't know nothing!"

I watch the top of his head, the long hair dangling and wavering from side to side as he continues shaking his head.

"You got any brothers and sisters?"

He stops shaking and looks up. "Yeah," he says with a grin, "that kind of stuff I know. Three. Two sisters and a brother. I only know about 'em, though, cause outside of my youngest sister I never got a chance to meet 'em except for when I was still a little kid. They were born in Japan and live there with my old man's side of the family. My old man's there with 'em now 'cause he got caught in Japan when the war broke out. They wouldn't let him come back. Doesn't make much difference either 'cause we never seemed to have much of a family life. We worked all the time while my old man sat and drank his sake."

Kodama peels his shoes off, swings his legs over the edge of his cot and slumps against the wall. He crosses his hands on his chest, twiddling his thumbs. "Son of a

Gun!" he says. "If we're gonna live like this, we might as well do it for the right side. We could be getting medals, citations, back pay." He clenches his right hand into a fist and slams it into his left palm. "But shit! Somebody's gotta take care of my old lady and my sis. Can't just leave 'em in this nut house."

Ten o'clock taps blows through the barracks. When the lights go out, he is still slumped against the wall, thumbs twitching again, staring into space, still trying to figure out why he's in the stockade.

"Hey, Kodama. How did you get in here?" I ask. "I never heard of you. You hangin' around with those troublemakers?"

"Yeah," Kodama answers.

"And how come you didn't get out with the others?" Tomato asks. "Must be guilty by contamination!"

Blasts from the police whistle jar us out of bed and outside. The south wind whips snow into the compound, flapping our loose jackets and pants in the gust, forcing our heads into our collars. At a senseless roll call it is too cold to do anything but answer quickly and get back to the barrack.

It goes efficiently until the roll gets to Kodama. "Kodama!" the voice calls, starts to go to the next name, backtracks. "Kodama!"

There is a pause. "KODAMA!" The sergeant bellows as if shouting at a recalcitrant ass.

After the fourth time, I feel anger rising against Kodama, like a bubbling cauldron. He is responsible for the cold, for the wind, for our being in this camp and in this stockade.

A soldier comes up behind Kodama and pushes him stumbling to the ground, his hands still in his pockets.

"Get him on his feet!" the stockade sergeant shouts.

"It's freezing out here."

Kodama is pulled up. One of the soldiers grunts and mumbles the Jap should quit faking and get on his feet. They have him off the ground, knees almost touching, legs sprayed out, head sagging. They shake him. "Come on, you yella son-of-a-bitch. Damn you. Son-of-a-bitch. It's cold."

Kodama just dangles, and is finally dropped to his knees, then to all fours. One soldier jabs Kodama and another kicks him.

Kodama's head is facing directly at the rifle. Another jab, a kick, a curse. Kodama slips his hand around the barrel end of the rifle, and in the early morning blur, he turns and swings the stock hard into a khaki knee. The soldier slumps down by Kodama, his eyes staring blankly. The freezing wind wheezes stiffly through the stockade fence.

Kodama is enraged now. He gets to his feet and swings again, wildly, the weight of the rifle pulling him in full circle. He spins, loses his balance, and falls. Another soldier rams a rifle butt into Kodama's head. From behind me in the semi-darkness there is a rifle shot, then another, and some one falls to the ground. The Japanese fling themselves on the guards, swearing, shouting, wrestling. A soldier stands astride Kodama's body, raising his rifle to crush Kodama's face. He pauses for a moment, undecided, and in that moment, I am on him.

He grunts and spins, his rifle discharging inches from my ear. We stagger and fall.

Chapter 25

A voice, muffled as if it were coming from inside a stuffed linen closet, says, "Benn-nn . . . ," pauses, "Benn . . . , Benn-nn . . . ."

Knock . . . knock . . . . The soft sound of knuckles tapping against gypsum board. Over and over again. Tap . . . tap . . . "Benn-nn . . . , Benn-nn. . . ." Calling, pausing, tapping, calling.

The board bed that I have been lying on for some time is built into the wall where the tapping and calling persists. I am right below a small barred window, its eight inches by eight inches the only light.

I lift first one leg, then the other, bend and straighten my fingers, move my arms a few inches.

"Benn-nn . . . ," the voice calls. Tap . . . tap. "Ben!"

I lift a foot, let it drop. After a few thuds, the voice asks, "That you, Ben? Hey, Ben, that you?"

I raise and drop my other foot.

"Hey now, just give me an answer, okay? Just give me an answer with a coupla' thuds."

I try to speak, producing an unintelligible croak. Tomato says in muffled excitement, "Okay. Okay. At least you're not a ghost!"

He pauses for a few minutes. Tap. "Now listen. One thud means yes," he says, sounding distant. "Two, no. Okay, you got that? You okay?"

Thud.

"Good," the voice says reflectively, "Good. Now, nothing seriously wrong, nothing seriously hurt, no serious damage?"

I think about that one carefully, then answer with a thud.

"Had to think about that one for awhile, huh? Know what you mean. Know what you mean."

The voice stops a moment, then continues. "We've been here twelve . . . twenty-four plus eight . . . equals thirty-two . . . thirty-two hours. All this time you've been quiet. Now I want to know if you can talk, if you can make use of your voice box. Clear your throat, take your time and don't worry about me. Like you, I got a lot of time. These past years are teaching me about patience like I never woulda' dreamed existed."

The window casts a small square sunbeam on the opposite wall. I watch it climb for a few hours. In mid afternoon, Tomato begins to ramble on about his cell.

"They painted the cell black! The only light they got in this place is from a tiny window. When the sun sets, everything will be so dark, the walls will vanish!"

At that moment a slot in the door opens up, and a tin tray is slid into the room.

"That's supper," Tomato says. "Bread and water, twice a day." He lets out an irate snort. "Boy, flop house accommodations! Oh well, I guess we can't expect the Waldorf Astoria!"

I think back to the violence, try to remember what happened to Kodama. I remember him lying on the ground beneath a rifle butt. I lean towards the wall and whisper softly, "Kodama . . . where is he? What's happened to him?"

"He's alive. But it'll be awhile before he'll be doing any talkin' or gettin' around. If he were in uniform, he would be getting a purple heart and permanent disability for his face. But you did it, Ben. As close as anyone coulda' come and still be on time. Kodama's gonna be okay, but you're implicated up to here." I can almost see Tomato's index finger against his neck.

"What about you?" I ask. "What are you doing here?"

"When I saw someone knock down that soldier just before he rams Kodama, I think there's only one guy with that kinda quickness. So when someone was gonna rifle butt you, I laid him out." He draws in deep and says with his breath half held, "Hoo boy! It was wild! Shouting, shooting, clubbing, blood running around the ground, melting ice and staining everything ketchup. Hoo Whee!"

He lapses into silence and instead of talk coming through the wall, there is a scraping, gnawing sound. I try to figure it out and conclude that Tomato is doing something to the wall.

"That you Tomato? What are you doing?"

"Got it!" he says triumphantly. "I just cut through my side o' the wall. Three-quarter inch gyp board and half-inch plywood. I just about got the hole big enough . . . there . . . I can see into your side of the wall." There is another long pause. "Now if that don't beat all. We're public enemy number one, in maximum security, and they've got interior and exterior walls a guy can carve through with a pocket knife. Hey, they forgot to check me for weapons!"

Tomato quiets as he clicks open and shut the blade of his knife. "Nothin' makes sense," he says, thoughtfully. "We get put inside flimsy jails in concentration camps inside a country that puts us here in the name of freedom and liberty and democracy. And here we are, nowhere, no place, with faces like full moons."

He jabs the sharp blade into the wall several times.

"And why not gyp board and plywood? We could cut our way through the walls, through all the layers of fences, and where would we be, where would we go? Some of those Hakujins out there say they could recognize us from five miles, smell us from four. And maybe they got their evil senses so honed up they can. You know what? It's like trying to find freedom in an air bubble at the bottom of the sea."

Splintering glass and a loud crash comes from Tomato's cell.

"What's going on?"

"Seems like the whole camp's marching around. They been picketing ever since the word got out about the fight!"

"Why are they angry?"

"Who knows?" Tomato says. "In this nut house there's no room for knowin' why or what you're doin'. Just go ahead and do it. They think a lot of things out there: that Kodama was beaten, that you bashed the soldier, that the soldier shot a soldier while trying to get a 'Jap,' that Kodama did the shooting. Et cetera! Et cetera!"

Tomato gets to his feet and steps on his rack to look out the window. "Easy now," he chuckles softly. "An inch or two at a time ... don't wanta catch a rock square in the kisser."

I imagine him peering over the bottom of the window.

Very slowly, so I don't black out, I get to my feet and lean against the wall. I work myself to the window and look outside, to the three fences that enclose the jail. There is a large crowd of people carrying signs and posters and wearing arm bands.

A prominent sign reads:

"WE DEMAND PRISONERS SEE ACLU LAWYER!"

"American Civil Liberties Union?" Tomato says loudly. "Here we are already behind barbed wire and the ACLU's involved. Civil Liberties, Hooray. An accessory after the fact -- or something like that."

"We might be needing them yet. They've been fighting the Denationalization Act in Congress," I say. "They lost, though. But I have a feeling we're going to need all the help we can get."

"Denationalization Act? What the hell's that?" asks Tomato.

"A law. A special law just passed in Congress specially for Japanese, so we can renounce our American Citizenship."

"Hallelujah!" Tomato exclaims. "That's what the Resegregationists have wanted for months, so they can become 'true Japanese.' Interesting they should suddenly pass a law like that just because crazies like Honda and Togasaki want it."

"I don't think it was because of them. There's never been any provision before for an American citizen to renounce his citizenship. I think there are other reasons."

"Yeah," Tomato says thoughtfully. "There's been talk lately about needing trade bait for American prisoners of war. You think that might have something to do with it?"

"Who knows?"

"Say," Tomato says, "how much do you suppose we're worth? I mean, how many of us would it take to equal one white guy?"

"Who knows? I guess they make decisions like that in the White House."

"Denationalization Act," Tomato mumbles. "Denationalization Act. Sure hear a lot of new things in camp. Speaking of 'true Japanese,' how is it we're behind bars and guys like Honda and Togasaki are running around free? I mean, relatively free!"

Across the way, Tomato sees a new sign saying the stockade detainees should be allowed to see the Spanish Consul.

Tomato's voice reaches me now from outside. "Hey, they still trying to get those Spaniards involved? Think those guys can help us?"

"I doubt it."

Tomato pauses as if he were looking at me through the wall. "Yeah?"

"They might be able to help the Issei but not us. We're citizens. No foreign government's got a right to interfere in domestic affairs."

"Domestic affairs!" Tomato exclaims. "So that's how it is! And the only recourse we got is to the government that put us here in the first place? Talk about a stacked deck!"

Tomato rams his fist and I hear gyp board crunch. "Say . . . how is it, Ben, that we got stuck with these faces anyhow? Sometimes I think I'd like to trade mine in on a second-hand Frankenstein from the Salvation Army."

From the moment the gavel pounds the hearing to order, Tomato and I and the others put our minds to reconstructing the riot, to dissect frame by frame, word by word, the curses and shouts, the running about, the stabbing and shooting.

The administration personnel and the military preside at the inquiry. Behind them an American flag is pinned to the wall. Facing them and flanking us on our other side is the Japanese Committee of Arbitration, made up of respected members of the Community who are investigating stockade conditions and working for "justifiable releases" of detainees. Father is one of the representatives. It is the first time I have seen him in a long time. Since that day somewhere between Halloween and Thanksgiving and now beyond Christmas, New Year's, and Lincoln's and Washington's birthdays, I have been a fugitive, buried, arrested, stockaded, bullpenned, jailed, and now, brought before another kangaroo court.

Father's face is bruised, and he wears a patch over his right eye. Although he sits straight and attentively, he does so with much effort. I wonder about the bruises and what there is -- or isn't -- behind the patch. For a long while I watch him, but when I close one eye, I immediately lose perspective: everything is in the same dimension in space.

Among the Japanese there is one white man, very thin, with glasses that nervously perch on his nose or hang from his ears or swing between his fingers. He is an ACLU lawyer who is fighting for our abrogated rights as American citizens. They say he cares about our unjust imprisonment, for he understands that what may befall one of us may befall anyone. Among us who have been tanned from this shadeless camp, his face stands out like a white playing card in a coal pile.

People move in and out of the witness chair, each giving interpretations of what happened. The stockade sergeant sits at attention in the chair and tells us what could be seen early in the morning. "When you got right up to him, you could see from his eyes the kind of guy he was. He had the kind of expression that causes concern about Caucasian women whenever Jap men are around. His eyes were wide open, hardly blinked, and yet closed off. You understand how impossible it is for us to teach them to communicate to us on our level. The white man's got to step down."

"You are describing Kodama?" the stockade lawyer interrupts.

"Yes, Sir!" the sergeant says, nodding. "It's difficult to be able to know what they're thinkin' from the looks on their faces and eyes. They're different in a funny lookin' way that isn't exactly stupid but more tendin' to sneakiness. A man wouldn't want to have money lyin' around when one . . ."

"Objection!" our lawyer shouts, leaping to his feet. "The witness is dealing in subjectives -- his own prejudices and images."

"Objection sustained!"

"That may be so," the sergeant says heatedly to our lawyer, "but it's been my responsibility to take care of these people for months. I see 'em and come in contact with 'em several times a day for weeks. So I get to know 'em. What they do in their spare time, how they act, how they think. We guys in the stockade have gotten to know 'em like few other white guys, and if you could see what we seen, you wouldn't hardly believe it."

The sergeant stops, breaking attention and shaking his head slowly from side to side.

"Objection!" our lawyer shouts, standing up again. "That is not the point. What should be of concern to us is what happened to Habeas Corpus. We can't hold people for months without charges or a hearing. They have been held," he says, pointing to us, "and denied private counsel with their lawyer. Each time we have met, it has been in the presence of someone from Internal Security. All these things are in gross violation of constitutional rights!"

Burrell is framed by the flag; from the stars clustered around his head, he answers in a self-righteous, annoyed voice, "It's done for the welfare of the majority. We have done nothing in violation of constitutional rights by holding these men. It is nothing more than an 'administrative procedure' necessary to maintain order by keeping them from having contact with the majority of people and inciting discontent."

"And it is a small price to pay," Mr. Moore of Internal Security says defensively. "Only thirty men out of a one-time high of two hundred and eighty. That's only ten per cent of the original number of detainees. To preserve order and the rights of the vast majority by keeping a small troublesome group under lock and key makes good sense."

"Good sense!" our lawyer shouts again, waving his papers at Burrell and Moore. "You seem to forget you're dealing with citizens of the United States of America. Your prejudice has blinded you! If your intentions were so lawful, why were United States Army soldiers allowed to steal valuables from the detainees and truck away food and gifts from their families during the holidays?"

Burrell clears his throat and says, "Well, that may be true, but it doesn't have anything to do with Kodama. Together with the Arbitration Committee, we have diligently worked towards all 'justifiable releases.'"

From a section of a hearing room set aside for the public, Reverend Togasaki unexpectedly stands up and says loudly, "That's the problem! 'Justifiable releases!'"

He points accusingly at the Arbitration Committee. "You do not work for release of 'unjustifiable releases.' Until there is no one in stockade, you are traitors to our people, to detainees, and in some cases, traitor to family members."

Father's head twitches, the skin on the back of his head creases. The purple bruises on his face turn black. He suppresses the urge to touch the sores, to finger the patch, to turn 180° to look at me, see me, decide who I am, who I may have become in the months I have been imprisoned. But fingering, touching, turning would be conspicuous; instead, he shudders in his chair.

Colonel Griffin suddenly stands up angrily, glaring at the lawyer, and orders Togasaki's removal from the hearing room. When our lawyer says that had Due Process of Law been followed none of us would be here, the Colonel pounds a large gavel on the table for silence. "It's not our intention," he says, "to deprive anyone of their constitutional rights. And in almost all situations it has not proved necessary, due to the cooperation and willing spirit of ninety-five per cent of all the Japanese who have gone cooperatively into relocation centers. But obviously, in every barrel there are always some rotten apples! And when this happens, it becomes necessary to separate them lest they infect all the apples!"

"Rotten apples!" Tomato exclaims softly, inadvertently touching his temple as if fingering a juicy bruise. "Rotten apples? Now I been called a lot of bad things since all this happened, but I gotta admit, that's the least bad of them all. Barrels of rotten apples! Holy shit!"

He thuds his foot against the table leg. "Gettin tired of names and categories . . . 'loyalees' . . . 'disloyalees' . . . 'detainees' . . . 'justifiable releases' . . . 'unjustifiable' . . .

'stockadees' . . . 'bullpennees' . . . 'domestic affairs' . . . 'apples.' Sometimes I think I got a bubble stuck up my ass, making me confused." He leans over and whispers, "Why don't we just hang it all up for one title . . . Private Senzaki . . . Private Tomita?"

He closes his eyes, shuts out the talk of rifles, of busting bones, of Kodama's face being smashed into the center of his head. For the next couple of testimonies he goes into a trance, his head bowed, the only movement the slow rising and falling of his breath.

"He was a 'troublemaker,' a guy always complaining and bitching about conditions," another guard says about Kodama. "He was asking for what he got." Then the guard looks over at me and points, saying, "And what's more, it was because of him the other prisoner got shot. If he'd stayed out of it, there wouldn'ta been no more blood spilt."

Tomato's face turns red. He hops out of his trance onto his feet, protesting my innocence. "The guard was gonna ram Kodama when he was already smashed in the face and lying out colder'n a mackerel." Tomato's voice is loud and vehement.

The Colonel bangs his gavel and threatens to remove him.

"It wouldn'ta been possible," the guard answers despite the banging, "cause he was just standing there."

"That's a lie," Tomato says, looking around the room, searching for someone who will listen. "And even if it weren't," he continues, "What the hell you suppose the guard was gonna do? Break some more bones in Kodama's face? As if a concussion and caved-in cranium weren't enough."

Tomato suddenly seems pained by sharp blows. He cups his hands and puts the palms against the sides of his head. He sits this way through another half hour.

"Shit," he whispers finally. "This is getting hard for me to take. Gotta think about more pleasant things before I get dragged through the slime of this garbage can." He lets his eyes drift upwards until they rest on the ceiling where he conjures up pleasantries of the past. "I guess I'm just a San Joaquin Valley Boochie," he whispers, "cause when I think about the good ol' days, I think about hot weather, about sweat bubblin' outa the skin . . . and cold water . . . and swimming. There's nothing like cold water on a hot day." He takes his hands from his ears and rubs them down his pant legs. "Say . . . remember that time we had class swimming party at William Land Pool when it was 108°?" he asks, wrinkling his face. "Remember that ticket seller looking down at us -- sayin' we can't go into the pool because the oils we secrete might contaminate the water? Sure made me feel creepy . . . like I wanted to wash down with a bar of lava."

Tomato suddenly sits up and socks himself with his fist a couple of times. "Shit! Now why'd the hell I have to go and think about that? I was supposed to do some happy thinking. How come? Huh?" He looks at me as if expecting an answer.

"I guess when the mind's been slogging around in the gutter so long, it's kind of hard to get it to go anywhere else."

"I suppose you're right," he replies. "Suppose you're right."

Father stands up and from a sheet of paper reads the "Final Recommendation" of the Arbitration Committee. His voice, like his back, is weak and tired. "Committee has always worked for 'justifiable releases' from stockade. And it is true that ninety per cent of original prisoners are now back in camp. But there is still great unhappiness. There is strong feeling for the men in the stockade. Many of them have not seen families for many months. Some have had children born and have not seen wives or new babies. Mail is pried into and censored. There is no privacy of lives, and plight of detainees weighs heavily on shoulders of Tuleans. It is the recommendation of the Arbitration Committee that stockade be closed and all men returned to Tule Lake and families. It is not possible to live in peace under such circumstances."

"Rotten apples," Tomato mumbles. "Rotten apples."

For many nights I lie awake with the image of Father's weary voice and patched face resting in a dark plane. I try to think of reasons for the patch. Another ambush? A beating? Did he fight back? Was there anyone to help him? The darkness draws more lurid details from my imagination.

During the day the sounds of washos and banzais drift through the barrack windows. Next to me Kodama lies sleeping in his cot, a snoring mummy covered with a white sheet. The unbandaged fragments of his face look like dark stains on the gauze.

A couple of days after the hearing he was given medical clearance and returned to the stockade. I feel a relief, the warmth of reunion with a long-lost friend. He has changed since becoming the focus of the riot. He is no longer the unobtrusive individual he was. He has a new found sureness, a cockiness, a new sense of self-importance. I am happy for him, yet I miss the quiet, sensitive Kodama.

Kageyama sits down on the wooden crate between

the cots. He listens to the rowdy voices outside. They are so bitter and so ignorant. "Look," he says, with his index finger pressed against the glass, "they are running around the compound, and the wind is blowing. They freeze!"

"They are learning to suffer hardships," a voice intrudes from the other end of the barracks, "for when they go back to Japan to fight for mother country."

"Mother country?" Kageyama says, his eyes fixed outside. "What do they know of mother country? And hardship? Because they have sprouted goose pimples?" He stops to laugh. "I will tell you story about hardship my father used to tell me, and he would say that until I could have greater hardships, I couldn't complain. He said there were Japanese who came to America who had only enough money to eat rice balls and umeboshi. When he does not have enough left for that, he rolls pits around in his mouth for months while he works long hours in fields."

"Ha-ha, ha-ha," Muratani laughs from across the center aisle. "Old people always have funny story about great hardship. Ha-ha, ha-ha!"

"Umeboshi pits! Living in dirt floor shacks with rain leaking! World War I!" Horie calls across to Muratani. "You've heard same stories too?"

"Sure thing!" Muratani answers. "Same stories like the Hakujin. Hard work, big hardships! Big struggle!"

"But weak mind!" Horie says. "Hakujin say jump through hoop . . . white-Japanese jump through hoop. Stand on hind leg, Hakujin say . . . white-Japanese stand on hind leg. Piss on hydrant. They piss on hydrant. Lick mud off shoe . . ."

"Turn skin white, Hakujin say, and they try. Huff and puff, and skin turns pink, red, blue, blue-black,

black. Many colors but never white. Only funny colors."

"Ha, ha! . . . Huff and puff," Horie grunts and
laughs, slapping his knee. "Red . . . blue . . . black . . .
funny colors . . . but never white!" His laughter becomes hysterical. His arms crossed over his stomach, he
wriggles like a box full of baby snakes.

Muratani joins Horie and they roll on the floor,
laughing convulsively. "Tanuki . . . Tanuki!" Muratani
squeals between grunts and guffaws. "Cheat and
change . . . Cheeee . . . and sometime Japanese turn so
white, father deserts son. Cheeeeeee . . . Senzaki . . ."
he begins and dissolves into unintelligible laughter.

The faces of Muratani and Horie expand like inflat-
ing balloons. I want to poke a hole in them to bring
them wrinkled and aged back to earth. I have seen the
Hories on Fourth Street and in the pool halls, talking
about getting into girls' pants. He is weakness, strength,
anger, hatred, meekness, happiness. I go outside to the
wood pile and bring in the long handled axe. Before
Horie realizes what is happening, I am at the foot of his
cot. He stops laughing when he sees the axe. In three
violent chops his foot locker is splintered plywood,
bleeding out clothes, shaving instruments, toothbrush
and other personal belongings. I whack the axe head
into the side of his cot, lift the end of it and jerk violently, dumping him head over heels onto the floor. Slowly
he regains his senses.

He turns purple with anger. With a black-belt's
quickness, he charges me, his head lowered. I easily
side-step the charge, and Horie trips, feet flailing. Off
balance, he lurches across the floor and rams his head
into a four-by-four post.

A large knot forms immediately on Horie's head,

and for a long while he just sits there, his big body slumped against the barrack wall as if it were too weary to continue struggling. It is the calmest I have ever seen him. With a distant look on his face, as if he were pushed back into the past, he starts to talk slowly about his life as it was, and how it led up to the lump on his head.

"What the hell," he says disconsolately, "they won't let me even get in contact with my mom or she with me, but I know she's out there waiting. That's the way she's always been. She kind of hounds me because the old man always stays out and drinks a lot. She used to push me around a lot but then I grew big, and she couldn't do it any more, so now she leaves me pretty much alone."

Horie laughs softly and shakes his head and says, "When she got to leaving me alone, I got to running around a lot, so she used to always say that I was just like my old man. She stopped saying that, though, when I got a steady job as a fish scaler in a fish factory. I made a lot of money but sure as hell no one sat next to me on street cars. I used to know a lot of girls from the country. They were pretty simple, worked in rich Hakujins' houses as domestics. I used to try and get 'em to take me upstairs or downstairs to the basements, but they never let me. I guess they knew better."

He leans over with his elbows on his knees. "But things got better, when I got canned from the fish factory and started working in the drug store. I didn't get as much money from it as fish scaling, but there were fringe benefits that sort of made up for the pay loss. I would cop a lot of things. I probably had more hair oil, more toothbrushes, and maybe the best medicines of any Jap in the country. I'd take things for girls, like bobby pins, hair rollers, things like that. And other things I'd sell, so sometimes I could make thirty-five dollars a month extra. That plus what I saved on tooth-paste and aspirins pretty much made up for the pay cut, plus the fact that I didn't smell like fish anymore."

Horie laughs softly and stares off into space. "One thing I couldn't get in my drug store, though, was rubbers. When I got the chance I'd look all over trying to find 'em. Then one day it occured to me that the owner was Catholic. I always tried to understand those guys but could never figure out why they felt so strong about it. What's the difference whether a guy's got a rubber bag on or not? It just don't seem any different than wearing a jacket!"

Several guys laugh. Horie looks around, surprised. He goes over each face, relieved that they are laughing. He smiles too, until he comes to Hiura, a fellow evacu-ee from Poston. Hiura is sneering as he laughs.

"What're you laughing at?" Horie says to Hiura.

"Ha hah, hoo ho!" Hiura laughs. "Stealing tooth-brushes and bobby pins! You a small-time petty thief!"

Horie sits with his arms crossed, frowning. His face lights up. He looks at Hiura. "At least I'm not such a yellow Jap that I steal from Nihonjin. At least when I steal it's from Hakujin."

Now it is Hiura's turn to frown. "Whaddya mean?" he asks, unsure of the implication.

"Yeah," Horie says confidently, feeling the sureness of the aggressor. "Some Japanese aren't so chickenshit they're afraid to steal from the Hakujin. Some Japanese steal from Japanese because they're afraid to steal from Hakujin."

"Whaddya mean?" Hiura repeats, his face turning red. "What're you trying to say?"

Horie smirks. "I'm not trying to say anything, ex-cept . . . the Japanese who steal from Japanese outside of camp steal from Japanese inside. Some people are only interested in making money. Some men belong to the Cooperative Enterprises so they can steal sixteen dollars a month from others."

Hiura bristles at the mention of the Cooperative. "You talking about my father and Senzaki's father? Come on, you two-bit phony. That what you trying to say?"

"Put on right-sized shoe," Horie says with a big grin.

"Why, you copper-plated bastard! If it weren't for the Co-op, none of us would get anything. No candy, ice cream, cookies, toothbrushes, toothpaste."

"You the two-bit petty thief now." Horie's voice is hard and accusing, all humor gone. "We live in concentration camp and you talk about candy, ice cream, cookies, toothbrushes, toothpaste. Nihonjin who steal from Nihonjin deserve to be beaten."

"You small-time nothing," Hiura says. "Stealing drug store crap . . . and . . . and silver ware!"

"Silver ware? What the hell . . . ?" Horie says, perplexed.

"I heard you talking before, about when you were a domestic and working for this Hakujin lady who thought she was so superior to you, so you stole from her and when she found out, she fired you, but only after you finished the supper dishes."

"Supper dishes? Fired?" Several voices chime in, then laugh.

Horie stands up, red-faced, sputtering. He disappears out the door.

Chapter 26

It is warm and pleasant, and when the sun's rays move up over my knees, it is a half hour or forty-five minutes before noon. I have grown flabby and pale from long hours of lying on my cot, thinking -- the only way I am able to escape the staggering boredom.

Two pin pricks of light turn to eyes. They fade, draw near, hover, vanish into a single pale face. I know the eyes: yet, I am unconvinced. I spend hours, years, waiting -- looking back. On the last day of my schooling in Japan, in the courtrooms, the hearings, in the barracks, and interviews, the faces peer at me but they do not see me. They listen, but they do not hear or understand.

Lying here, I am a jelly fish out of water, waiting for forces beyond my control to nudge or kick me back into the freshness of the sea. The normal barrack sounds suddenly cease as heavy footsteps approach my cot. I keep my eyes closed, the light filtering through my eyelids.

"You Senzaki?"

I nod my head and open my eyes. Two soldiers stand at attention.

"On your feet," one says. "The Project Director wants to see you."

A secretary announces me, and when I enter his office, I am motioned to a chair. "I have a couple of things for you," he says, uneasily, and hands me one of them -- an already opened letter that has been in the hands of a censor. 2ND LIEUTENANT GORDON SENZAKI, the envelope reads from its upper left hand corner. Ignoring Burrell, I begin reading immediately.

"Killed a couple of guys recently," the first sentence begins, "and saw a friend die. Three deaths in a week and any one of those could have been me. But I am sitting and writing to the family in Tule. One guy I killed almost at point blank range, the muzzles no more than a few rifle lengths away from each other. We were hunting around in ruins when we popped up face to face. He was slower than I was because he was so surprised to see a Jap. He was white, so I wasn't surprised. I thought a lot that night of what the final outcome might have been if I had been Caucasian. I guess it isn't always bad being a Nihonjin.

"Not so lucky though for this good friend of mine, Kenji, whose family is in Topaz. We were walking together, and he was telling me about his girl friend in camp when there was a gunshot and he fell beside me.

"There is no advantage in being Japanese from a distance. I dove helmet first into a ditch and remained there for a long time, afraid to move. Through the grass and weeds I could see Kenji's body. The sun was getting hot. Why was it him instead of me, why had he been on the right and I on the left?

"I guess a couple of hours went by, then something occurred to me. There wasn't one shot, but two, that I had felt a whine go by my ear a split second after Kenji had crumpled. I thought maybe the German didn't know whether or not he got me because he was shooting into a field of weeds. I had the advantage because he knew *where* I was but not *if* I was, and I knew *he* was even if I didn't know where.

"I could change one of the things he knew about me. I moved a hundred yards or so up the ditch. It was a relief in more ways than one because it had been quite a few hours since Kenji died and he had started to smell.

"It was getting dusk, so I figured the German was beginning to worry. I felt it too, but I kept telling myself the longer it went, the more the advantage shifted to me. The shadows started to make things fuzzy. It was hard to tell one tree from another or one weed from another. I started to feel panic because he was waiting too long, and when it got dark I would lose the advantage it had taken all day to gain. I saw a movement, then I saw him crawling. I wouldn't have seen him from where I originally was, but here, he was clear, so I shot him. Twice. I felt kind of sick, so I stayed in the ditch until dark."

"Almost mail time," the letter continues in a different shade of ink and under a new date. "The latest letter from Mom tells me you are still in the stockade, that they haven't seen you for several months, and you are not allowed any communication or letters. I put my title on the envelope in bold letters so maybe it will convince someone it is safe. Mom says Dad was beaten pretty severely, and he is blind in one eye. I mention this because I don't know whether you know or not. I hope it doesn't come to you as too big a shock."

"So often since I left camp, I've wondered whether what I was doing was the right thing. Perhaps I had made a mistake. Sometimes I'm so weary and depressed, I think I can't cope any longer, and I wish I had remained in camp where things are safe and sane. But I hear about the stockade, what's happening to you and to Mom and Dad, Kageyama, Obasan, and I see there is insanity everywhere, no matter where we are, each of us has to rise to our own particular situation, and ultimately, we will have to be judged by how well we coped. As you read this letter, I want you to know that

I don't believe anything that is happening to you is a result of whether or not you are disloyal or loyal, whether you are a Japanese nationalist or an American patriot. You are caught up in the same forces that I am, that Mom and Dad are, that Uncle Mas is. I'm praying for the day this insanity comes to an end. With love, Gordie."

I re-read the last paragraph several times and try to understand.

Burrell has waited patiently for me. Now he shifts in his seat. "Your father is all right," he says, "under the best medical attention."

"My mother?"

"Under protective custody. She was moved from the colony to a barrack near the administration area where she and the elderly women can be under protective guard twenty-four hours a day."

"I want my release out of the stockade. I have responsibilities to my family."

For a few moments Burrell's eyes are distant. Weighing many things, his frown turns rigid. "The stockade is being maintained indefinitely. It is necessary because the troublemakers have succeeded in creating havoc while they were free in the colony."

"We are in the stockade, and in the camp it is worse than when we were arrested."

His face empties of expression, dispelling the compassion and understanding that for a moment threatened to surface. "If you people were released, it would only get worse. It is bad enough the way it is."

I stare at him. He looks away, uneasily clearing his throat. Nervously he opens the top drawer of his desk and takes out an envelope, thrusting it quickly at me as if by handing it away, he is cleared of responsibility.

The envelope is trimmed in black. It has been open-ed. I stare at it, at the black bordered rectangle, at the frayed edges.

I slide my finger nail on the edge, unable to speak. After an uncomfortable silence, he says, "I am very sorry. You should know the envelope wasn't opened for censoring by any of us. It was first delivered to your parents who requested it be passed on to you."

I rise from my chair and walk out of the room, leaving the envelope on the desk.

Father appears in my phantasm to comfort me. He tells me I should not be concerned. "Long ago I have put mind over matter to survive. In the winter time when it was wet and cold, when the fog was heaviest and longest, I would think about going back to the old country. But each day I put it off, until finally it would be the warmer weather of spring when there was no longer time to think of other things. But it is past spring now, and since there are no plants to tend to, no medicines to take into the valley, no customers in the drug store, we will work to bring back what there is left of our family. Your brother . . . he is gone . . . a young man. Your mother does not say anything, but it is not necessary, for it shows in the dark lines in her face. It has not been worth it. Everything has gone wrong. I am still working to get you free, but it is getting harder because all members of the Committee have resigned, as have all the camp policemen. Some ways it is better for you to stay inside the stockade because here there is no law, only law of violence."

For a while a confused look comes across him then changes to a tiredness. "This relocation of Japanese is part of growing pains of a young country . . . . Just have to close my eyes for a moment . . . ."

Chapter 27

As temperatures go up, sweat cakes clothing, blankets, canvas, layer drying upon crusty layer, beginning to stink. Men on both sides of the aisle open windows. But outside of occasional small swirls caused by someone walking by, the musty smell of human mold sits in the room, waiting for a wind or breeze or gust to blow it elsewhere. We sit or lie idly, separate, distant from one another except for smell.

Baba says in an annoyed voice, "Something funny going on. All winter there is lots of soap, but now, when it is summer and weather gets hot, there is soap ration."

"What do you expect?" Kato says. "More people taking showers, so more soap is used. Water shortage doesn't come in the middle of the rainy season!"

"I know about water shortage and rainy season," Baba says, sniffing the air, annoyed at Kato's sarcasm. "But that's not the point. The government put us here, so they should give us enough soap to keep clean, summer or winter."

"And what about sugar ration?" Shiozawa says, stirred out of his lethargy by the conversation. "One bowl a week for thirty men. That's pretty funny."

"And fruits," Baba says.

"Fruits, sugar, soap?" Kato answers. "We prisoners of war and everyone outside have ration."

"Ration of rotten fruits in bottom of box!" Shiozawa answers angrily.

Koike is lying down on his cot, gazing distantly at the ceiling, his fingers interlaced under his head. "Eight months," he says, unconcerned about the legitimacy of the soap ration. "Pretty soon we'll rot and the sun will dry us up like smelly old fish. I thought I would die like a worm when I lived nine days in the ground. I didn't like the rot in the darkness, but now I think maybe the dirt wouldn't be so bad!"

A pained look spreads across Kato's face. He says in a depressed voice, "Better we were still buried. If we had stayed down there, all our troubles would be over now."

"All over," Koike says, "except for maggots and rot and dampness."

"Hey, Koike," Hiura says, from on top of his foot locker, "How come you always talking about rot?"

"Aw, leave him alone, Hiura. He was one of the guys that was buried for nine days."

"Yeah, Hiura, if you were buried alive that long, you'd think about rottin' things like that too. And besides, it's so dark down there after a while there isn't such a thing as Monday or Sunday, just dirt."

"Well," Hiura says, holding his hands up, "Maybe so, but there was four other guys buried too and I don't hear none of them going on and on about rotting. How come the majority's gotta listen to the misery of the minority? Reversing justice ain't no way of bringing about justice."

"Amen!" Tomato says, emphatically. "AAA-MEN!"

Just then footsteps patter quickly across the compound and a head comes into view through the door. Kodama announces they are having a mail call.

"SHIT!" someone calls out in surprise. The barrack

comes out of its lethargy. We run to the door, heat and rot forgotten. Outside is confusion, no one knowing where the announced call will take place. There are no guards out there, nothing in the yard. We are escapees running madly into the daylight, and suddenly, with all barriers removed, we stand in a patch of freedom, not knowing what to do or where to go.

It is a murky day. The watch towers seem distant, a vague form suspended in water, the skinny legs non-existent. We stand bewildered until finally, Hiura says, "What the hell! What's going on around here?" He looks around for the person who shouted out the mail call. His eyes light on Kodama, and he accuses him of falsely exciting everyone. "Hey Kodama, you like that guy who runs around calling 'wolf!' I don't go for any of that baloney."

Everyone jumps on Kodama, his head bobbing back and forth as if it were fastened to his body by loose stitches. At the moment it seems the stitches will tear, there is a commotion at the gate of the stockade. A squad of soldiers stands outside while the squad leader rattles the gate and locked chain, trying to get it open. "Okay," the squad leader announces, taking a step inside the gate. "All of you birds over here! Single file, four feet between each of you!"

We obey without question and march through the gates, to an open field in the middle of the military settlement, where a platform is built on four-foot high stilts. "Okay, you birds," the soldier on top of the platform shouts. "Mail call!" He reads out the names on the envelopes.

"Senzackey," the soldier calls, and hands me Gordie's death notice. Attached to it is a cursory note from the Project Director informing me I had left it in his office and he was returning it to me. I finger the envelope while the mail call continues. I close my eyes and run my fingers over the edges and feel the blackness, the fine line where white and black abut. It is a sharp edge, and I can feel it on both sides, along the entire perimeter. It cuts my thumb and index finger, the blood bonding the paper to my fingers.

I am vaguely aware of the twenty-nine other stockade detainees moving away from me, shuffling, depressed, towards the gate. They move thirty or forty feet, then with puzzled expressions turn around and look at me, my fingers fastened to that envelope. By the time I hear the command to move on, I realize by its rage that it has been repeated three or four times. But I am unable to move. The soldier becomes more enraged at my immobility.

He pushes me. I stagger a few feet, while everyone curiously watches. He prods, shoves, bumps me until I tumble into the dirt. A round leather boot slams my kidneys, but I grab the ankle before it can kick me again. Then I am struck on the head.

Chapter 28

There is no wind blowing through the bullpen. My tent smells of dust and heat. It is dark, as in the middle of the night. But it is too warm to be night. I open and close my eyes, but nothing changes. It is so still I can hear my breathing echoing off the canvas. I reach around in the darkness to find the tent flaps. On opening them, I can barely make out the dark brown color of beaverboard. Odors, body temperature, sounds, and feelings are caged in a large box nailed as tight as a waterproof coffin. Nothing can reach me here, or escape, neither cold nor pain, nor hate, nor death, nor sunlight.

A slot is opened, letting in a shred of light. Two pairs of eyes peer in on me, study me for several moments, then disappear. Suddenly a whole side of the enclosure opens up and a tin rattles onto the ground.

"Chow time!" someone shouts.

The boots step back and shuffle outside on the rocks and hardpan. Two voices come through the beaverboard. "Son of a bitch," one says. He leans against the wall, scratching a match on the rough grain. "For someone who raised so much hell, he's sure quiet now." He taps his knuckles on the side, indicating his reference to me.

"Yeah." There is a long, uncertain pause.

"How'd we end up here!" one voice inquires of the other. "Everytime I hear from friends overseas, I wonder how come I'm here."

"Well, somebody's got to watch these creeps," the

other answers in an annoyed tone. "Unless you watch 'em and keep 'em under lock and key, they're Japs, you know."

They pause to consider the prospects, then come around to the front and push aside the tent flaps. They study me carefully, noting my food tin. "Plate full of food again.!"

"Yeah! You know, he's lookin' kind of sick."

"Now I know why they says Japs is yellow. Kind of a dirty yellow, but yellow just the same."

"Not eating sure ain't helping him any."

"Well, that's the way he wants it." A shoulder shrugs, a head dips to one side. "That's his choice."

"Yeah." The other soldier reaches for the tray of food and slides it over the ground. "Nothin' we can do about it 'cept keep bringing it like we're ordered."

"Yep," comes the curt reply. "If they want us to stuff food down his mouth, they'll tell us."

Both stand up. "Better eat it . . . you ain't gonna make it long this way." A foot nudges the tray. I feel it lightly touching my ear.

The wall is swung back into place and everything becomes dark. The shuffling and voices fade.

A loud thump bangs against the outer wall, followed by another and another. There is a pause then, and a voice slightly worked up from the physical exertion says, "Would sure like to kill me a Jap or a Kraut! And here I'm stuck out here in the middle of nowhere."

The final billows of dust expand beneath the walls, up into my enclosure, and settle slowly back down. The other soldier says, "Well, let's go back. Can't stand around here all day. Gives me the creeps staying around here too long, anyway."

"Yeah," the other soldier answers. "Know what

you mean, kinda gives you the crawls, the way this guy looks."

"Right." Their conversation grows dimmer and fades with their footsteps.

Chapter 29

I awake in a steel framed bed, in the midst of a doctors' conference about my condition. I suffer from jaundice, hence, my color. I have malnutrition from going without food and liquids for three days and eating only rice for three weeks before that.

The older doctor takes my pulse. Watching me expectantly, he cocks his head to one side and asks the time.

"Twenty-eight minutes."

"Very good. This is the longest he's been conscious now for the past thirty hours."

"He looks a lot better too . . . his eyes are much clearer." He presses his finger on my lower eyelid and pulls down. They bend down to study my eyeballs.

The senior doctor's skin is loose and wrinkled. "Amazing tenacity," he says. He stands straight up, rubbing the shiny metal tubing of his stethoscope. "Isn't this the same young man who was in here last year when he almost suffocated?"

"The same man," the younger doctor answers, letting go of my eyelid. "It is amazing! I always sensed these people were hardy . . . even so, such tenacity! Look at this report . . . then he was put into the bullpen, the stockade, the bullpen again. And he's still alive . . ." He looks at me with genuine admiration. "And it was a very cold winter, too."

"It would help if we could keep him here, keep him from doing himself more harm."

"I wish we could," the old man says, "but we got word this morning that he's not to be coddled, and as soon as he's well enough, he's to be sent back to the stockade."

He notices that I am listening. For the first time since I have become conscious, he addresses me directly, "You'll be okay. You have a lot of resiliency. We can't keep you here, but we've made arrangements with the stockade to see that you won't have to do any clean up, drills, work, mustering for roll, or any other unnecessary activity."

They wait for me to respond. For me . . . the soft heavy summer silence. An eternal fly buzzes around the room in aimless frenzy.

I return to the stockade on the fourth of July. The same thirteen faces greet me. For the first days they leave me alone to think, to lie on my cot and study the despairingly familiar view of a piece of ceiling directly above me. There is a perpetual sound of breathing and snoring, fitful bodies trying to find rest, the harsh clacking of geta on the floor. I hear only my lungs pumping fetid summer air.

On the third day there is unusual early morning activity. In the dim morning light, Kageyama watches me, his arms folded on his knees. He starts to recite to me in a soft voice. "Shiozawa, Horie, Ansai -- 270. Moriuchi, Tomita, Baba -- 269. Senzaki, Funo, Kato, Koike, me -- 260. Muritani -- 239. Hiura -- 213. Kodama -- 205. Abe -- 200.

"We have staged strikes, presented petitions, written a protest to Spanish embassy, tried to get government of Japan to intercede because of inhuman treatment, hired lawyers from ACLU, requested repatriation back to Japan."

Puzzled, I roll my head to look at Kageyama.

He reaches out as if he means to smooth my fore-head, but hesitates and places his elbows back on his knees. "Be patient," he begins, then smiles wearily and shakes his head. "We have seen winter and spring and summer and we are still here, unable to see our families, friends, fellow Japanese. Ansai has become a father and wishes to see his newborn son." At the mention of his name I look past Kageyama to Ansai, lying on his stom-ach, mouth open, arm hanging over the cot's edge.

"Maybe we will be here until the war ends -- 1944, 1945, 1946, 1947. Maybe many of us will rot here and die. We are unjustifiable releases and Spanish consul cannot do anything. We have seen a lawyer only once and there is little he can do against the government."

Kageyama's expression seems relaxed, his muscles hang loosely from the bones. He is weary, his resiliency fading. His brows are heavier, the shadows across his face deeper and darker.

"There is little we can do," he continues, "so we have decided to stage a hunger stike to be carried out until we are released . . . or until we die."

He looks at my color, the redness of my blood, the tint of jaundice. "We have heard reports about you, and we know you are weak and sick from lack of food. But you are young and strong, and recover quickly. Under circumstances, we cannot ask you to join strike; however, if you wish to do so, we would welcome you."

I roll my eyes back, look up again, and consider the alternatives: of fasting, of eating in the midst of thir-teen starving men; of the ceiling above me unchanged for 1944, 1945, 1946.

Kageyama pauses to watch Kato bending stiffly

over to pull on his aging, yellowing long johns and snap them weakly around his bony waist. Kato puts on his getas and disappears out the door on his way to the wash house. "Time has come when anything is better than this."

The bullpen, the canvas, the bumpy inhospitable ground grinding into my back, and now this again. Kageyama is still sitting on the edge of the cot. Moriuchi drops his hand basin and kicks it across the floor and out into the compound.

I nod yes. Kageyama looks wonderingly at Moriuchi, then shakes himself, suddenly broken out of a stupor. He stands slowly and waits for the blood to rise into his head. Kodama takes a small Japanese flag out of his locker, and ties it to a pole protruding from the north gable of the barrack. From his own foot locker Kageyama takes a note book and hands it to me. "It has been voted upon, he says "that you keep diary of strike."

It is a hot day. I look at the crude barracks calendar on the east wall and count the groupings of fives that mark the number of days we have lived here. The calendar covers most of the wall to the right of the door. To the left of the door, Kodama has begun to mark four slashes in crimson. Rain thuds softly against the roof and steams off the heated earth. I can't see the vapor, but it penetrates my skin. I lie dripping and naked, listening to the sounds of others.

"How many days now?" Abe asks, as distant as if he were underwater.

"Yesterday three, today four." Moriuchi answers. He looks suspiciously at Abe. "You always asking that. How come?"

"This is funny way to die. Many times I dream of dying in Imperial Army . . . many times I dream of dying for America. Now I kill myself. Four days is the longest time I have gone without food."

"Ah shit!" Horie spits out. "No one's going to die. Resegregationists are working to get us out of this pig pen."

"Resegregationists?" Kageyama says. "Bah! If we wait for them, we will die for sure. We are in stockade *because* of them. We are pawns who will rot away waiting for friends to help us."

"Nine months," Tomato says angrily. "Nine months they been working on it."

"It takes a long time," Moriuchi says. "They have to work underground to avoid arrest."

"So far underground, no one knows they even exist," Tomato says, "except for the guys who get beat up by their goons."

"Ah hah!" Moriuchi exclaims knowingly. "You're talking about beating of Inu. Yes, sometimes beating is necessary."

"Inu," Abe says. "Resegregationists kill Inu. It's simple. Japanese kill Japanese."

This time Moriuchi does not raise his head, but lies motionless, focusing his eyes on a point between himself and a rafter. He smirks. "Ah shit! Too much talk about dying. I don't plan to die. Maybe you do, but not me. My old man says we should all die in the old country and be buried with the ancestors. My old man's seventy-five years old."

"Seventy-five?" Abe scratches his head. "And he talks about dying in old country? When he is behind barbed wire fencing? He can't get back to the old country now!"

"Hah!" Horie scoffs from across the aisle. "Many will never get back to the mother country because they don't have 'Yamato damashii' spirit. Spirit of Japanese! You think of dying, not why you're proud of Japanese blood."

"Hey," Tomato says, "you getting to sound just like Togasaki and Honda and the rest of the crazies."

"Tule Lake Japanese," Abe answers, "kill each other, beat each other, become vandals, thieves."

"For the good of people . . . ." Moriuchi begins in a distant tone. He lapses into silence.

On a dark overcast morning Kodama struggles to a sitting position on his cot and very carefully takes up a small brush. He dips up bristles laden with paint and unsteadily marks a seventh red slash. He finishes and sinks back on the cot like a pole in soft mud.

All activity grows slower, but noise increases in proportion. Each breath, each profane oath, each rustle of clothing is nerve-shattering. It is difficult to move. Those who can no longer walk lie in a stench of sweat and urine. When the smell becomes intolerable, Tomato and I overcome our own weakness to help those who cannot reach the toilets under their own power.

We are visited daily by administration personnel. This morning Burrell walks briskly in and looks around uneasily. Five others are behind him. Between two of them hangs a stretcher. Each day Burrell's voice becomes more nasal. He tries hard not to breathe through his nose. "What you are doing," he announces, "will not affect our decision as to whether or not you will be released from the stockade. Each individual's case is being studied, and if he is given security clearance, he will be returned to the colony."

Tomato props his head on his crossed arms and answers a non-existent question. "Why should I be patient? I've been here for 258 days . . . eight months and eighteen days."

Burrell moves past several cots until he comes to Shiozawa's, turns to the opposite wall and announces, "Following this procedure, we have taken the case of Shiozawa. Shiozawa has been cleared by Internal Security. He will be taken to the hospital and will subsequently be released. I think this is something the rest of you should keep in mind."

He motions to the stretcher bearers, who shuffle about removing Shiozawa from his cot and depositing him onto the stretcher. Hazy figures, kago carriers, struggling under a heavy load up a steep mountainside on the Tokaido, carry Shiozawa out of the stockade.

I get to my feet, bumping my cot. I trip over the end of Kageyama's and smash my head against the floor. I want to get that son-of-a-bitch Shiozawa for deserting us. I want to pound him and the carriers black and blue.

But somebody picks me up and rolls me back into the canvas-lined peach pouch. I float gently, bobbing down the rocky stream bed. My sensitivity and serenity return.

Ansai says what we must all feel, "Son-of-bitching Shiozawa! He has gone out of stockade!"

"What're you son-of-a-bitching about?" Tomato asks, as antogonistic to Ansai as Ansai was to Shiozawa. "You only pissed because it isn't you."

"We made a vow to stay together."

Several voices join in a chorus of throaty laughter.

"Fight to stay here?" Tomato says. "You trying to tell us *you* would?"

Ansai hesitates a moment. "Yes. We agree to live or die together in spirit of 'Yamato damashii.'"

"You fool no one," Kageyama interjects. "If you

had chance to get out, you would be gone now. And be-sides," he adds, "you and Shiozawa have been here long-est. That is why you think it is unfair."

"Shit!" Ansai mutters, his teeth clenched. "If I wasn't so weak, I would come over and give you punch."

Kageyama laughs, a paper-fish-in-a-breeze flutter. "It is over nine months now, and we are weak, cannot even stand up, almost cannot talk, and you want to punch me. Why do you wait so long?"

"Son . . . of . . . bitch!" Ansai mutters with finality and rolls over on his cot.

It is an appropriate prelude to the subsequent si-lence, to being swamped by sweat and flatulent, satu-rated air, of hearing muscles twitching and lungs suck-ing in and out the moisture of a rainy summer after-noon. Sweat glues my cot to my skin, and when I roll, the cloth peels away, taking my skin with it.

"God! But it stinks in here!" a voice exclaims. "Open the windows, air the place out!" Men in white coats with black bags enter the room.

I feel the cross currents, watch them float by a foot or two above me.

"That's a big improvement," the voice in command says. "Now," he continues after a pause to survey the situation. "We should begin by checking the worst ones first." He rotates, swinging slowly up one row and down the other. "You and Elliot work that side, Robert and I will work this side." He points first at one and then the other.

They move up and down the rows of cots, intently looking us over, trying to discern signs of decay or infestations of maggots and vermin. The two doctors finish my row and stop to discuss the person who is the worst looking. "Him . . ." An arm thrusts out in some vague direction. "Number three." The two men move to the foot of a cot. "He should be temporarily admitted to the hospital."

"At least two from this side," the head doctor says from the other row. He grabs a thumb and finger full of someone's cheek. "I don't like the looks of this man's color." Arms extended, he straightens up. "We'll take these three. THREE STRETCHERS!"

Six kago carriers bound into the barracks, their fleshy buttocks shining sweatily out of black loin cloths. I consider the odds of being among the three out of twelve, try to remember in which direction the doctors had moved and pointed, think about standing on my canvas and signaling two of the bearers to remove me, to take me involuntarily to spare me any decisions about myself, that I may not be judged by others -- or myself -- to be weak or strong, brave or cowardly, loyal or disloyal. The carriers jostle in the space between Kageyama's cot and my own, grab legs and arms and jockey Kageyama's limp body onto a stretcher. He breathes in wheezing gasps and grunts.

The head doctor is busily moving up and down aisles, lifting and looking at charts as if he hadn't heard. But he answers, a concerned look on his face. "Yesss . . . the same three for sure." He picks up another chart, glances at it, then lets it slap against the cot's legs. "But what I'm really wondering is whether we should do the same for all of them." He looks at the other three doctors one at a time, but they just stand there with blank, relieved looks, happy they are absolved of responsibility.

"Well," the head doctor says, in a hesitant voice, "They're all pretty listless . . . low blood pressures . . .

dehydration . . . low temperatures. We had better take them all."

The room floats up and down. We are bobbing along the Tokaido, up the steep footpaths of Mount Satta. Sunlight washes across us and forms shadows across lava. We pass through the stockade gates for the first time in over nine months, borne like a feudal daimyo. We are a billion dandelion parasols floating in the wind.

Nurses touch and examine us carefully, dribble liquids down us that we absorb greedily. Where they have touched us, a softness remains that lasts the two days we lie in the hospital. The fleeting interval is over and we are carried back to the stockade. In panic I roll off the stretcher and collide with earth. The stretcher clatters down, and four bodies pile on me. I am rolled along the ground and back onto my stretcher and onto my smelly cot. The stink is suffocating. I try to slow down my breathing.

"Shit heads!" Tomato curses. "We're back!" He shuffles around on his piece of canvas and takes a deep whiff of the stench . "Don't got to worry any more about fouling the nest!"

I laugh with the soft chorus around my head "Ha . . . ha . . . ha . . . ."

The chorus laughs and fades into an exhausted silence.

When the Project Director comes into the room to make an announcement, no one stirs. We lie immobilized, staring vacantly or with eyes closed. Burrell raps on the wall a few times with clenched fist. "From the people of Tule Lake I've been asked to be merciful, to do something about your situation. So I've told everyone you've brought this on yourselves, that we bring you food every day, and of your own choosing you do not eat. We can only take horses to the trough, we cannot make you eat. I was asked how I'd feel if this situation were reversed, and it was Americans starving instead of you."

"Americans?" Tomato asks, his head poking up from its exhaustion. "Americans! Hey, I thought that's what we were. That's how we got into, and can't get out of this big pen. Say . . . just who the hell are we anyway?" He stares for another few seconds, then his head drops back.

Burrell waits for Tomato to finish and continues as if he hadn't heard him. "Of course, there's no way to evaluate such a comparison, because if there were Americans prisoner in your country, they wouldn't be given choices. After all, you are given alternatives and what you choose to do is of your own making."

More days and nights fade into each other. In a dusky time of the day, Kodama rolls over to the edge of his cot and pushes himself to an upright position, where he sits for a long time mustering his strength to perform his daily task of marking the days of the strike. From under his cot, he takes out a paint can and with a screw driver pries the top off. With a brush dipped in red, oblivious to droplets plopping onto the floor, he staggers up and moves to the calendar between the door and the foot of his cot. He is about to make his mark when he grimaces suddenly and shrieks. His brush hand runs up over his heart and a blotch of red paint splatters over his chest. He tips to one side, his free hand groping vainly for a horizontal surface to grasp, but there is only a screen door which flies open, pitching Kodama out into the daylight. He disappears, his bag of emaciated flesh and bones thumping down the wooden stairs onto the jagged lava.

He lies there in silence, alone, waiting patiently for someone to chase away the flies from his half naked body, to examine him, to decide what is the matter with him and react accordingly. There is no movement inside: we are too weary to get up, too overcome by futility, knowing that even if we were able to get to him, we would be unable to drag him back up the stairs. In the ensuing wait, we concentrate on sounds.

Footsteps move up near the barracks. Someone brushes the flies off Kodama, then rushes off for help. Within minutes the stretcher-bearers arrive and drag Kodama from lava to canvas. They carry him off, grunting under the strain of his weight.

Chapter 30

Gordie appears to me in my dreams, his face colored a pastel wash, his arms waving back and forth to attract my attention. He calls to me, a frosted smile chiseled in ice. Beneath the frozen surface, webbed nerve endings lace his distant face. "Polychromatic capillaries," he announces, catching me staring at him. "Black, dotted, dashed, red, solid, double, blue . . . like a road map. When I got innoculations, they reached a kind of . . . flood stage . . . like rivers, and I had this feeling I was going to die. But someone tells me that being sick will make me stronger, more impervious to sickness and disease." He looks amused, as if there is something inane about his efforts to order and understand.

He looks around him at the earthly but still indistinct figures of Kageyama and myself. "We sweat, we muck around, we don't wonder who of us is going to come back, because wondering about it reminds us that someone else won't. Better the decision is out of our hands."

He backtracks, and dwells on the disconcerting array of color running through the veins and vessels of his face. He spreads his hand and pulls down the skin of his temples, his face stretching grotesquely. I wince.

"Count your blessings. You don't have to see the rest of me. But you can be sure that what you read here," he points first to his face and then to his body, "is what's happening all over the rest of me. You just can't see it, because I'm covered with mud from slipping and sliding and crawling. You see, it's been raining, so there is mud. We spend hours, days on end, groveling like moles that forgot to hibernate. We're used to oozing through anything. We just hope deep down we're doing something more than simply slipping and sliding and crawling."

His shoulders slouch at a resigned angle, and his wet, muddy uniform hangs heavily. He suddenly looks uneasy, as if he has talked too much, too openly. He changes the subject and asks about me, our parents, the camp.

The abrupt change catches me unprepared, but I try to visualize, to see the frenzy and chaos of camp from a different viewpoint, like trying to see the difference between brightness and saturation. It is difficult to explain or visualize. He waits while I speak cautiously. "What we fear most, we give creation to, for we are only the product of our fears. All I have heard," I tell him, "is about patriotism, sacrifice, community, and yet all we have is hysteria, violence, hatred."

As he listens, Gordie nods his head in rhythmic, rocking affirmation. But his eyes are distant.

I try to explain. "You understand I don't envy the mud, the physical conditions, the blood-shot skin, but at least you have some idea about why and what you're doing, even if you don't know if you'll be one of the ones coming home. And you have some clear-cut alternatives. But in Tule, we don't even have what we believe to hold onto."

Gordie interrupts, "The hunger strike . . . did it get you freedom? If you had died, there would have been no freedom in a box six feet under -- only the glory of some kind of perverse martyrdom! The same six feet under, but the glory of war over here." His eyebrows raise skeptically.

Kageyama suddenly speaks, a complacent look on his face. "I believe I understand," he says kindly. "They're trying to make us believe what they believe, after we have spent a lifetime knowing what is right. But it is late in summer," he laughs sarcastically, "and at this time of year, things are not giving birth or rebirth. Watch them carefully. Don't be blind to the colors." He begins to laugh and his face and laughter fade away.

"You trying to understand him too?" Gordie asks. "Wearing this uniform and fighting and seeing people getting killed, I've thought a lot about Kageyama, bitter and angry, a soldier in one part of his life and ending up in a concentration camp in another. How do you understand it, how do you justify what you feel about it all?" His voice is abrupt, disjointed. He shrugs his shoulders. "You have reasons, some justification, don't you? After all, that's what this is all about, isn't it? That's what we talked about so long ago, wasn't it? Understanding? Reason? Justification?"

"Of course. I remember. But it doesn't seem to be working here. It is like using the wrong law of physics to solve a problem in dynamics. Everything's coming out twisted, as if all this is taking place for patriotism. We look in the mirror when we are shaving the coarse black hair, and we see the peculiar tinge of skin, and we feel guilty because we are here."

I check Gordie's reaction, anxious for him to understand. "But it could be worse," I continue, "we could act what we feel, and *we* would end up killing everyone of different opinion, beliefs, skin color. Then where would we be?"

Kageyama interrupts again. "These rocks," he says, kicking at the lava, "scorched dead long ago. They uproot me, transplant me into wrong kind of soil. This is not kind to grow cabbage, peas, lettuce, daikon, tomatoes, nasubi." He kicks again, sending the pocked lava flying. "Of all seasons, I enjoy late spring most!"

Kageyama's face twists angrily. "We are victims. We are not responsible for what is happening. They are at fault, their hatred, their believing they are so innocent, so righteous. We only do what we have to survive."

He jumps into the foreground of fields, where in the distance, a small cluster of men wearing white shirts hoe, weed and irrigate in long rows of crops. They look frail, transitory and irregular. "Us -- in spring and summer, in Florin, in Sacramento Valley, in Willamette Valley, and now this . . . ." He points to the double fencing, the barbed wire, the machine gun towers high above the barracks. "And now they have turned us against ourselves."

"Chaos!" Gordie exclaims, shaking his head in disbelief.

"Chaos?" Kageyama says. "It is madness. Hooligan gangsters from southern California camps cause endless trouble. Administration with full backing of U.S Army cannot control camp. But it is only round five, only half the fight. And I understand the white man better then he understands me. I have always watched and studied him. But he does not even know I exist."

Gordie shakes his head slowly and sadly. He says, "Some day we must forgive just as we must fight now."

At the periphery of my vision are two faintish tinges of orange, like the tip of a short candle flame. From the background comes the sound of 18,000 people in Tule.

The air has the taste of late summer. A woman kneels by a hibachi: My Japanese mother broiling fish.

Her eyes are shaded and indistinct; when she looks up, I can feel her warmth and gentleness. But it is distant.

Chapter 31

The stockade is closed when Burrell realizes the hunger strike will end in death. After a week in the hospital on liquids and vitamin supplements, I am released back into camp. I walk slowly through the maze to my parents' barrack.

I am blinded by the change from sunlight to the dimness of the interior. When my eyes adjust to the inside, I see clearly the grotesque features of Father's face. His blind eye is covered by a patch held in place by a black strap around his head. I envision a young and beautiful woman of my childhood, but I see a tired old woman standing before me. Mother's hair is prematurely grey, the lines around her eyes have spread to the rest of her face.

They stand rigid at their first glimpse of me, unable to smile or speak. I have lost almost thirty-five pounds; I am pale and weak from sickness and atrophy. I hug Mother first. Her eyes smile. I take Dad's hand. He gently holds my arm.

"We are happy to be together," Dad says.

"Yes, I am happy to be home," I answer.

Mother quickly puts water on for tea.

Our new quarters are near the military compound, where Mother and Father could be closer to the stockade during my confinement. Inside the room is identical to our Block 46 apartment. The wall common with Obasan's is reserved for a single object, the silken flag with the star in the center, its white now turned a dusty grey. The windows are covered with new rice paper that has translucent bamboo leaves pressed into it.

The apartment is stifling. Flies whirl around the stove and cupboard. The chairs we sit in are the same ones Gordie and I built when we first came to camp over three years ago, a reminder of our optimism that Tule Lake would become an equitable substitute for the lives we left behind. Could we have foreseen the months in the stockade, or the hunger strike, or Gordie's death?

During the ten months in the stockade, I thought often of returning to the privacy of our home, but now after several days, I feel crowded and irritable. "Three summers in camp, and we're stuck here. Three people in a twenty by twenty room."

Father looks at me and says, "What about the families with five or six people who have to live in one room?"

"Flies and heat and dust." I comment, frustrated.

"This is not the first time we have lived like this," Mother says calmly. "It was this way when we first came to this country, except we didn't have wooden floors. I didn't think it was possible to live like that, but we got used to it.

"Maybe it is more difficult when you are *forced* to live like this."

"No matter what the circumstances, it is not easy," Mother says. "I was nineteen years old. I was very lonely. I thought only of Japan, wishing I could go back. I learned a lesson I have always remembered: it is not so much the number of rooms that is important, but the sounds of voices. When a baby was born, I never felt the same loneliness again. It is the same here. When we are together, even though it is crowded, I feel at home, and content. When we are separated, like during the past ten months, it is very lonely."

When Mother talks about the past, she lapses into both Japanese and English, sweeping easily from one language to the other like a seagull on the wind.

"What I miss most," she says, "then and now, are the little birds, the sparrows and chickadees. There are no trees here, there are no birds. In the middle of the fields there is no singing, except for the geese that pass overhead, and they are so high in the sky."

She stops for a moment to listen to the children's voices coming in through the open window and door. "Sometimes I could not understand why we came to this country . . . I do not understand why we were sent here. Maybe it was always a mistake, our coming to this country in the first place."

"Bakatare!" Father yells. "It was difficult choice to come to this country, but we came! How can we say something we did so long ago was mistake!"

The sounds of hopscotch abruptly turn to imitations of barking. Outside, children dance around an old man brandishing a bamboo cane. From behind the shoulders of a girl, Uojiro's face appears momentarily.

For a moment Father sits watching, then quickly he is on his feet and out on the porch, shouting and waving his arms. The children disappear between the barracks.

Father motions for the old man to come in. I am surprised to see Atsumi-san looking so old and frail. He is very thin, his eyes are weary and dark. His brown face is sallow, a shadow of the sociable proprietor of the Nihonmachi music and electrical appliance shop.

"Ben, it is so good to see you again," Atsumi says, laughing warmly and nodding his head. He grabs my hand and shakes it. "I hope you are recovering easily."

"Very well, thank you. I'm glad its over."

"Yes, yes, we are all happy it's over," he says, in Japanese, shaking his head.

"You are a young man . . . your body is still strong and resilient. It was hard on you, but I know you'll soon be strong again." He sits down on one of the hand-built chairs. "Your dad and I and many others worked hard to get that stockade closed up. It caused a lot of trouble and grief. The administration wouldn't give in an inch. It was the hunger strike that did it. They got worried, and I think Washington got upset too."

He takes a handkerchief out and wipes perspiration from his forehead and face and looks at the dust and dirt. "Bah, those children! What is becoming of them? Barking at people and calling them names! It is disgraceful."

"There is no more discipline," Father replies. "Young people now raise their children differently from my day."

Mother sets an earthen ware tea pot on the table with four matching cups. With the tea she serves a green tea-flavored yokan, a sweetened bean desert made in a gelatin form.

When everyone is served, she too sits down. "They are not at fault," Mother says. "The children are like mirrors. They reflect what the adults are doing. The children do not make up the names they call people. They repeat what they hear."

Father and Atsumi sip tea, looking curiously at Mother.

"We are living in fear and hatred and violence," she continues. "Children do not make or change the world they live in. They are the result of what is made for them. If we wish to change them, we must change ourselves."

Mother and Father and Atsumi continue their discussion about children. I keep thinking about Uojiro's face behind the shoulders of the little girl jeering at Atsumi. He is now about the same age I was when I first came to this country. Yes, she is right. The children are only a reflection of the world we, grownups make.

I want to know about Alice. The early days of Tule seem so far away.

"How does Alice enjoy her school?" I ask.

"Fine, Ben. She is very happy with school. We are grateful she did not have to stay here through all this trouble. We have not told her much about the stockade. She has little time for anything outside of studies and practice. She is doing very well. The Hakujin family she has been living with have been loving and kind to her. She is lonesome but not lonely."

The confinement of the apartment is oppressive. I excuse myself and head for the main firebreak. It is almost a year since I last saw Asoo and Goto. Before I reach the firebreak, I hear the sounds of nationalistic exercises. Several hundred youths prepare themselves in body and spirit for a triumphant return to the mother country. There are small groups of spectators watching them around the perimeter of the field. I spot Goto's tall, powerful frame immediately. With him are Asoo and Tomato.

Coming up from behind, I hear Tomato say, "Look at those clowns. Jumping around and exercising like some kind of fanatics."

"It's time for fanaticism," Asoo says. "How else you going to fight wars? You *got* to be a fanatic. We *all* got to be fanatics."

"Yeah," Tomato agrees, "you can't just stick a rifle

in a guy's hand and send him off to become a killer. You got to train 'em like those clowns, except they're on the wrong side."

Goto says, "War's that complicated, huh?"

"For some of us," I interject. "For others, not so complicated."

They turn together at the sound of my voice. Goto and Asoo throw their arms around me, their faces smiling and kind, showing no surprise or shock at my emaciated state.

"How you been?" Goto grabs my hand.

"Okay, I guess. And you?"

"Real good!"

"How goes it, Ben?" Asoo grabs my hand and pumps it with both of his.

"We been wanting to come around and see you, but we thought we better give you some time with the family. Sure miss seeing you in 46."

"When you moving back?" Goto asks.

"We seem to be pretty well settled. Guess we'll stay there for a while."

Japanese nationalistic music blares out of the loudspeakers. Kendo sticks are brought out for the young men to do kendo excercises to the music. The loud clacking of sticks sounds across the fields. Tomato says, "Looky that. Any of you guys do that kendo stuff?"

The others shake their heads. Tomato looks at me. "You do that stuff when you were a kid?"

"Yeah," I smile. "When I was a kid in Japan."

"Were you any good?"

"As a matter of fact, because of my size and quickness, they thought I was pretty good. The secret is how quickly you react."

"Oh?" Tomato says. "So that's how come you took

up baseball one year and ended up hitting almost .400."

"Yeah," Goto says. "But his fielding, remember? Like a lost duck squawking around in a flock of sheep."

The kendo activity on the field quickens pace. When the clashing of sticks gets louder, Asoo's face hardens. "It was funny for awhile watching those clowns do their stuff, but sometimes I get this urge to go out there and wipe 'em all out. That garbage makes me disgusted."

"Hold on there," Goto says. "They got sticks right now . . . besides, one thing this camp doesn't need is more violence."

"The goons," Asoo says.

Tomato says, "I think it's time to go. After ten months in the stockade, Ben and I need some time to get ourselves in a decent state of mind. There'll probably be violence enough coming up without us going around asking for it."

We walk slowly away, the frenetic battle sounds fading behind us. Tomato says in an unexpected change of voice, "It's been over three years now. I feel like I been moving backwards. I guess I've really been standing still, but when I think what I could have been doing, accomplishing, like working, going to school, marrying maybe, it sure seems like these years have been wasted. We been living in some kind of underserved purgatory. Hell, I might as well of stayed in the stockade until the war ends."

"How about the family?" Asoo says. "Nothing's that simple."

"Yeah," Goto says, "they still need you. Like my folks and Asoo's here and Ben's. That's really why we're still here, standing still in time, or moving backwards like Tomato says. Waiting for the conquering army of the rising sun to liberate us." Then in a disgusted voice he says, "What a human garbage heap this place's become!"

"It's a lot worse than I want to admit out loud," Asoo says. "But you know," he continues, a tone of wonderment coming into his voice, "in a strange kind of way Mom's grown to love this place. It's not so much that she sees us shut in, but that the hostile world out there is shut out. She feels safe because she knows the outside crazies can't come in to hurt anyone. She knows if she keeps her mouth shut, nobody inside these fences is gonna bother her. Sometimes I think she would gladly stay here the rest of her life: no worries, pressures, no financial troubles, meals three times a day, all of us Japanese. She says, 'America sure knows how to run a concentration camp.'"

"Holy shit!" Tomato exclaims. "She must've swallowed their whole line!"

"Well," Asoo shrugs his shoulders, "What do you pick to believe? We've heard it all, haven't we? Now that she's heard the rumors about closing the camp she's really upset. She's afraid they'll kick us out. She is afraid of Hakujin violence outside. I think this is the most secure she's felt since Dad died."

Tomato shoves his hands in his pockets and shakes his head. "I don't know what's heads or tails either, but I do know when I came to this place I was twenty-two years old, and now I'm almost twenty-six. I'm an old man with three wasted years behind 'im. To top it off we got to sit around and stew instead of doing something constructive. People who want Japan to win don't feel any great attachment to Japan. It's like they want to get even with this country for what it did to 'em. But none of that stuff for me. I'm still an American trying to figure out how to survive and how the hell to get out of this camp."

"We always have that ace in the hole, though," Goto says. "The sure one-way ticket out of camp, the U.S. Army!"

"I've thought about that a lot," Tomato says. "And been thinking about it more and more lately."

"Me too," Asoo says. "When the war first broke out, I wanted to go so bad. But now I'm not so sure. I never thought about dying, but now I'm considering it. I just know I don't want to be one of those guys who gets killed on the last day of the war."

"Never thought much about death," Tomato says. "But with so many friends never coming back. . . ."

After a few moments of an awkward silence, Goto says, "Ben . . . I'm really sorry about Gordie . . . I grew up with him . . . it's like I lost a brother too."

"The same goes for me," Asoo says softly.

"And me." Tomato grips my shoulder suddenly.

I return to the stockade to help Kageyama remove the last of his personal belongings. Already the walls smell not of man stink and bodies, but of aging. I try to imagine ten years from now. The colors will be faded, bleached by dust and winds and summers and winters, the window glass broken by boys passing by, doors will hang from rusty hinges, squeaking in the wind. It will not be easy to believe that here we once lived out an issue we did not understand.

Out of the stockade, I know a freedom that Kageyama does not share. We live closely now as a family, as neighbors, eating together, visiting, talking often of the past. Kageyama spends long hours on his front porch, in the shade, watching the gathering migrations overhead.

A feathered hourglass, the Pacific flyway stretches from Canada to Central America, narrowing into the neck of Tule Lake refuge, where flocks of geese and ducks sound faintly over Tule lava as they move swiftly past.

Kageyama's complexion has changed. He no longer has the healthy, out-doors tan. His skin is loose and pale, a frail casing for the bitterness and pain festering within.

Bugles call in the autumn dusk, a plaintive answer to the winged travelers overhead. Kageyama looks up, his shoulders for a moment firm. A year ago the Meiji Setsu ceremony marked the loss of our last remnant of freedom. Soon will be another Meiji Setsu where we ex-stockade prisoners will be honored as camp heroes for our ordeal and our survival. In a departure from tradition, the Meiji Setsu will be combined with the late summer Bon Odori dance festival for the single largest celebration ever held in Tule Lake.

I think it will please Kageyama, but his shoulders droop again, his face is impassive. Only his shadow moves, a dark caricature on the barrack wall.

Chapter 32

Young men with Bozu haircuts strut onto the fire-break to the sounds of drums and bugles, their thin layers of loose clothing flapping in a soft wind, a harbinger of an early winter. In honor of the fourteen of us, we and our families are seated on a center platform overlooking the eastern and western halves of the firebreak. On the east field young men dressed in white judo clothing line up in rows and exercise to Japanese military music.

The long serpentine lines form, and a man in his late thirties climbs up on the platform. He unrolls a large scroll, proclaiming, "Hissho Kigan Shiki." He pauses to explain in English so everyone will understand. "We along with all people of motherland will offer fervent prayer for victory on eighth day of each month. We purify minds and body by exercise, cold showers on mornings before prayer, and classes to teach the ways of Japan."

The loud shouting of banzais temporarily drowns out the rhythmic, slowly beating drums from the west firebreak, where young and old, women and men move slowly across the firebreak like a giant wheel, dancing the shovel dance of the peasant farmer. The women are dressed in colorful kimonos, and the men, heads tied with bands, wear the traditional light coats of the peasant. They move from side to side, shoveling in pantomime into the soil, stepping to the right, then to the left. Drums boom from the hub beneath lanterns swaying in the wind. They lift unseen shovels lightly over their shoulders, then move again to the soil.

We sit mesmerized, the firebreaks transformed into a valley, green between rolling hills in a Japanese countryside, the barbed wire gone. The ceremony goes on late into the evening. The fields are lit by thousands of paper lanterns.

With darkness, the dancing and military exhibitions end. Reverend Togasaki, now the acknowledged leader of the Saikakuri Seigan, the Resegregationists, takes the center stage. "We are proud," he says in Japanese, "of what we have seen for the past few hours, of those who have sacrificed to prepare themselves for returning to motherland to serve in spirit and body. Soldiers of motherland die and make sacrifices. True Japanese of Tule Lake give up luxuries and show willingness to sacrifice also."

When he finishes, Honda, now second in command of the Resegregationists, gives a report of the war. "Japanese Navy is mounting a counterattack and sweeping across the Pacific in an irresistible force that will soon end upon the shores of the Pacific United States to liberate those of us held as political prisoners of war by racist and imperialistic America!"

A thousand young male voices reverberate across the field. They are members of the Hokoku Seinen-dan, an organization of Japanese men dedicated to serving their motherland.

When the cheers die, Honda talks about our ordeal in the stockade, of how we have suffered persecution unjustly and yet in the face of hardship survived, exemplifying in our behavior "Yamato damashii." We have endured indignities, unjustified imprisonment, beatings, isolation, and finally have achieved freedom from the stockade by a death-defying, self-imposed hunger

strike. We are introduced to the multitude accompanied by drums, the booms echoing across the silence of
the fields. When we are all introduced and standing,
thousands also rise, cheering, clapping, shouting over
and over, "Banzai! Banzai! Banzai!"

"And we have worked hard for their freedom!"
Reverend Togasaki shouts between cheers, "and the or-

PN
3448
D4
D8
1974

Dupuy, Josée.
  Le roman policier / Josée Dupuy. —
Paris : Larousse, 1974.
  191, [1] p. ; 25 cm. — (Textes pour
aujourd'hui)
  Bibliography: p. 189–[192]
  ISBN 2-03-038002-4

  1. Detective and mystery stories—
History and criticism. I. Title

o new paths we
and and not to
put us behind
st prepare our-
ue Japanese re-
est repatriation
The youths rise
.

s face. He sur-
of Japanese na-
d impassive ex-

e heroes we are,
whistles softly.
asked me three
nods his head in

so firmly muted
He jumps to his
abbing Togasaki
e hurls him back-
ki stumbles into
against the wall.

listen to crazies!
Outside world has destroyed old communities! These
crazies are trying to destroy camp! Tule Lake has be-

come nest of gangsters! We are behind barbed wire with fellow Japanese and must fear for our lives! We were ruled by Japanese crazies while we were in stockade for ten months!"

"This is not true tradition of Japanese!" he shouts in staccato Japanese, his voice booming over the jeering of the judo-clad youths. "We have forsaken unwritten law of Japanese community. We have always been strong, but now there is contamination from outside society. Do not become blind to violent fanatics who try to run community by fear, rumors, and threats, who try to make us believe Japan is winning war!" He pauses. The jeering of the Hokoku youths grows louder in the rolling winds.

Kageyama talks louder and faster, buoyed by the accelerating voices trying to drive him from the stage. Above the shouting, his voice is audible in sporadic bursts. "Tyranny of minority . . . violence . . . gangsterism . . . destruction."

My friends, my family, my stockade comrades stand dumbfounded and silent at the spectacle of 13,000 people screaming and shouting. For ten minutes it continues. As it threatens to boil over onto the stage, a change sweeps through the crowd. The anger is no longer directed at Kageyama but at the youths who have become the strong arm gangs of the camp.

Togasaki and Honda and other Resegregationist leaders, sense the shifting anger, too. They disappear behind the stage, leaving their young army to face the accelerating anger of the crowd, who for the first time find themselves united against the minority who have run the camp. As the insults and jeering grow to a dangerous, angry level, the Resegregationist youths back away across the firebreak until they reach the safety of the barracks and disappear.

The crowd suddenly quiets. For the first time since the early days of camp they have been able to make their feelings known.

My long confinement has estranged me from the camp. I decide to take an evening walk again, from fence to fence to fence. Passing through the Resegregationists' section, I hear the sounds of Japanese music, voices teaching classes in Japanese history, bodies thumping in judo classes. Despite the setback at the Meijisetsu ceremony, the Resegregationists have evolved from an underground pressure group to a formal, institutionalized organization, exhibiting their nationalistic and disloyal program in open defiance of the camp administration and the WRA. Their stated goal is renunciation of American citizenship by the young men and women of the camp as a symbol of their complete rejection of America and their allegiance to Japan.

I reach the fence below the face of Castle Rock, and follow it until I come to a corner watch tower. From there I can see down two lines of fencing. As in the early days, the camp again assumes immense proportions. I walk the complete perimeter of the camp and return to the barracks.

Approaching the northeast quadrant of camp, Uojiro's block, I think of his thin face appearing in a crowd of children taunting an old man. Near the supply center of camp, I hear the sounds of children's voices at play. Intermittent shouting accompanies the kicking of a tin can. As my eyes adjust to the shadows, I am surprised to see Uojiro alone, kicking at the ground, looking expectantly at the corners of barracks, into the darkness below them. When he moves away from the can, boys emerge from the shadows, dart across the opening, kick the can and disappear, Uojiro vainly pursuing. When Uojiro slows down, the boys slow too, until they all stop, leaving Uojiro alone by a battered can.

I take him by the hand and lead him out into the light. He looks up and smiles broadly.

"You still living in block 64?" I ask him.

"Yep."

"Pretty far from home, aren't you?"

"Kind of far. But it doesn't make any difference. We're still in camp."

"That's true. But the last time I brought you back, your mother didn't seem to like your straying so far from home, especially at night."

"Yeah," Uojiro agrees.

"I saw you earlier this week. You and some other children."

"I didn't see you."

"You were busy barking at that old man."

"He's an Inu."

"A sixty-five year old Inu?"

"That's what everybody says."

"Everybody?"

"Everyone knows who the Inu are from the list that comes out every month."

"Yes. I'm familiar with that."

"But I never barked at your father," he says, looking quickly up at me. "And the other children too. They would never do anything to hurt your father."

"Well, I think maybe it would be better if you didn't bark at anyone."

"But we never hurt anyone, really. All we do is bark at 'em. Only at the Inu -- Atsumi, Okada, Nakajima -- all those other Inu."

"Hold on, Uojiro. Atsumi, Okada, Nakajima and all those other Inu. What do you mean by that?"

"Those guys who run the canteen and movies and rob everyone of their money."

"Where'd you hear all that stuff?"

"The *Saikakuri Seigan* newspaper."

"Do you remember that first time I met you, when those guys were leading you around blindfolded and calling you Inu? You asked me what it meant."

"Yeah," he says subdued. "I remember."

"Do you understand that what they were doing to you is what you're doing to other people?"

"Yeah, kinda."

"Well, you'd better think about it carefully. And it would be best if you stopped barking at anyone and encourage the other children to stop too."

"How come, Ben?"

"Sometimes things go wrong and nobody seems to know why or how to make them right. If we want to make it right, the only way to start is by not taking part in actions that are wrong. Like barking at an old man and spreading lies and rumors about people. Do you understand?"

"Kinda . . ."

"Some day you will understand completely. Right now I want you to promise me you'll do as I ask."

"I promise."

I knock on Uojiro's door before he opens it.

"Who is it?"

"Ben Senzaki. I brought Uojiro home."

The light shines across the porch as the door opens, shadowing the profile that I saw the night Gordie was ambushed. The hair is fixed differently. I do not remember what it was like before, only that it was different. Jeanne takes Uojiro by the hand and pulls him inside. She invites me in. "It's so late," she says, closing the door and motioning me to sit down. "I was worried. He's usually home before nine. Where did you find him?"

"He was playing kick the can near the supply store warehouse, and the older boys disappeared."

"It's so hard," she says hesitantly, "to be alone . . . to raise children in camp . . . running around like slum children."

A girl of thirteen or fourteen silently observes me from a table with an arithmetic book open before her.

There are children's drawings of camp life on the wall, along with a sumi wash of the surrounding hills and Castle Rock done in an adult hand. In all of the drawings there are no fences or watch towers. It is the first time I have seen the surrounding environment that way. Clothes hang from a line stretching across the room, and below them on a small table is a piano keyboard drawn on a piece of cardboard with color crayons. I look at Jeanne's hands, hands that once played the piano. They are delicate but strong.

"I thought about you so much while you were in the stockade," she says. "Uojiro talked about you often. News kept seeping out about the stockade. Then we heard about the hunger strike. We held family prayers for you. We were so worried, sometimes we couldn't sleep." She shakes her head. "When we got word you were going to be released, we were very happy and relieved. Uojiro wanted to come and see you, but I thought he should wait."

"He should come anytime. Until his father comes back, I'm willing to help in whatever way I can."

She stares at me a moment, her mind suddenly

elsewhere, eyes filling with tears, then turns and tells the children to get ready for bed. She wears her hair in a bun in back of her head, more like a middle-aged farm wife than an attractive young woman. When she disappears behind the curtain that divides bedroom from living area, I glance at my own clothes, at the dusty shoes, the faded levi's, the worn-out mackinaw; we have all become a reflection of camp, of its starkness, its monotony, its desolation where surface appearances are secondary to the struggle to survive. Perhaps we will care for such things again when we return to a life that values personal appearance.

When the children are settled, Jeanne comes back and carefully closes the draw curtain as if it were a door.

"Would you like something?" she asks. "I have some cookies. I could warm up some tea." She goes to a crudely constructed shelf covered with the same material as the one over the bedroom compartment and takes out a box of cookies and a cannister of green tea.

"Have you heard from your husband recently?"

"Bob is not the writing kind," she says, her voice rising. "But it's just as well. His letters are full of anger and bitterness."

"It's happening to a lot of us."

"Maybe when the war ends, the anger and bitterness will end too."

"Will he be coming to Tule sometime soon?"

"He doesn't want to come here. He says he would rather remain where he is and have us join him. He wants me to renounce my citizenship and the children's so we can bring the family together at Crystal City."

"Isn't that the detention center for families?"

"Yes. He says we should repatriate to Japan after

the war ends, that we have no future in this country after what they've done to us."

"Do you feel that way too?"

"After three years of living in this room, I don't know what I feel. So many people tell us conflicting things. Bob telling me the children and I should renounce our citizenship. They're eleven and thirteen-year-old American children, and they're supposed to prepare to go back to Japan and become Japanese? He's been saying I should have renounced six months ago and joined him in Crystal City. He's angry because I refuse.

"He's become a stranger to me and the children. He never used to talk about anything except his radio business and about how bright the future was. He was warm and happy in those days, and he was close to the children. Now he talks about them as if they were Japanese children raised in the old country. He used to speak highly of America, the land of opportunity, he called it, and said what a fine place it was to raise a family. Now all he talks about is racism and imperialism. He says we are the negroes of the west coast and the camps are really what this contry is all about. I don't think he knows who his family is any more. He's forgotten all the good people we used to know back home. All he can remember are the rednecks who broke into his store during the spy scare, and destroyed and stole everything he owned. The local law enforcement people would do nothing."

I study her face while she talks. Her eyes occasionally cloud, staring into another time, another place. She speaks rapidly and openly as if I were an old friend. And perhaps I am: members of the same community for a number of years, enduring struggles that only those who shared them could understand.

From behind the curtain, I hear occasional rustling and creaking of cots, a reminder of the children's presence in the room. Perhaps it would be better if they did not hear the conversation, but there is little we can hide from each other.

Jeanne looks at me. "Do you think Japan is really winning the war?"

"I know for sure they're not."

"Uojiro tells me you lived in Japan until you were ten. Do you think it's possible for Japanese Americans to go back to Japan and live happily?"

"When this war is over, Japan will be a war-torn country. Even if it were not, it would be difficult. In a defeated Japan it would be that much harder."

"What do you think it would be like for the children?"

"They're Americans of Japanese ancestry, not Japanese. It would be very hard on them. The Japanese nationalists are painting a deceptive picture."

"Bob is so angry with me. In one letter he even threatened me with physical violence if I didn't do as he said. This war -- and the hatred and violence -- have changed him. He is a stranger. In all the years we were married, he never threatened me before."

She fights to hold back tears, looking suddenly older. She puts her face in her arms on the table. Directly behind her are the children's drawings of Tule Lake without its fences.

On the way home I hear scattered voices of men and women visiting as they walk through Tule. A chilly but gentle wind blows against the barracks. Near the center of camp, fifteen minutes from our apartment, is written on the walls:

BE TRUE TO THE MOTHERLAND!
SHE HAS NOT BETRAYED YOU!

In a thoughtful way I agree. Time and location at the moment of birth hold top priority. But what about the nine years of my life in Japan? There comes a time when because there is insanity, we do little except wait patiently.

Gordie's voice calls to me from the darkness. I turn quickly, unwittingly sparing my head a crushing blow from a club which strikes my shoulder, knocking me to the ground. In the darkness I am aware of two hooded shadows kicking, grabbing, hitting me. Three new figures rush in. The attackers escape.

"All you would have had to do was listen to me, and you could have avoided this. We average two beatings a week, so you might of guessed you'd be a sitting duck walking alone in the middle of the night!"

In spite of the pain I laugh at Tomato's lecture. I gasp weakly, "You bastard."

Tomato says softly to Goto and Asoo, "He's gonna be okay."

"You're lucky we were patrolling near here," Goto says. "Let's get you to the doctor."

To hold my shoulder rigid while my broken collar bone heals, the doctor straps a small wooden brace across my shoulders. I tire easily, and spend my days sitting on the porch, watching the last stragglers of the winter migrations overhead.

"The birds. Free as the sky itself. Buggers!" Tomato reaches over and raps the cross on my back. "And me? Head of the Ward IV Tule Lake Police Department, protector of the people, protector of the people's rights, defender of law and order, standard bearer of justice. All that because nobody else in Ward IV is willing or crazy enough to take on the risk."

"Lucky for me."

"Yeah, lucky for you. Lucky you were in Block 45. One of these days someone's going to get killed, and I'm just happy it wasn't you."

"Me too."

"Well, back to duty," Tomato says as he leaves.

Father and I sit together for hours on the porch he built while I was in the stockade. He shifts his weight from one buttock to the other, and clears his throat. He says, "Worry is unnecessary. All life is adaptation."

"What do you mean?"

"I adjust to the trouble in Tule just the same as adjusting to new country. All things run their course," he says, "and always when the wind no longer blows, the trees are motionless."

I find the analogy a strange one, for he and I and Mother have not seen the dark trunk of oak or the feather softness of spring poplars for over three years. There is nothing to cease moving, for the barracks and fences are stationary. Only weeds poke from the stale crust of lava and dust. Inside the small room, we hear with foreboding the calls of the winged stragglers closing in on their wildlife refuge. I wait until their cries fade in the night before I reply . . . .

"But when a man has a choice," I tell him, "and knows the alternatives, he would be foolish to choose the more difficult way."

"Nothing is more difficult," Father says, "than to acknowledge *after* what we have done, that it was for the wrong purpose. Even if that is true, we would be foolish to admit it, for we are not given wisdom to determine absolute truths."

He breathes heavily and shifts his weight. "Department of Justice representatives have been in camp for two days setting up the machinery for renunciation. Approved by Congress, the process for giving up American citizenship is now ready. The machinery for clearance is also perfected. You can be out of here and on your way to Denver, or Minneapolis, or Chicago, or elsewhere within a few days."

"There is no shame in being wrong," I answer, "for our lives consist as much of error as of being correct. The only real error is not to learn from the times we have chosen wrongly."

"All things are within our control," he says.

Rothke is a man I have come to recognize in three years as a close friend. He has greyed prematurely but even in the harshness of life in this camp, there is still a kindness that softens his eyes, and a gentleness to his voice. "Your mother and father registered loyal a year and a half ago and have had the option of leaving camp." Father, Mother, and Rothke scrutinize me, seeking an understanding that I do not possess. They ask again why I do not change my stance on registration, and depart this camp for the freedom of the outside. Now it is my time to feel the weariness. One month after the hunger strike, and they've already forgotten.

"You have done nothing during your residence at this camp to fully justify your being classified as disloyal," Rothke says. "This is particularly true in your case, for your status derives not from a disloyal registration but from simply failing to register. All that is being suggested is that you commit yourself on paper to what you have already committed yourself in action."

I do not answer.

Father is immobilized in his chair. I know his question: Why can't we leave as a family? Many years ago he left me in Japan. Now he will desert me again, I think, for hidden in his weariness is a desire to escape. Rothke's voice is hollow. He leans his elbows on the desk and looks at me directly. "If this is carried to its ridiculous conclusions, have you thought about where this can end up . . . for you?"

"I have thought of it much."

He waits, but when I do not continue, he says, "Please . . . explain more in depth what you are thinking."

"Have you thought," I ask, "about where this can end up for you?"

He slumps back into his chair. "Nothing different," he says softly. "My position here is voluntary. I'm here because I choose to work here . . . free to leave now if I so choose . . . the same option open to you."

I repeat after him, "Nothing is different. The same holds true for both of us. You are free, past or future. But whatever you may believe, *we* are not -- inside this camp or out. It makes no difference whether the gate is opened or closed. What matters is that it is there, and we have been imprisoned behind it."

"But not to move away from the heat, when you are being scorched by the fire!"

"To escape what has taken place is not simply a matter of moving away from the fire."

On his face, on Mother's, on Father's, there is the same question. Why?

"I have known you for three years," Rothke says. "We have become close friends. But I do not understand you."

Rothke I cannot help, but Father I must try to help

understand.

I wonder if this is the way it always is. Each closed within himself, never touching. To myself I try to answer what I cannot to others. I remember faces of two sets of parents on the distant day of a sad reunion. I was led to believe it would be a joyful time. Instead, the faces are lifeless.

Chapter 33

Long ago I was told there is no direct relationship between the seasons and the distance we travel from the sun on our eliptical orbit. It is the angle of radiation that causes summer, fall, winter, and spring. I feel the first chill of autumn in the evening turn to the persistent cold of winter. I remember the fanning of charcoal in an hibachi in Japan. Frail silhouettes of pines stand quiet against a deep orange sky. Each evening in Tule mountain shadows race across the valley floor until we are submerged in blackness.

Along with loss of understanding, there is loss of time. It makes little difference what day of the week it is, what season, except Sundays are days off. The rooms are the same and the camp is deadeningly familiar. Any other way of life is too remote and unreal to contemplate. In another year or so I might adapt unquestioningly to a lifetime in a concentration camp.

I look at the interior of the apartment that Mother has so carefully tended. "It is not so much the size of what we live in, but what is inside it," she says. For three years she has made camp our home. Our barrack is immaculately clean: the floors are swept daily; shelves and table, window sills and furniture are dusted every day. The paintings hang in perfect alignment. She changes them the first of every month. Sometimes they are her own, sometimes they are painted by her friends. The table and shelves are covered with a bright print cloth that matches the curtains. The room in its simplicity is like a formally set Japanese dinner table. It is a Japanese order of beauty that Mother brings to this barrack, to the drabness and colorlessness of our lives.

Despite Mother's efforts, Father continues to deteriorate. From the moment he set foot on the shores of this country, his whole world -- his work, his tools, his time -- was defined by order and schedule. He imposed his own structure on whatever hardship he encountered. In this way he found his strength, his source of survival.

His world is outside this camp; severed from it, he is bereft of function and worth. He is apathetic and irritable, unable to direct himself in the simplest of hobbies or crafts or games with his friends. Now he has received another of the periodic letters from the people who are managing the family property in Sacramento. A year ago the house in Florin was broken into and ransacked. Four months ago the fifth family who occupied our house on X Street moved out, but the house was not rented again because of its deteriorated condition. A month ago word came from the local law enforcement agency informing us that confiscated family heirlooms had mysteriously disappeared, along with many other families' things, from the place where they were being "safely" held until the end of the war. The latest letter concerns Father's business: the man who had leased the drugstore and printing shop recently went bankrupt, and all the inventory, machinery and equipment was being taken over by the man's creditors.

When the news was first received in camp about the loss of property in Nihonmachi and the outlying areas around Sacramento, a group was organized to contact lawyers and law enforcement agencies to demand investigation and apprehension of the lawbreakers. Petitions were circulated and signed stating that further steps should be taken to protect our property.

It became apparent to Father that nothing would be done, and at each new missive of disaster, he would fly into a rage, cursing the government, the law enforcement agencies, and the people who were managing his property. Watching him read the latest letter, I prepare to leave the apartment to avoid another of his tirades, but this time a look of resignation and defeat comes across his face. He gets up, throws the letter in the stove and goes to his cot, where he lies staring blankly at the ceiling. I decide I need a haircut.

I watch the barber. His dark face perches on his white smock like an olive. He moves away from the chair with a square sheet and shakes it violently, bits of black hair tumbling to the floor in tiny sommersaults. He nods to me to take the barber chair.

On the opposite wall there are two signs: one small, saying in black type, "HAIR CUT 20¢." The other sign has a picture of a wavy-haired man in a Marine uniform looking affectionately into the adoring eyes of a young blond. It says, "WILDROOT HAIR OIL FOR MEN!"

Scissors clip busily; the barber chatters about camp and baseball. There is sudden silence as a burly bozu-headed youth enters the shop. He goes directly to the wildroot sign and rips it off the wall. A smaller youth, equipped with hammer and tacks, bangs another sign in its place. In English and Japanese it states, "All men who are true to their motherland will cut their hair in the bozu style and become honorary members of the Imperial Army." More toughs push their way into the small two-chair shop. The sign-ripper announces that he will supervise all haircuts, to make sure everyone wears the proper style. One man tries to rise but is shoved back into the chair. There are ten customers in the room. Nine are forcibly given bozu haircuts. Short, frizzly, black carpets sit squarely on their shiny skulls. I am the only one left unmolested.

The Resegregationists disrupt our lives openly and unrestrained now. Even at the movies, as we laugh at Costello pulling fistfulls of money from a head of a moose, the lights suddenly flash on. Bozu-headed youths pour through the doors. The windows of the theater barrack slide open, attended by hostile faces.

When the room is quiet, Honda enters. He moves to the small stage in front of the screen, followed closely by the sign-ripper. Honda clears his throat and reads from a paper held at arm's length. "It is urged that all Japanese who love and feel loyalty to the motherland sign petition to separate disloyal Japanese from loyal Japanese. Resegregationists have been working to do what WRA has decreed: that Tule Lake become center for disloyals. Those who are true disloyals sign petition to send loyal Japanese out of this camp! When this is done, camp will become peaceful place to live."

Uojiro jabs his elbow into my side. "What's he saying?"

I bend my head down to Uojiro, whispering, "There's going to be trouble." He looks at me disconcerted. "I want you to help me. Think you can?"

"I think so. What should I do?"

"I want you to try to get out of the barracks. If someone tries to stop you, tell them you're scared and have to go home. They'll probably let you through. When you get out, go to Tomato. You know where to find him. Tell him there's trouble, to get help as soon as he can. Think you can make it?"

"Sure thing," he says confidently.

A voice from the movie audience shouts, "I've already heard all that stuff! This is Sunday movie night. On with the show!"

The youths at the windows lean into the room waving clenched fists and shouting down the protestor. In the commotion Uojiro slips through the door unnoticed.

When the room is quiet again, Honda continues, "Everyone here and in all areas of camp must register yes to renunciation and repatriation petitions, or yes to loyalists list. Then we will know where everyone stands!"

"On with the movie!" someone shouts, clapping his hands and stomping his feet. In moments the building vibrates with the pounding of feet and hands beating in unison. The faces disappear from the windows and reappear in the doors. Several of the youths carry kendo-style clubs which they bang on the interior posts.

Honda knots his fists into a tight ball. Someone hurls a folding chair from the middle of the room. Honda ducks and the chair catches him across the back of his shoulders. People begin shoving and pushing, some heading for the exits, others toward Honda and the youthful Hokoku members. The crowd shoves me with it, up to one of the kendo stick wielders.

He is bumped from behind and knocked over. His stick drops to the floor. I grab it and begin hitting at the other sticks descending on me. I retreat to a long table against the wall, crawl underneath and turn it on edge, clouting my attackers as they clamber up on it. Tomato runs in. He spots me and battles his way across the room.

"For such an easy-going, unperturbable guy, you sure are always pecker-deep in a heap of garbage!"

Good old Tomato. Even in a brawl he keeps his wit as well as his wits. Still swinging my stick, I realize suddenly how deeply I have come to care for him. He joins me, dealing blows with foot and fist. We are both laughing. "Who says that I'm easy going and unperturbable?" I shout over the noise.

Together we are invincible, and enjoy the battle thoroughly. It soon ends, but not at our hands. Soldiers surge into the room shooting into the ceiling. The noise and fighting subside.

While the combatants are separated and lined up, I turn to Tomato. "Thanks for saving me again. I don't know what I'd do without you."

Tomato eyes the approaching soldiers. "You remember that time when we were kids and I got the cramps and you pulled me outa the river?"

"Yeah, I remember."

"Well, as the Japanese always say about 'on' and 'giri' and all that indebtedness stuff, if you hadn't done that then, I wouldn't be here now. I've owed it to you for a long time."

The riot squad herds us out to the trucks with rifles, and drives all of us including the Resegregationists towards the military compound.

Chapter 34

I am taken to a room encased in sheetrock. The shadow of the hooded light hangs in perfect symmetry along the four walls. It is one of the two adjoining rooms Tomato and I shared following the stockade riot. I do not know for sure which room it is until I see the hole that Tomato carved into the wall with his pocket knife. Through the barred window, I see again the watch tower. The moon, hangs above the hills like a marble, luminous and mercury soft. Slightly to the south of it, the distant horizon floats like a slab of ice on a sea of earth.

I am awakened in the morning by a door slamming and footsteps echoing down a corridor.

It is a shock to see Mother walk in, her color as drab as the old overcoat she wears, her face wan and weary.

"What are you doing here?" I blurt out.

"I heard about the fight. They said you were seriously hurt, so I went to the hospital. I asked around until I found you were here. Are you all right? Were you injured?"

"I'm fine. No injuries except a few bruises. Tomato came just in time."

Tears of relief flood her eyes. I take her arm to sit her on the cot. "I was so worried I couldn't sleep," she says, her voice shaking. She covers her eyes with her hands and begins crying, a gentle sobbing that accelerates into uncontrollable spasms. I hold her fearing that something has happened to Father.

Finally her crying subsides. She says in a halting voice, as if reading my fears, "Your father is all right. He is in the hospital, but he is not hurt. It is Atsumisan," she says, struggling to control her voice. "Late last night he was stabbed in the neck . . . he died immediately."

I feel Mother's shoulders sag as she says it. My parents, Atsumi, and perhaps a half dozen others were among the first Japanese immigrants to have settled Nihonmachi. I contrast the small, energetic vibrant man I knew from Nihonmachi with the man I saw a week ago. The three years of evacuation and incarceration had worn him down and broken him, and now this, killed by his own people.

Mother says, "How can we live here any longer, with our family and friends getting hurt and killed? Alice wants her mother to come and join her while she finishes out the year. I think she will go. She is alone now. We can't stay here, Ben."

The following morning two men enter the room. One is the project director, Burrell. The other is Turpin, the representative from the Justice Department. His glasses magnify his blue eyes.

"I'm sorry we had to lock you up here," Burrell begins, "but it was done to ensure your safety. You are one of those on the Resegregationists' blacklist. As of now you are free to go. We kept you here this one day so we could talk with you this morning."

Turpin says, "The Hokoku Seinen-dan, the Resegregationists, are a well-organized, powerful influence in the community. They are made up of the instigators and troublemakers of this camp. Now, as you may have heard from rumors, we are approaching the time when Tule Lake will no longer exist as we have come to know it, that is, a detention center for all Japanese Americans. Before the week is out, we will issue an official statement announcing the rescinding of the Western Defense Command exclusion orders of Japanese Americans from the West Coast."

"Does that mean that we will then be free to return to our homes on the West Coast?" I ask.

"Exactly," Turpin replies. "And in conjunction with this, the War Relocation Authority will force resettlement by liquidating all relocation projects within a year, with the exception of Tule Lake."

"What do you mean, with the exception of Tule Lake?"

"For some this will mean returning to West Coast homes, for others resettlement in the interior of the United States, and for a minority, the true Japanese nationalists, continued detention in Tule Lake until such time as arrangements can be made for their repatriation back to Japan. And this is where the Justice Department comes in, defining and categorizing who these people are."

"Do you realize for many people there is nothing else?"

"I don't understand."

"Many of those who you say should leave camp have nothing else left. Their homes are gone, land gone, families broken up and scattered. For many there is nothing left but this camp."

"What are you saying? That people shouldn't leave this godforsaken place? That they should remain here as wards of the government?"

"I am just pointing out a reality. Many people, particularly the elderly, have lost everything. Their hopes are diminished as well as all material possessions, and in many cases they have lost the sons who would now be taking over their responsibilities."

"It is a hardship being experienced by other American families, preparing for a post war life."

"It is not the same. We have been robbed of everything and put into a form of purgatory, while others outside have prospered from the war. It is deceitful to make any analogies with us and the rest of American society."

"What do you want? To make this camp a permanent reality for your people?"

"The reality is, there is a great deal of hatred for Japanese Americans outside these fences. Many people do not want to go back out there for fear of their lives."

"The reality is, innocent people have suffered needlessly. Those of us who have the responsibility to aid in preparing others for a new life, must do so. We cannot view these camps as sanctuaries where we can hide from the real world."

"You are trying to tell *us* of the real world?"

"No. I am trying to convey to everyone that when the war ends, there will be no more Tule Lakes, Manzanars, Heart Mountains, Gila River, Minidokas. However much the Japanese Americans have suffered from injustice, the camps will be no more and the Japanese will have to take up life anew."

"The war will end, and we will be assured that the racism and hysteria that put us here will exist no longer? The acts of recent violence against Japanese outside these fences will not be repeated?"

"Why are you asking me this? Perhaps you feel I am responsible for what happened?"

"We are all responsible."

"I do not understand you, Mr. Senzaki," Burrell

says. "Your stance, your stubborn refusal to register, your refusal to resettle, when these things would make your life immensely less complicated. During the past few years I have learned much about you people. Much of which I have come to admire and respect. Who you are, your philosophies of life. That it is the Japanese way to bend in the wind, never breaking. What you are doing will break you. Why do you resist when it is most logical to bend?"

Turpin says, "You are young, well educated, possessed of all things that will ensure success in the future. Why do anything now that will jeopardize all that?"

"Perhaps. But what of those who are less educated, the elderly who cannot speak English, the parents now penniless without American-born sons? What are they to do? Where are they to go? Already I have friends and acquaintances who have moved to Chicago to live in tenements and slums, making their livings as janitors and dishwashers. This is the fulfillment of the promised land?"

Turpin sighs. "Your brother who died for this country has not died in vain. What he has given, what those others of the 442nd are giving is an acceptance throughout America which might otherwise have taken generations to accomplish."

"It is a perspective you as a white man can have, free to enter or leave camp any time. For those fenced off by watchtowers and barbed wire the perspective is of fear and disorientation and insecurity. We cannot suddenly be dumped into a hostile society without any guarantees of safety."

"It is dangerous to judge all white people by the actions of a few," Turpin says. "Doing so would be reversing the discrimination that brought about evacuation."

Burrell says, "That is why we are opening the hearings to determine who should remain in camp and who should leave. We are concerned with what is happening in this camp. We believe a lot of innocent people are going to suffer, as some already have. There is a strong movement towards renouncing American citizenship, which must be reversed. The Resegregationists are terrorizing the people with violent tactics. We are going to initiate grand jury proceedings against them to decide whether there is ground to try them on treason. But we need cooperation. We need people who would be willing to testify against them."

"Why are you telling me this?"

"You have refused to register, yet you have done nothing overtly that could be construed as disloyal. Your family has a history of Americanization. All of you are Christians, your father is a successful businessman, you and your brother were Eagle scouts. Your family was among the founders of the First Presbyterian Church, you and your brother attended American colleges. Your entire history is one of Americanism, more so than most Caucasians. In the years of knowing you in this camp, Rothke says you have never once spoken disloyally towards this country. Need I go on?"

The angle of light on Turpin's glasses changes the silvery surface. He scrutinizes me with the pinched Tule Lake look that characterizes all who have endured the sun, the dust, the snow, the smoke filtering through the barracks.

"We are willing to make you a deal," Turpin says. "You register loyal so you can get leave-clearance, testify in the hearings, and without returning you to the camp we will make arrangements for you, your parents, and the Kageyamas to be out of the camp and on your way to the midwest before any -- uh -- recriminations."

Burrell says, "We have taken the prerogative of talking to your parents. They are in agreement. Your parents and aunt will be removed from camp ahead of time and lodged in Newell where you can join them after the hearings. You will all be on the train the next morning."

From somewhere within the Army compound come faint sounds of a phonograph playing Christmas carols. It is the first time during their visit I have heard the music, although I am aware that it has been going on for some time.

Burrell takes a paper out of a briefcase and slides it across the table towards me. "All you have to do is sign this, declaring that you are loyal to the United States."

I stare at the paper for a while. That piece of paper, clearly, concisely typed out, when signed will make all the turmoil, the bitterness, the wrongs of the past three and a half years disappear.

I push it back to them. I cannot sign it. "But I will testify against the Resegregationists. They have committed much that is wrong."

"What are you doing?" Turpin asks. "Are you bent on self-destruction?"

Burrell adds, "Things may not be the way you want them, but you can't ignore the way things are. And even if you won't look out for yourself, you should look out for your parents. You owe it to them."

"Perhaps you don't realize," Turpin says, "that your life is in jeopardy."

"I want my parents removed from the camp and sent to Colorado. They have friends already settled in

Denver who will help them get settled. The war cannot go on much longer. I will join them when the gates of Tule Lake are closed . . . forever."

"Why?" Burrell asks."

"Because I have to see this through to the end."

"Why?" Turpin asks.

"I owe much to my parents. They are my parents. But I owe much to the Japanese of this camp. They are my people. Because of my work, there is much that I can do for them . . . . There will be much to do."

Chapter 35

I am back in our apartment, waiting for the first snow flurries of my third winter behind barbed wire. Father spends most of his time on his cot, sleeping, reading accounts of the war from different newspapers, taking breakfast and lunch in the apartment and going to the mess hall for supper. He reads and re-reads Southern Pacific schedules of trains that will take him and Mother to Denver where they will move in temporarily with friends until I join them, or until we can return together to California.

Father picks up a week old California newspaper and reads a byline on the front page. "Listen to this. "President Roosevelt, Western Defense Command, and the War Department yesterday were strongly urged by the State Senate's Committee on Japanese resettlement not to permit the return of Japanese to the Pacific Coast, and particularly California, for the duration of the war. We believe because California is required to make an all-out war effort, to allow the Japanese to return during the war is inadvisable because it would cause riots, turmoil, bloodshed, and endanger the war effort.

"'Return of Japanese Americans to the West Coast is apt to result in wholesale bloodshed and violence, Representative Benson, Democrat of California said today.'"

"I'm glad we are not going back to California," Mother says. "I hope it is safer in Colorado."

"We have heard nothing bad from Colorado," Father says. "The Onishis have had no trouble. Some people are very unfriendly, but no one has threatened them or hurt them. The Onos are there and so are the Tsudas. They are all saying that it is a good place to be, that there are many Japanese going to Colorado because the governor of the state said that the Japanese would be welcomed and would not be harmed."

"I think I will like it there," Mother says. "It will be strange to go outside these fences -- to see trees and birds again and hear them singing." She smiles, and suddenly she seems ten years younger than the woman who came to the jail cell several days ago. "When will we be leaving?" she asks.

"You and Father and Obasan will be leaving within two weeks," I answer. "As soon as all the papers are finished, and travel and other arrangements are made."

Mother turns quickly, looking at me with wide eyes. "Your Father, Obasan and me?" She pauses as if afraid to ask. "And you and Masahiro?"

"As soon as certain matters are cleared up . . . we will come . . . when it is possible."

"As soon as it is possible? What are you talking about?"

"There are certain matters that have to be cleared up."

Mother's face clouds. "When we made plans to go to Colorado, I thought it was for all of us. No one said that some of us would go and some of us would stay. Why wasn't I told?"

Father interjects, "We thought it would be best not to upset you."

"You knew of this," she says, looking angrily at Father. "And you did not tell me?"

"It is a very complicated matter."

"Complicated matter? What is a complicated matter?" she demands, looking first at Father, then at me. "You are hiding something from me. I want to know what this 'complicated matter' is about!"

Reluctantly, Father says, "Masahiro . . . has decided to renounce his American citizenship. He cannot leave this camp and does not want to."

"He has joined the Resegregationists?"

"No. He would not do that. But he is very bitter about the past three and a half years, about this camp, and he does not wish to remain in this country. He wishes to return to Japan so he can build a new life free from these bitter memories."

"And you," Mother turns to me. "You are going to renounce your citizenship too?"

"No."

A look of relief spreads across her face. "Why is he doing it? He has only been to Japan once, for a month. How can he go back there and be happy?"

"We have tried to talk with him. We have said everything, but he will not listen. He has already filed his papers."

Mother turns to me again. "And you are going to stay here with him?"

"Yes. I cannot leave him here alone."

"Then I will stay here, too!"

"You cannot. You and Father are going to Colorado where it is safe, and when everything is cleared up, I will join you."

"How can such a matter just be 'cleared up?' You are trying to tell me that it is a small matter that Masahiro is going to renounce his citizenship, and all he is going to do is return to Japan while his Mother stays in

Colorado?"

"It would not be good to stay here. For the matter of your safety it is best that you and Father and . . ."

"Safety?" Mother interrupts, suspiciously. "Why are you talking about safety? We have lived in this crazy dangerous place for three and a half years. You have been involved in fights, you have been beaten, Gordie was beaten, your Father was beaten, you and Masahiro spent ten months in a stockade and now you are telling me that something is happening to make this camp too dangerous to live in?"

Mother's face colors angrily. "I am not being told everything. Do not deceive me any more. I want to know what is going on!"

"We have tried to talk Masahiro out of renouncing his citizenship," I tell her, "but he refuses. Because he refuses, he cannot leave camp. It will become dangerous for us to stay here because Masahiro and I have been asked to testify against the Resegregationists to stop them from forcing other people to renounce their citizenship. Many young people who have never been outside this country are considering renouncing. The WRA, the administration and the Justice Department are trying to stem the tide, and they want our help. We are going to cooperate, which will be dangerous for us. Because of this, we want the family out of camp."

"You *have* to do this?"

"Yes."

"I will talk to Masahiro," Mother says, moving toward her coat.

"No!" Father says. "We have talked to him for many hours, and he has made up his mind. You cannot change him."

Mother hesitates, hangs her coat back up abruptly,

then walks to the window and looks blankly at the dull barracks wall opposite.

In a determined voice, she says, "I have lost one son. He was in the height of his youth, in the height of his promise. We have seen violence and disruption. And now I am being asked to split up my family."

She hesitates, and a far-away look comes over her face. "Long ago, after one year in this country, we returned to Japan. When I was there, I was asked to give up my son who was born in America, so that some other family who did not have a son could carry on a family name. They said I was young, that I would have other children, that life in the new world was too difficult, and that for the sake of the other family, I should do so. But most importantly they said I should do it for the sake of my child. I was young and there was a lot of pressure put on me. So I did it. I was wrong. They were wrong. I should not have been asked to do such a thing."

"But we came together again," I answer, tears filling my eyes.

"Yes, for that I have thanked God over and over again. I am thankful. But those nine years . . . never, never, do I wish to live through such years again. No," she says slowly, "I will never go from this camp while any member of my family remains here. I could not live with the fear and the uncertainty, of waiting for mail that might someday tell me that my son or my cousin was seriously hurt or killed. If any member of my family remains here, I will remain also. We will leave together, or we will not leave at all."

I look at her profile. Her resolve gives her a new serenity, a new dignity. Her decision may not be logical, but more important, it is right. Father looks at me, relief in his eyes. In a rare gesture of respect and affection he bows his head to the diminutive figure at the window.

A gavel is hammered on an oaken block, accompanied by a voice announcing the opening of the grand jury hearings. It is now the New Year, the time of driving away of evil spirits, when long handled mallets pound soundlessly the steaming rice into a smooth sticky dough for mochi.

Kageyama wears the black suit that he wears only on Sundays, at festive occasions, at funerals and on that morning in early 1942 when he was arrested and taken off by the FBI.

For a long while I pay little attention to the proceedings, but study, instead, the faces of Holmes and Cardozo flanking the "Great Seal of the United States."

"The activities being practiced by the Resegregationists verge on treason." Turpin points toward Togasaki and Honda and two others sitting at a table at right angles to the judges' bench. "Persons disloyal and antagonistic to the U.S. are coercing others, with threats and violence, to renounce American citizenship and repatriate to Japan. Because the Resegregationists are so vociferous and aggressive, more and more families are urging their citizen children to renounce."

"Bah!" Reverend Togasaki interrupts. "You are from Washington. What do you know of what is happening to Japanese families?"

"I have been working with the Japanese in these camps for over three years."

"Who is representing us in Washington? There are Japanese in Congress?"

"You have the same protection that all residents of this country have."

"Then why are we here?"

There is a long pause. A weary pause; he has endured this conversation numerous times. He is from Washington, from the outside world, but he is as tired as Kageyama, as all of us, struggling within the confines of the barbed wire fencing.

"Mr. Togasaki . . ."

"Reverend Togasaki!"

"Reverend Togasaki," Turpin says in a wearily patient voice, "What is your definition of disloyalty and loyalty?"

"By honor people pay to what flag. Whether man wears hair cut in bozu style of Japanese motherland. By paying honor to things Japanese and not to things American."

"How can you determine the basis of a man's loyalty on such factors as these?"

"Bah!" Togasaki replies. "It is as good a way as answering fifty-four questions about family, political beliefs, relatives, investments -- questions from Washington where there are no people representing Japanese."

"What about those people who are not committing themselves to either side?"

"Fence sitters, and disloyal to motherland because they profess no loyalty. They are opportunists waiting to see what will happen so they can choose winning side. They are cowards!"

Kageyama's face flushes, as dark as the maroon carpet in front of the bench. He jumps to his feet, roaring, *"Cowards!* You are the coward! Attacking people in the dark. Murderer, gangster! You and Honda and all the rest. But you are worse than that. You are hypocrites! You are alien who encourages Nisei and Kibei to renounce citizenship, but you yourself have not yet signed for passage aboard Japan return boat."

The judge rises from his bench and says angrily, "Such outbursts are outrageous! Any further such behavior will result in disciplinary action."

Horie and Moriuchi rise from the audience and wave denationalization papers over their heads, exhorting others of like mind to renounce. In their free hands, they wave small white silk flags. "We are loyal to Japan. We do not care about American justice and courts that have put us here!"

Marshalls close in on the two and remove them shouting from the room.

A second chair is set on the witness platform and Kageyama and I are sworn in simultaneously. The ACLU lawyer, Wayne Collins, who has taken on a personal crusade for the Japanese Americans, reviews for the record Kageyama's and my involvement in the political surges and countersurges of the camp. After a lengthy report, he says, "You are difficult ones to categorize. Overtly you have done nothing treasonous, yet Mr. Kageyama has renounced his citizenship and Mr. Senzaki has steadfastly refused to register loyalty to this country, and whenever something takes place of a notorious nature -- I speak here of conflicts, the stockade, military and police roundups, violence -- you seem always to be near at hand. However, because of your past histories and the fact that you are on the Resegregationists black lists and are known as public Inus no. 1, we know that you do not belong with the Japanese nationalists who want Japan to win the war."

The judge raps his gavel on the oaken block. "Mr. Collins, for the record and for those who are unfamiliar with camp terminology, please explain to us the terms 'black lists' and 'Inu'."

Collins says to Kageyama, "Perhaps Mr. Kageyama will explain it for the court."

Kageyama looks down, rolling his eyes upward. "Dog. It is the word for dog."

"That is the literal translation? Perhaps you could explain it in the context in which it is commonly used in the camp."

Kageyama says, "If you do good for the people, you get put into stockade. If you do good for the administration, you get called Inu." Kageyama then adds with bitterness, "So we should all play baseball."

"Baseball?" the judge says.

Kageyama stares at the floor, expressionless. "Like the Italians who play baseball, so do not have to go to concentration camps."

Turpin looks at me uneasily. "Mr. Senzaki, will you enlighten us further?"

"What Kageyama has said is an accurate explanation. Many of us who have worked for the welfare of the people of this camp were put into the stockade and oppressed by the administration when our views did not coincide with theirs. Those who tried to work with the administration on their terms were labeled in the colony as Inu -- traitors and informers against the people. It is a device to control social behavior within the Japanese community."

"In other words, it is the Resegregationists' way of trying to divide up the community into loyals and disloyals."

"Yes," Kageyama says loudly. "It is crazy way like Washington who wants to divide loyals and disloyals by questionnaire."

Turpin checks his documents. "I think it is safe to characterize the loyals as 'Those to whom Japan as a symbol of allegiance or a future place of residence holds no attraction. And in spite of the discrimination they have met, they still prefer the prospect of a future in America to a future in Japan.' However, it is not so easy to characterize the disloyals. In an effort to understand them and their behavior, and the beliefs that led them so far as to commit murder, we have called the two witnesses."

"They are crazies," Kageyama says.

"Crazies?"

"Crazies, nuts, fools, bakatares, cowards, booby hatches."

"Bakatares! Cowards! Booby Hatches!" Honda suddenly shouts out. "You are the bakatares, the cowards, the booby hatches! And worse you are a Inu, a traitor to the Japanese."

Kageyama looks up to the judge. "You wish to see a crazy?"

Honda turns red and begins shouting obscenities. The judge pounds his gavel on the oaken block. The marshals drag Honda struggling from the room.

When it is quiet again, Kageyama says, "And if you do not understand still, there is always the governor of California, who as attorney general helped put us in these camps. He is a crazy too."

The judge raps his gavel once more on the block and admonishes, "I will warn you again that my courtroom is a place of law and justice. I will not tolerate words or behavior that bring disgrace to this court."

"Getting back to the definition of disloyal vs. loyal," Turpin says, "I think the official explanation defining disloyals would be, 'Those who are extremely bitter towards America and aggressively vociferous in their expression of loyalty to Japan.' 'True Japanese,' would then be an accurate characterization, would it not?"

Kageyama looks up at Turpin. "That is very good explanation. Washington is very good."

"Because of your stance," Turpin says, "it is safe then to assume that you and Mr. Senzaki do not fall into either category. Is that correct?"

Kageyama throws his hands up in a shrug. "Those who had made no hard and fast decision favoring either America or Japan as a future place of residence or symbol of allegiance. Postponing the choice of America versus Japan until after the war is over. Very ambivalent towards a future in Japan *or* a future in America. See," Kageyama says, "I have read same directive, but I do not mind what Washington says when it is well put."

"Considering your understanding of the situation, Mr. Kageyama, why have you chosen to remain in this troubled place? With the lifting of exclusion orders, we are coming to the final stages of the relocation program and the prime objective as always is to restore all of you to private life in normal communities. You can help fill the demand for workers in plants, farms, consumer goods production. The employment opportunities are plentiful. It is, therefore, a good time to resettle."

"Normal communities? Bah!" Kageyama says. "Why should we? It is coldest part of winter now when everything frozen solid. It is time that all things become hard and immovable. If you squirt ice with water when it is so cold that water freezes, you make ice bigger, stronger, immovable. Midwinter is not time to chip away ice."

On the opposite wall are two large windows. The light shining through the icicles outside makes shadows of barred windows on the walls.

"Your honor." Burrell looks towards the bench. "Perhaps I could interject here that the lifting of the exclusion orders does not necessarily mean that people have to resettle in the midwest. The Japanese are free to go anywhere in the United States, including their former homes in California."

"What homes in California?" Kageyama asks. "I have received letters from Caucasian acquaintances who have said those of us who still hold property there have had our homes broken into and robbed of everything. Some have had their houses burned down. The land has sat idle and grown over with weeds while we live in purgatory for almost four years. Now we are told we can return to our homes as if nothing has happened. It is terrible joke," Kageyama says bitterly. "Like justice and white man's law, like this courtroom."

"Restrain yourself," the judge says from the bench, "or you will be held in contempt of court."

Reverend Togasaki gets noisily to his feet. "Contempt of court! What do I care for such things? What can happen to me worse than what has happened? I do not have fear of such threats anymore. You talk of justice and law for behavior in this room. Well, what of vigilantism and violence that is happening to Japanese who have returned to California?" Togasaki takes newspapers out of his pocket and points to headlines. "Here, home at Yamato Nursery burned down. The third building owned by Japanese to burn down in Placer County last week because of opposition to Japanese returning. And here, three ruffians accompanied by fourteen people attack Nisei soldiers and their friends and relatives in train station. Those who have fought for this country. This is why many people wish to renounce citizenship. They do not want any part of this crazy country. After all that has happened to us and is still happening, what do we care for justice and honor of this courtroom?"

A score of young men rise in the spectators' gallery, shouting and waving flags. The judge pounds with his gavel, and marshalls pour into the courtroom, grabbing people and dragging them out.

When order is finally restored, the judge angrily orders the room cleared. The following day a notice is issued: "The hearings have been postponed because of blatant disregard for justice."

Two days after the hearings, Turpin announces through the *Tulean Dispatch* that seventy members of the Resegregationists will be sent from Tule Lake to the internment center in Santa Fe, New Mexico. On Thursday morning I awaken in the darkness at 5:00 A.M. The removal will take place at the main gate. It is a clear cold morning, stars still bright and twinkling in the total blackness of the sky.

Through the quiet of the early morning, I can hear truck engines warming up from the motor pool and heading towards the pick-up point.

When I arrive, the seventy members of the Resegregationists are still several blocks away from the gate, but I can hear them, shouting banzais and washos, the bugles blowing marching rhythms. They are a strange sight coming from the barracks corridors into the flood lit compound at 5:15 A.M., ghostly figures in the artificial light. They march in doubles to the center area and begin forming seven long lines of ten men.

They are all dressed alike. The older men, the leaders, march in the front ranks; the younger strong-arm boys bring up the rear. I see many familiar faces: Horie, Muratani, Moriuchi, and others whom I have come to know and recognize during the past few years. Among the older men, there are Honda, Reverend Togasaki and all the other officers that run the Resegregationists. The group will soon be separated from their leaders -- the Justice Department's effort to break the power of the Resegregationists and stop the movement towards renunciation.

"Ben," a voice says from behind me. "Been looking around for you. Thought for sure I'd find you." It is Asoo. "Wouldn't miss this for anything."

"Me neither."

Army trucks roll into the compound, and a company of armed soldiers fall in, opposite the Japanese.

Asoo says, "Almost as many arrestors as arrestees. Very impressive."

The Resegregationists continue singing patriotic Japanese songs, blowing their bugles and shouting intermittent banzais.

As in past arrests the officier in command of the military reads off the names of all the Japanese who will be arrested. When the roll call is finished and each of the seventy are accounted for, the Army lieutenant orders the Japanese to board the truck peacefully and of their own volition, or they will be arrested by force.

There is murmuring from the young Japanese when force arrest is mentioned, but without incident they march to the trucks and climb aboard. There is loud cheering from the crowd. From behind me, a woman cries out loudly. "My child has now become a true Japanese!"

"Ben," Asoo says, "do you suppose we'll ever see anything like this again?"

"I think we've seen it all. But if there's anything left in the Frankenstein grab bag, I would just as soon let someone else have the pleasure."

"Amen! I think we've served our time."

The trucks begin pulling out through the gates of Tule Lake. Their headlights move away from the camp onto the highway and disappear to the sounds of cheering.

When the last of the trucks disappear, Asoo shrugs his shoulders. "Well, that's the last we'll ever be seeing of those guys. I hope they like life in Japan."

We head back to the canteen. Walking quickly on the perimeter road to warm up, Asoo abruptly states, "I renounced my citizenship."

The announcement stops me in my tracks. "What did you say?"

"I said I renounced my citizenship, my American citizenship."

"Why? I don't understand."

"Lots of reasons," Asoo answers vaguely. "Lots of reasons. And no reason at all. Who knows?"

"You've never let on you were that bitter."

"Bitter? Who knows what that means by now. No, that isn't the reason. I've swallowed the bitter pill and passed it."

"To stay out of the Army? To stay in this camp like so many others are doing?"

"Sure," Asoo says. "That's it and that's it and that's it."

"You're an American. You've never been anything else and never can be or will be. You'd never be happy in Japan."

"Whoa! Hold on there! Who said anything about going back there?"

"I thought . . ."

Renouncing and repatriation are two different

things. I don't plan to go back anywhere except where I come from, Sacramento Nihonmachi. I'm not crazy or stupid you know."

Asoo smiles at the obvious relief on my face. He says, "I plan to go back and try to pick up the pieces after this crazy bit of history is over."

"Aren't you afraid about your record of loyalty to this country?"

"Put it this way," Asoo says, walking down the road towards the light of the canteen. "If you're a Hakujin you take this matter of soiling your loyalty record seriously and would never say or do anything to dirty it up. But if you're a Jap and nobody believes in your loyalty to this country anyway, you think more about your future and your family. I've talked this over with Mom and the family at great length and at this stage of the war we don't want to break up the family. I would have been willing to go to war, but now I don't feel that way. Mom's a disloyal just so she can stay in this camp. There's a possibility they would separate family members if some are loyals and some are disloyals. So if we're all disloyals we can be assured of staying together and staying right here until the war ends."

"You're beginning to sound like everyone else around here."

"Well," Asoo says testily, "that's what I am, aren't I? You something different?"

"No, I'm not. I'm just like everyone else, caught up in the same forces. But I don't think it was necessary to go so far as renouncing to make sure family members could stay together."

"And I should take the gamble? For three years we run around trying to smell like roses and end up smelling like you know what. At that stage of things no thinking man would count on anything. You won't see *me* trying to fill an inside straight. You gotta give me better odds than that."

We walk into the warmth of the canteen, and voices immediately call to us. Sure enough, it is Tomato and Goto sitting at a table with four coffee cups steaming and two empty chairs.

"Knew you'd make it," Tomato says. "What took you so long?"

"Talking," Asoo grabs his cup with both hands and sips.

Goto says, "You look kinda greenish, or whitish, or something like that, Ben. Kinda like those goons they took out this morning. You got a problem or something, or it is just the god-forsaken cold?"

"Well, I am kind of in a state of shock. Asoo just dropped a bombshell on me."

"Oh?" Goto raises his eyebrows.

"Just broke the news about renouncing."

"Oh," Goto says in a funny voice.

I eye him suspiciously. "Don't say it! Not you too?"

Goto takes an unnecessarily loud suck from his coffee cup. "There's nothing like a good hot cup of java in lava land early in the morning."

"I can't believe it! Asoo -- and now you, too -- renouncing your citizenship? You guys gone batty?"

"Aw, come on," Goto says, "don't take it so seriously. This here's make believe land. It's all a fairy tale -- democracy in a concentration camp, constitutional rights, loyalty to anything that sneezes, soldiers and tanks sent to guard a bunch of Japojins in a cage. The only way for anyone to keep their sanity is to develop some make-believe of their own. My mom's not well these days. When she says Japan's winning the war and we're gonna be liberated by their conquering army, why argue? I have to go along with her."

"Maybe they'll deport you when the war ends," Tomato says.

"Not likely," Goto says. "We can change our minds any time, just like the registration. Right now we got to do what we can to keep the family intact. Later, when that threat's gone, then we can change our renouncing."

"You're taking this thing pretty lightly," I comment. I turn to Asoo. "That the way you feel too?"

"I'm not taking it like a joke, but I sure to hell don't plan to go back to Japan. I renounced, but I didn't request repatriation." He pauses, then says in a concerned voice, "You don't suppose they *will* deport us, do you?"

"I'm sure not going to take a chance," Tomato says. "There was a time not so long ago when nobody could've convinced me an all-American citizen could ever end up in a concentration camp on American soil. So now I'm where you might say, I believe anything is possible."

Chapter 36

A mantle of clear, cold sky settles down to the valley floor, then rises over ridges and peaks and thins to sub-zero sunlight thousands of feet above. I try to recall faces, but the features begin to blur, eyes become indistinct. Barracks empty of people in a reverse evacuation, doors and windows left open to the cold as if departure had taken place in great haste. Not everyone chooses the stultifying life of concentration camps over the uncertainties of the outside. The camp will soon become a ghost town: the young, the bored, the adventurous, the weary depart for other places, for jobs, for schools, for beginning anew where life had been left in limbo three and a half years ago.

I come to Block 64, and go to Uojiro's barrack. The door is open and the inside emptied of all personal belongings. The clothes line is still up. The table is gone, but the cardboard piano keyboard lies face up on the floor. Where I once saw Uojiro's sister studying, there is writing on the wall. In the small tight hand of a young girl is written:

> Dear God Please Don't Make Me Go Back To Japan.
> Dear God Please Don't Make Me Go Back To Japan.
> Dear God Please Don't Make Me Go Back To Japan.
> Dear God Please Don't Make Me Go Back To Japan.
> Dear God Please Don't Make Me Go Back To Japan.
> Dear God Please Don't Make Me . . . .

I run out of the barracks. From the next-door neighbor I learn that the Yoshimuras are due to leave the camp at 10:00 this morning, that they had left the barracks about an hour ago.

I sprint the half mile to the administration offices. As I run into the compound, Uojiro spots me and runs to meet me, throwing his arms around my shoulders and hugging me tightly. He starts to cry softly and says, "How come we got to go? Where they gonna send us? What they going to do to us?"

"Hold on, hold on." I pat him softly on the back. "Slow down." I look over his shoulder at Jeanne, who is watching us apprehensively, her eyes moist with tears.

I take his arms from my shoulders and hold his hand in mine. "Come on, Uojiro, I want to talk with your Mother.

"I saw the empty barrack just now, and was scared I would miss you. Why didn't you let me know you were leaving?"

"I'm sorry, Ben." Jeanne says. "I did send Uojiro to find you yesterday, but he couldn't locate you. And you've been so tied up with the hearings, I thought it would be best not to burden you with my troubles."

"Where are you going?"

"Santa Fe, then to Crystal City, I guess."

"To join up with Bob?"

"Yes. I had no choice."

"What were the conditions?"

"The conditions?"

"You know what I mean."

"I renounced . . . my citizenship," she says, looking down at the ground to avoid my eyes.

"And the children?" I demand.

She hesitates. "Yes . . . they renounced too."

For a moment I want to grab her and shake her until her head rattles. In an irrational way I feel she has betrayed me. I try to control my anger. "Not *they* . . . renounced. *You* renounced . . . *for* them. I hope you know what you've done!"

Tears roll down her face. Uojiro and his sister watch with wide, unbelieving eyes. "Don't do this to me, Ben . . ."

She cries uncontrollably now, like a child. And I see suddenly how small and young she is, how alone she has been these three and a half years: alone she has raised two young children in the violence and degradation of a concentration camp. Somehow, with her husband thousands of miles away in another camp, she has kept her integrity, and provided strength and stability to these two children. I wonder if I could have done the same.

Abruptly, my anger fades. With new respect for her, I take her in my arms and hold her tightly, feeling her gentle sobbing against my chest. "I'm sorry, I felt so angry for a moment."

"I didn't know what to do . . . I don't understand what's going on . . ."

"I know, I know." I hold her, feel her hair against my face. I glance around at people watching us.

Her sobbing subsides. I tell her, "You're doing the right thing by going back to Bob. I know that he needs you and the children very badly. You need each other and the only way you'll survive will be to do it together."

Her arms at her side, her face buried in my chest, she says, "What did we ever do to deserve this?"

"Listen to me," I tell her. "Don't start looking back and trying to understand now. It's too close for us to understand ... sometime, somehow, maybe it will make sense a little. Don't waste your energy. Just remember it is because of people like you that we have a chance of coming out of this without permanent scars."

"But maybe I have done permanent damage by renouncing the children's citizenship."

"You've already signed the renunciation papers, so you can't undo that now. But don't go a step further by requesting repatriation, or you may end up an American in war-torn Japan. Don't let Bob do it either. But no matter what he does, don't *you* go that far."

"What will happen to us?"

"I don't know, but I recently met the American Civil Liberties lawyer, Wayne Collins, who is a true friend to the Japanese Americans. He's already talking about the unconstitutionality of the evacuation and the renouncing of American citizenship. He feels that such an unprecedented thing as passing a wartime law permitting people imprisoned without charges to renounce their citizenship is unconstitutional. He wants me to work with him to lay the groundwork to undo all of this. Perhaps it will take a long time, but he thinks it can be done."

I release my hold on her. "Promise me you won't do anything further that would jeopardize you or the children."

"I promise."

I look at her carefully. Her hair is down, with a ribbon in it. She is wearing her best clothes, a dark dress with a white collar; the lace around the wrists flutters from her coat sleeves. Despite her swollen eyes, she is very beautiful this morning.

"You should smile now. You'll be going through those gates."

She looks at me timidly.

I tell her, "You look very beautiful."

She smiles and blushes. Uojiro and his sister smile happily. I take both of them by their hands and tell them to help their mother wherever they live and try to take good care of her.

The bus is loaded, waiting for the three of them. The doors close behind them, and the bus moves towards the main gate of the camp. Before it disappears, the sounds of departure die away. I watch the bus until it vanishes behind a point on the valley floor.

Suddenly, I am very tired and weary, left behind to the monotony and depression of Tule Lake. I wish to escape the camp, the fencing, the watchtowers. I remember the drawings of Tule Lake and the mountains that the Yoshimura's left tacked to their wall. I go back to retrieve the pictures. They will be the one thing I will take from this camp to the outside world. In these drawings of the camp and the hills without fences and watchtowers there is a strange kind of beauty. Not the beauty of the trees and birds that Mother has come to miss so deeply, not the beauty of lush growth, or of trees outlined against winter skies, but the beauty of a landscape that embraces earth and sky, that draws distant horizons to one's doorstep. On this finest of lines, space and earth connect . . . and the spirits of God and Man unite.

I search for a place to go within our prison, to escape, to dispel the heaviness. I think of Tomato. His gift is to see, and to see truly: what he sees is not oppressive, but reassuring.

I go to his block, to the canteen, to Goto's and Asoo's, but cannot find him. I return dejected to the area of our barracks. From the fence I look again to where I last saw the bus carrying the Yoshimuras away.

Peripherally, I see movement. A cart is wheeling along the hard ground, dishes and utensils drumming a rhythm on stainless steel. It rumbles to a stop behind me, and someone shoves me into the cyclone fencing.

It is Tomato, dressed in khaki. He stands at attention, arm up in a mock salute. "Joined up so I could get a uniform, be loyal, visit a disloyal friend. My ticket to decency, good red-blooded Americanism." With his salute hand he raps himself gently on his chest. He points to his arm. "And wouldn't you know it too, corporal stripes from the beginning! None of that private stuff for this ol' Boochie."

"How did you get that uniform so quick? You haven't been to boot camp yet."

"Travel uniform. Makes it easier for a Japojin to get from place to place. Army don't want any of their doggies getting lynched on the road."

"And corporal stripes?"

"Had to work for it. When I bring up the matter of age and a year of upper education they just sort of look at me like I'm some kinda pesky mosquito. They being too lazy to get up and squish me, they try to do it by lookin' as evil as they can. Then further down they come to my record as master welder, rivet rupturer, fillet weld wielder, metal melter . . . that's me, I tell 'em. Proficient in all them arts. So they give me rank. None of that rags-to-riches-startin'-from-the-bottom stuff."

I look him up and down, noting the distance between shoe and pants cuff. He looks quickly at me. "Hey! What're you smilin' about?" He then looks down. "Oh! The pant legs. You got to excuse my old lady for that. She ain't exactly had long and meritorious service when it comes to washing and ironing doggies' uniforms. She tossed the whole wool works in extra hot water and by the time we got the wet molecules to dry out, they done shrunk things up a little. To compensate I try to keep the waist at half-mast without losing the whole works!"

He yanks his waistband lower. "But can't get 'em to regulation level. When I bring the pants in, a guy at supply says we got the shortest pants in the whole damned U.S. Army for you monkeys and first thing you do is go out and make 'em even shorter. Pygmy length, the guy calls it. So that's me -- Corporal Tomita reporting in his pygmy pants."

"Hey," he says, changing the subject. "You had lunch?"

"No."

"Great! Let's get this stuff inside before it freezes up." He takes a covered tray from the cart.

"Freezes?"

"Surprise," he says. Inside the barracks, he lifts away the white cloth. There are two sets of ohashi and covered bowls with steam weakly drifting out. "The Boochies have the right idea," Tomato says. "Whoever heard of 'tough udon'?"

Engrossed in our food, we suck and slurp in Japanese style. Tomato's eyes dart furtively above the rim of his bowl. He sets his bowl down and with ohashi still in hand stretches his arms out and sighs, patting his stomach. "Really enjoyed that one . . . noise and all. Got to make the most of it when you can. Not proper in the army mess halls. Besides, the day when this man's army serves udon with ohashi is yet to dawn."

"Where'd you get it?"

"You got to remember, the guys behind the pots and pans in this place are ancestral rice eaters, not potato munchers. I just told 'em I wanted some udon today for a special occasion instead of spam and mashed potatoes. I told 'em it might be a long time before I get a chance to be eating this kinda stuff."

"Thanks. That was a real treat."

"Our last meal together for some time."

"Where you headed?"

"Monterey Army language school. They need interpreters for the Pacific theater. Want to help America win the war, but don't want to end up killing any relatives."

"Leaving soon?"

"5:00 A.M. tomorrow morning."

"Now you can stop marking the x's on your calendar."

There are no traces of humor now. "Yeah," he acknowledges. "I'm a real short-timer now. Over a thousand x's and I'm standing on the last one, looking over the edge to see how far the drop is before I start working myself back up the other side."

He adds thoughtfully, "It's time to move on, but it'll sure feel strange to leave this place and become an interpreter against my own relatives and ancestors."

"You don't have to worry about the ancestors. Besides, the war will end soon."

"I think you're right. And then maybe, I'll get a chance to find out for myself what this true Japanese business is all about. Maybe I'll end up a soldier in Japan."

"A lot safer way of going back than renouncing."

"Amen. This way I can be sure of getting back where I belong.

"This place is getting out of hand," Tomato continues. "I didn't think things could of gotten any crazier

than those stockade days, but now look, people renouncing their citizenship like it was some kind of holiday celebration."

"Over 3,500 people already renounced and the number's still growing."

"Goto, Asoo and his entire family, Kageyama, kids
under fifteen, whole families. I hear from some friends
in the administration that the figure might climb to 70%
of everyone who's eligible," Tomato says.

"The administration and Justice Department are
trying their best to stop it. There's going to be another
mass arrest of the Resegregationists."

"Too little, too late," Tomato says. "There's no
stopping it now until it carries out its logical consequences. What you going to do, Ben? Stick it out
here?"

"Have to. There's going to be a lot of broken lives
to help pull together."

"There'll be that, okay," Tomato says. "Lots of
questions to be answered, for us, for our kids. Well, it's
going to blow over some day, and we're gonna go back
where we came from and start all over again."

Tomato gets up as if he were preparing to leave, and
walks over to the east window. He is profiled on glaze,
his hair a bristly army brush. "I've gotten to know you
real good these past years, like I never would have
gotten to know you otherwise. If there's any one thing
of value that came from it all, I guess I would have to
say that this was it." He breathes deeply.

"If they gave out purple ribbons for hazardous duty
in Tule Lake, you'd be crippled from the weight of Purple Hearts pinned all over you. They'd have to give you
a Purple Heart for the Purple Heart wounds. When I
come back, I'll find you. I got a nose for honesty no

matter where it is."

He is gone. Through the door passes the last vestige of pre-war Nihonmachi.

Eventually, we will be back, try to begin where we left off, take count of those who will never return. Life will continue, it will change, we will adapt but not forget: the tenements of Chicago, the battlegrounds, trials and hearings, the anger and bitterness, the violence, the unmasking of many facets of ourselves that we would not have otherwise come to know, and the shame. It will take time for all the wounds to heal.

In the sky there is less glare, the blue tempered by an early spring. I can see it through the windows that line the walls. I expect to feel better than I do, to enjoy the fragrance peculiar to this time of year. But I don't.

And so we wait. Mother and Father, Obasan, Kageyama and I. Kageyama . . . a citizen by birth, become an alien, now ineligible for citizenship in his homeland. We are here because of him . . . because of me . . . because of reasons beyond our understanding.

We are here, lava still dusts our feet, while early migrants gabble overhead, seeking refuge on the voyage to summer nesting grounds.

Glossary

Bakatare: A colloquial term for stupid.

Banzai: Cheers, hurrahs.

Biwa: A Japanese lute, mandolin.

Bon Odori: The Lantern Festival to remember the dead. A summer dance.

Bozu: A soldier's haircut similar to a crewcut.

Bukkyo-kai: A Buddhist association or gathering place.

Daikon: Japanese white radish.

Daimyo: A feudal lord.

Genmai: Unhulled rice, brown rice.

Geta: Wooden clogs.

Giri: A duty, an obligation, justice.

Gomen Kudasai: Excuse me, I am sorry for this.

Go: A table game.

Hai: Yes.

Hakujin: A caucasian person.

Hashi: A pair of chopsticks.

Hibachi: A charcoal brazier.

Hissho Kigan shiki: Ceremonial prayer for certain victory.

Hokoku Seinen Dan: An organization of young Japanese men dedicated to serving their motherland. In Tule Lake they used pressure tactics to influence others.

Honshu: The main island of Japan.

Hyogo-ken: Hyogo prefecture in Japan.

Inu: Dog. Slang for traitor in Tule Lake camp.

Issei: First generation immigrants to America from Japan.

Judo: A Japanese art of self-defense.

Kago: A chair or basket for carrying a person.

Kagokaki: One who carries the kago or chair.

Kanji: Chinese writing character or ideogram.

Kendo: Fencing, swordsmanship.

Kibei: A Nisei who is sent to Japan for part of his education during childhood.

Kimono: A garment; the traditional dress of Japan.

Koto: A harp or a lyre.

Meijisetsu: The anniversary of the birthday of the Emperor Meiji.

Miso: Salty soy bean paste.

Mochi: Pounded rice made into a small cake.

Nasubi: Eggplant.

Nihon: Japan.

Nihonmachi: Japanese town.

Nippon: Japan.

Nisei: The second generation, American born children of Japanese immigrants.

Obi: A tie around the waist worn over the kimono.

Obasan: A grandmother or aunt.

On: A kindness, favor; an obligation; a debt of gratitude.

Sabishii: Lonesomeness.

Saikakuri Seigan: A Resegregationists' group.

Sake: A rice wine.

Sandan Judo: Third class judo.

Samurai: A warrior, of high class in Japan.

Shamisen: A three stringed guitar.

Shamoji: A wooden rice scoop.

Shakuhachi: A bamboo flute.

Shigeru: A boy's name.

Shikata ga nai: It cannot be helped. That's the way it is.

Shinbashi: A railroad station in Tokyo.

Shogi: A chess game.

Shoyu: Soy sauce.

Sumi: Black ink, charcoal, or Indian ink.

Sumi-e: A sumi on rice paper painting.

Sushi: Special rice dishes flavored with vinegar, sugar, and salt.

Tatami: A straw mat, matting.

Tendon: A bowl of rice with deep-fat fried shrimp or fish laid on top.

Teriyaki: Meat and fish marinated in soy sauce and broiled.

Tofu: Soybean curd.

Tofu-ya: A bean curd maker, a shop for buying bean curd.

Umeboshi: A pickled, salty plum.

Wasshyoi: A cheer shouted in a crowd, no specific meaning.

Tanuki: A badger-like animal in Japanese folk tales.

Tokaido: Highway form Tokyo to Kyoto. There are fifty-five stations on the road.

Urashima: A boy's name in a children's folk story from Japan.

Yamato damashii: The Japanese spirit.

Yokan: A bean jelly desert.

Chi Chi Pa Pa,
Suzume no gakko no sensei wa,
Muchi oh furi furi,
Chi Pa Pa.
Chirp, chirp, twitter, twitter,
Little bird school teacher,
Waving her baton,
Chirp, twitter, twitter.